Reading *Sweet Waters* is like taking a beach vacation from the comfort of your own living room. Julie Carobini paints a beautiful story of fresh starts, painful secrets, and the depth of a family's love. The small town beach setting is as soothing as the sound of waves, and so well drawn I could almost smell the salt in the air. Engaging, fast paced, and romantic. Highly recommended.

—Kathryn Cushman, author of *A Promise to Remember* and *Waiting for Daybreak*

As sure as the ocean ebbs and flows with the tide, so life changes take the characters from one adventure to another in Julie Carobini's latest release, *Sweet Waters*. Exhilarating, fresh and warm as the summer breeze, this book is fun from start to finish. Grab your tanning oil and beach towel, and immerse yourself in a great read that's sure to make a splash when it hits the store shelves!

—Diann Hunt, author of *For Better or For Worse*

Sweet Waters

Sweet Waters

An Otter Bay novel

JULIE CAROBINI

B&H
PUBLISHING GROUP
Nashville, Tennessee

978-0-8054-4873-3

Published by B&H Publishing Group
Nashville, Tennessee

Dewey Decimal Classification: F
Subject Heading: ROMANCES \ FAITH—FICTION \
FAMILY LIFE—FICTION

1 2 3 4 5 6 7 8 • 13 12 11 10 09

For my darling dad, Dan Navarro,
and your First Corinthians 13 kind of love!

Acknowledgments

A BIG HUG AND hearty thanks to family, friends, and colleagues who inspired me throughout the writing of *Sweet Waters*, especially:

Dan and our kids—Matt, Angela, and Emma—along with my parents, Dan and Elaine Navarro, for your forever love and encouragement (and willingness to endure seemingly random brainstorming sessions).

Steve Laube, my agent, for your tremendous tenacity and wit.

Karen Ball, for your wisdom and friendship. After more than a dozen years of knowing each other, I'm thrilled that we finally get to work together!

Julie Gwinn, for your humor and passionate creativity.

David Webb, for finding the Otter Bay Novels a home at B&H.

The rest of the terrific team at B&H Publishing Group—thanks so much for welcoming me aboard!

Tami Anderson, Sherrill Waters, and my husband, Dan—for critiquing this manuscript. Your faithful and honest feedback incited changes to these pages.

Author Jeanette Hanscome for sharing your research and knowledge with me.

Firefighter and fellow writer, Shawn Grady, for all your help, and especially for your patience in the face of my many questions. Thanks also to Firefighter Stan Ziegler for allowing me to pepper you with last-minute clarifications.

The many friends of ACFW who shared their personal stories of heartbreak with me. I won't mention you by name here, but please know I am grateful for your transparency. You made this a better book.

My God, though I'm not worthy to receive You, You love me anyway. Thank You for allowing me to live this dream.

Chapter One

Digest 19, Episode 90

Eliza Carlton knew what she must do. As always. She strode across Sapphire slowly, deliberately, like a cat flaunting its superiority. Though Eliza noticed the sway of diners' chins moving in her direction, nothing in her face showed her satisfaction.

Maurice Von Otto rose to meet her, his smile appraising, but his eyes altogether something else. If Eliza had to describe them, she would choose muddled. His eyes always shifted when he was trying to manipulate her. "Eliza, darling, you captivate me this evening."

Nicely done. Eliza paused, allowing Maurice to hold out her chair and then wait patiently behind her, until she had settled herself. She nodded and admired the way he hurried back to his seat. *She took in his features, noting his beauty, and for a moment, almost lost composure.*

Maurice laid a napkin across his lap, cleared his throat, and leaned forward, as if in hiding. "There is something . . . something I've been hoping to discuss with you, my dear."

And there's something I must discuss with you. Now, however, was not the time to reveal secrets. He wanted her alliance. As the boldest city councilwoman ever to grace the chambers of Quartz Point, Eliza knew her vote would be most crucial to the success of his proposed project.

"Another time, Maurice. Tonight"—she let a coy smile curl her painted lips—"is a night for lovers."

Maurice opened his mouth, as if to protest, but instead tipped his glass flute of champagne in her direction. A fiery grin found its way to his face.

No matter that she was much too nauseous for any such nonsense tonight. At the moment, Maurice was exactly where she needed him. Some may call it manipulation, but Eliza maintained it was simply taking control . . .

THE DOOR SQUEALS OPEN, and I slap my laptop shut. *Tell me I didn't just crack the screen.* My sister Mel leans through the doorway of the quiet office I had borrowed, her mouth twisted into a grimace. "Tara, you're being paged."

As usual. Mel darts off before I can answer. Cheerful voices drift in from the garden. Silverware rattles in the bustling kitchen. The pianist I hired warms up with a few bars of "The Wedding March," and I deflate.

Eliza Carlton wouldn't let a broken heart rule her.

I'm tempted to take one more peek at the weekly digest of *Quartz Point*, the daytime drama of which Eliza is the star, but really, there's no time left. All I can do now is hope that everything Eliza's taught me over the years will, somehow, help me make it through this long and trying day.

Chapter Two

She reminds me of you."

I glance across the lawn to the bride in her tea-length dress, her eyes dancing, the laughter on her face uninhibited. Considering I just said good-bye to my hopes and dreams yesterday—all six-foot-three of him—the resemblance is lost on me.

Anne, my mother's best friend, taps my shoulder. "I meant the little girl over there."

I turn to find a child of about six, blonde hair pulled up into a fountainhead, staring at the double-decker wedding cake, eyes hungry. Fat giggles escape from her child's body. "Excuse me a sec," I say, and race toward the little girl, arriving just as she reaches a small hand toward the mountain of whipped cream icing piled high upon the cake. "Uh-uh-uh. Please don't touch the cake." I pause, then add, "Sweetie."

She jumps back, her dimpled hand hovering in midair. Round eyes glisten as they gape up at me. Strange how that look touches some dried-up part of me. With all the preparations for this wedding, and my tenuous relationship with Trent finally broken beyond repair, my mind surprises me by wandering into old territory.

My cousin Camille swoops in from behind the girl and gives her a hug, all the while pinning me with a mock glare. "Oh, Tara. You're such an old maid sometimes." She reaches over the girl's petite shoulders and takes a big swipe of frosting with her finger. "Here, Katie. Let's show my cousin how to play."

With that, my moment of reverie, wherever it came from, has vanished. Camille just turned twenty, but she still clings to her rollicking high school ways. In some ways, I envy her. She's my cousin by blood, but since Camille's lived with us since she was an infant, she'll always be more like my sister. My not-a-care-in-the-world, flirt-with-any-man-in-range younger sister. I love her.

Camille stands beside me now, her new friend Katie tucked into her hip, and together we look to the bride—our mother. It's an odd sensation, sending off one's mother to begin a new life, especially when my only hope for love has just vanished like sunlight into the dark.

"Mom's happy."

At Camille's wistful comment, I give her a squeeze. Camille never knew her birth parents, so I've been happy to share mine with her all these years. Mom's new husband, Derrick, eight years her junior, plants a sloppy wet one on her lips, right here in front of everyone. I cringe. Camille giggles. Melanie, aka Mel, our middle sister, joins our triangle.

"Well, now my lunch is ruined. What say we sneak out of here and hit PF Changs? What I wouldn't do for a dirty martini with a side of calamari."

It's just like Mel to make an impossible suggestion like that. Maybe it's the relief of another big event done, but I consider taking her up on it. Well, for a brief second anyway. Restlessness like I've never experienced has gotten beneath me lately, and I can't seem to shake it loose. Whatever the reason for it, if I *were* to take Mel up on her jest-filled offer to get out of here, it just might put my sardonic sister into shock.

Why Daddy's words from the past sink into my heart at this moment, I do not know. "Take the girls home, Tara," he told me. His voice was nearly a whisper at that point nearly six years ago, and I knew the end would come soon. He'd wanted us to leave the hospital room, to not see him go this way. Mother had gone to find a nurse, so I did as he asked and began to lead the girls from that oppressive room with its gray walls and faded medical diagrams. But as we turned to go, I saw the morning light spill across his nubby blanket for one last time, and he spoke to me again. "Take the girls, and say hello to Otter Bay for me, will you, Princess?"

In that frozen slice of time, the word "home" took on an entirely new meaning.

The memory catches my breath, and I run both palms over my temples to smooth back wisps of hair that have pulled away from my updo. "I can't leave now, Mel. I still need to settle with the caterer, and pay the judge, and make sure the hall and grounds are picked up afterward so they don't try to keep our damage deposit. And there's that table of gifts to take care of over there, although why people just don't ship their gifts in the first place, I'll never know."

Mel's arms are crossed against the Cavalli suit she purchased from eBay. She rubs the nail of her ring finger. "Kind of uptight today, big sister?"

Camille cuts in. "As usual . . . she's just the saddest thing of my life sometimes." She giggles when she says this, softening the blow.

But I'd say that Mel's right, and why shouldn't I be? Mom decides to marry a man with seemingly thousands of relatives, and they insist that outdoors would be the perfect venue, which it would be if we lived in, say, California or somewhere west. But this is Missouri, and the spring's just ending. We cut it that close. That and all the work that still needs to be done before turning our home back over to the landlord, has made me more tense than wire strung across two poles.

Anyway, somebody had to take charge, and I'd say by the

silly smirks on my mother's and "step" father's faces, the day went over quite well.

Mel drops both arms and scans the crowd, looking bored, impatient. "All I can say is I'm glad I'll be heading out of here in a couple of weeks. Had enough of this small town living, know what I mean?" She swats at a mosquito. "I don't suppose you know what you'll be doing, now that you're out of a job. I've got two interviews lined up, but I'll probably get the first one anyway—shall I ask them to hold the other one for you?"

I ignore her cynicism.

Camille pouts and squeezes Katie tighter before the little girl breaks away. "I don't want you to go, Mel. I'll miss you way too much."

I link eyes with Camille.

One of Mel's hands finds her narrow waist, and she gives me the evil eye. "What? You don't think that when I get a job in Manhattan I'll throw every possession I have into storage and take the next plane out of here?"

"Maybe you will."

"Oh, but you think I won't be able to stick it out."

"I never thought that." Absentmindedly I comb my fingers through Camille's tangled curls. "I know you can do whatever you set your mind to. I just think that in the end you'll want to be near family. We've always been close—especially since Dad died—I just think you'll miss us all enough to find something closer to home. Besides, Mom will need us."

"Evidenced by the way she and the new hub were making like a couple of freshies only minutes ago."

A waft of Mother's "Beautiful Love" perfume makes my nose tickle as the bride approaches. "Girls, thank you, thank you. The energy surrounding us is electric—do you feel it? Oh, of course you do! This entire space has such a vibe to it. I've loved every minute of my wedding day . . . the flowers, the ambiance. Every sunny minute, and I thank you very much."

Mel's face still looks as if she's swallowed sour candy.

Camille crooks an arm around Mom's neck and pulls her sideways. "I'm so jealous of you. I hope that when I finally fall in love, we'll be as perfect together as you and Derrick are."

Finally fall in love? I'm twenty-six. The only one around here who can safely and honestly use the word *finally* in regard to her woeful love life is me.

Mel slides a look at our thirty-eight-year-old stepdaddy. "So when are you and *Dirk* heading off to Maui?"

Mom runs a hand down her chiffon skirt, her princess-cut diamond flashing in the afternoon light. "That's what I've come over here to speak to you girls about. We did talk about Maui, but in the end our hearts have settled on another site for our honeymoon."

No Maui? The honeymoon was the one part of this entire event where Mom told me I wasn't needed. Please tell me they went through a reputable agency. And did she remember to use her air miles?

Camille leaps up. "The Caribbean! I bet you're going to the tropics, aren't you? I've always wanted to go south."

Mom pats Camille's back and my cousin settles like a baby going down for a nap. "Not the tropics, Cam. Not this time anyway. We've . . . well, girls, Derrick and I have decided on Italy."

"Italy!" Our voices squeal in unison.

Derrick slides both hands around Mom's waist and rests his pointy chin on her shoulder. His goofy puppy-dog face peers at us, draped by a wispy tendril of Mom's hair. "You tell them, Marilee?"

Mom pats his hand, but her smile's not nearly as large as before. "Working on it, darling."

He smacks his lips against her cheek and, in one fluid movement, takes her hand and twirls her into his embrace. "Take a good look at her, ladies. This time next week your mother'll have a daypack strapped to her back and hiking boots hugging those lovely ankles of hers. And I can't wait to see it."

I can't fight the frown. "Mom?"

For once, Camille stands still.

Mom's eyes plead with Mel. *Mel*, of all people. "Derrick has planned this all by himself. We're actually going to be traveling throughout much of Europe. We'll spend a few nights in Sicily, and then . . ."

"And after a few days of luxury, we'll be off on an adventure through Germany, Switzerland, France, Italy, Spain, and if she's a good girl, Hungary."

Derrick's smile is almost as big as the sudden knot in my chest. I cock my chin. "How is all that possible?"

He pats the jacket of his tux. "I've got the Eurail passes right here, for safekeeping. I'll take good care of her, and don't worry. A year'll seem like nothing."

The voice gasping aloud is mine. "A year?"

Mom's eyes finally find mine. "It's a chance of a lifetime, Tara. Your old mom's going to recapture her youth." She chuckles softly. "I promise to write."

"You're kidding. Right? Mom, you wouldn't leave your family for a whole year."

Mom's hazel eyes sparkle like golden sapphire, and I find myself fixated on them. "I know it sounds silly, but when Derrick approached me with this idea, I don't know. I felt . . . I felt . . . oh, what am I trying to say?"

Mel cuts in. "Like a kid again?"

Mom glances at her, then back to me. "Well, not quite a child, but like a carefree girl. You may not remember this, but I was once very much that way . . ." She draws in a deep breath and continues. "I'm going to miss you girls so much, but something inside of me says that this is right. For all of us." She turns her attention to Camille. "Would you make me a Facebook page, darling? I thought it would be fun to post pictures from our adventures . . . when I find the time."

Camille straightens, her face animated much like a teen at the mall, instead of a young woman who's still mulling her options. "Of course! I'll teach you everything you need to know. You can do all kinds of things with it—set up groups, post messages and videos . . ."

Mom laughs. "Have fun with it, Camille. Just teach me to use it, and the project is yours."

Camille pecks Mom's cheek, squeezes her tight, then dashes off toward a flock of girlfriends flirting with the DJ.

Mel looks more amused than bothered by Mom's announcement, yet before she can express herself, our Uncle Joe trots over and pulls her onto the dance floor. I ignore her eye roll as Uncle puts on his disco moves to "Play That Funky Music."

Mother takes a quiet step toward me and reaches for my hand. "Tara, I'm depending on you to watch over the girls for me while I'm gone."

When haven't I?

"My things are already at Derrick's, and I hope you won't mind, but you'll need to call back the rental agency. Tell them you'll be needing something smaller, now that there'll just be the two of you. Tara dear, you are always so responsible with the rent and your sisters, but I need you to promise me something else."

All I can do is nod.

"Don't let bitterness guide you, Tara. Forgive and move on, and you'll be set free. Make a point to *love* your life, dear one."

Trent. Now why did she have to bring him into this? He was supposed to be here today, but it would have been pretty awkward considering how much I long to key his car.

Okay, not really. I'd never do anything so . . . so rash. Anyway, this isn't about my ex-fiancé. It's about my mother abandoning me and the rest of our family. And it's about how at peace she looks doing it.

Weddings often bring on tears, but not usually after the vows have already been said and the customary chicken dance long over. So I fight back mine, and straighten my shoulders in an attempt to lure air into my lungs. Derrick pulls Mom toward a group of friends who are set to leave, and she squeezes my hand before turning away from me.

Mel joins me again and purses her lips before letting out a long, low sigh. "What was that you were saying about Mom needing us?"

Camille returns, throwing herself into my arms. "What am I going to do without Mom for a whole year?"

I haven't the slightest. Trent left me for good yesterday— I gulp back that sting of bitterness—and now Mom's running away with her young husband for a year of dusty hostels and mosquito bites. They say that things happen in threes, and maybe the cursed *they* are on to something. For the past two weeks, in between filling Ball jars with homemade bath soap dubbed "Marilee and Derrick's Green Tea & Me Scrub" to give as wedding favors, I've been cleaning out my office at the auto parts store where I've hung my sweater since I graduated high school. Poor Woody, my boss and the owner of the company, died of a heart attack while out picking up a pack of stamps. His sons, Ed and Phil, sold the place quick as they could, and the new owners have brought in their own staff. Thankfully they gave me a nice severance package, but I'm still bothered over how easy it was for Woody's sons to forget everything their father built.

I hang on to Camille and glance across the lawn, vaguely aware that Mom left her bridal bouquet, teeming with mini-roses, on a chair near the DJ. Someone really should gather everyone around before all the single women have gone. Little Katie wanders over and reaches for the blossoms, the image sending my mind even further away to my vaguely recognizable past.

I'm five or so, and my father guides my hand into clear, cool water to touch the tentacles of a green sea anemone that's stuck to the side of a craggy rock. "Go ahead, Tara. Just be gentle. It won't bite." I brush my fingers across the sway-ing limbs of the flower-like creature, their softness tickling me. Apparently believing I'm lunch, the anemone attempts to adhere itself to my fingertips and I pull back, laughing as I tumble bottom-first into a shallow basin of sea water. Joy and laughter and fearlessness wash over me.

Mel cuts into my drifting memory. "Aren't you going to go over there and slap that kid's hand? For heaven's sake, Tara, you're losing your touch."

She's right, except I already lost it. Long ago. In Mel's eyes I see mockery and disappointment, maybe even some disdain mixed in. Such a shame. "Maybe you're right, Mel."

"All right then, go on over there and set things right. Make that girl cry."

I take a step back and an unexplainable sense of peace, like budding freedom, washes over me. Is this what Mom's feeling? Is this the awareness Dad alluded to in those last pain-filled days of his life? *Isn't this what Eliza would do?* As if of their own volition, words spill from my mouth. "Can't do that. I've got packing to do."

Mel loses the pinched expression. "What? Where're *you* going?"

"To California."

Chapter Three

 Mel stands in my bedroom, arms crossed in front of her chest. "I know we've been over this, but tell me again what made you suddenly decide to throw out all logic and head west. Were you digging through Dad's old Beach Boys records or something?"

"Beach Boys! Thanks so much for the reminder, Mel-Mel. We should download some of those old songs to your iPod for good luck." I fold my fourteenth pair of underwear. The rest of our things can be shipped later—we're putting them into storage—but at least I'll be prepared for the first couple of weeks. I don't mention that I too am wondering about the sanity of this decision to move.

"*My* iPod? You can't be serious. Don't you know my motto—let no one come between me and my iPod? Besides, our music tastes clash. Beyonce and all those *American Idol* contestants you listen to cannot coexist. Frightening thought."

I know she's trying to dissuade me, and it's rather ironic. I'm usually the one trying to convince her of this and that. But once I made up my mind to break free from the questions plaguing me since our father's death, endorphins kicked in like I'd just had a double chocolate malt over at Steak 'n Shake. It was exhilarating. From that moment, I knew this decision, out of character as it might seem to her, was right. At least I hope so.

Anyway, Daddy wanted this for us a long time ago. I slow my packing just enough to catch my sister's eye. "Come with me."

"No."

"Please?"

"Right. I have two solid job interviews lined up this week—in the other direction."

I tie a ribbon around my stack of blouses and set them into the deepest part of my suitcase. "You can storm Manhattan later."

Silence.

I look up. "Isn't that true?"

"What does it matter where the interviews are?"

I pause. "I thought working in Manhattan is what you've always wanted."

"What I want is to get out of here." Mel looks away, and

all packing comes to a halt. "So I'm not exactly headed to Manhattan for the interviews."

I lean my head to one side. "Where then?"

"Near Manhattan."

"Is that like off-Broadway?"

She hesitates before finally continuing. "More like Brooklyn."

I place a handful of hairpins and claws into my suitcase, then sink into the quilt stretched across my bed, carefully plotting out what to say next to my strong-willed sister. I've no intention of leaving without my sisters but am at a loss over how exactly to convince them to come. Still . . . I'm a leader; I can do this. They both thought Daddy was delirious at the end . . . I wondered sometimes too. "I'm sure it's a good starter job, Mel, but not your dream, right? There'll be other jobs. Better ones. So why waste time on these? Come with us. You'll love being in California again."

"What makes you think that? All I remember of the California coast is the cold wind and Mom's tears." She picks up a ceramic lighthouse from my dresser and scowls at it. "I've never even thought of going back there."

My chin snaps up. "Really? Never? I think about it all the time." I pause, a catch forming at the base of my throat. "Obviously, my memories of our life back then are very different from yours."

Mel sets the lighthouse down with a *thunk*, nearly knocking over my autographed photo of Eliza Carlton, and sending my deck of Hearst Castle cards tumbling. She turns and flips a lock of hair behind one shoulder. "Which makes you right and me wrong."

Why did she always accuse me of insulting her? "I didn't say that. All I meant was that I remember how happy Dad was when we lived there. Remember how he used to take us down to the tide pools all the time and point out sea stars and urchins and everything?"

"Barely."

"Well, I do. I want that feeling again—to smell that salty air and feel the bite of cool when we're at the beach."

"Yeah, well, you'd better stay out of that water or you'll be feeling the bite of something else."

I exhale a tiny laugh.

She sighs. "Does this have anything to do with your breakup with Trent? Maybe you should stick around and defrag awhile, so you can figure out the right way to patch up the best thing that ever happened to you."

"That hurt."

"Sorry. It just sounds like you're in denial. Why else would you be running off in search of this far-fetched serendipity? Really, Tara, take my advice and stay around to face your life."

Frustration, like bile, rises up, clawing at my nerve endings. For most of my life I've done little else but deal with situations that no one else wanted to face. Every family holiday, for instance, Mom has said, "Plan whatever you like,

Tara. I'm easy to please." Sure, she's easy—as is everyone else when they're not saddled with the tasks involved in putting together a dinner for a dozen relatives and their stray invitees.

I swallow my annoyance, the taste bordering on bitterness as it goes down. Yet I'm not about to allow my sister's poisonous attitude to ruin my new start. "I've never felt so free in my life," I tell Mel, "and I'm cherishing the moment. Besides, we have no reason to stay here now—no Mom, no job . . . no house. This is the perfect time to make a change, and frankly, I don't want us to miss out." I rub my hand over the soft quilted squares beneath me. "And another thing, maybe you remember Mom crying because she didn't want to leave. I know I didn't. Have you thought of that?"

Mel does that staring thing, code for "I'm thinking." She calmly draws in a breath before answering me. "How do you propose to talk Camille into this anyway? You didn't plan on leaving our baby cousin here, did you? If you think it's tough to convince me to take your little romanticized trip to the Pacific Ocean, you know she'll give you a hard time. That girl dreams about Friday nights at the IHOP, and losing that might just send her over the edge."

It's just not right to make fun of people, but Mel has something there. Camille's world revolves around her social life, and to question whether she's ever thought of setting her petite tootsies outside of our Dexton, well I'd say the answer would have to be "no way."

Actually it's her friends who'll suffer most when we leave. For the baby of the family who has no problem acting the part, when it comes to her many friends, she's more of a leader. She wants to go skating on Saturday afternoon? They go. Ice cream after dark? Sure thing. Back-to-back chick flicks? Let's.

I wind my hair into a ponytail, hold it on top of my head with one hand, and lean back, trying to shut out Mel's obvious skepticism. "I know it seems like this is a snap decision on my part, but I've been longing to rediscover our old life again for some time. Just never thought Mom could bear to see us go, so I always put the thoughts aside. As for Camille, she's been so aimless lately. How long can you hang out in your high school friend's garage without looking like you'll never amount to anything?"

Mel gasps. "That's harsh."

"Sorry. Just the way I see it."

"Actually, I agree with you—imagine that. Let me ask you, though, why move? Why not go for a couple of weeks, see some sights, then come on home to Missouri? Moving there, that's mighty adventurous for my big sister—my well-organized, logical, big sister."

"A year. Mom and Derrick will be gone that long, so I figured we could go . . . on an extended vacation. I've got enough savings to last at least a month, and then, if, well, then I'll find work." I don't mention the small trust fund Dad set up for each one of us girls.

"So even you're not convinced this will be permanent."

I hate it when she reads me. My enthusiasm's quickly ebbing away, and I consider just giving up on her. Might be easier on me, but I give it one more try. "We can fly to Los Angeles first, take a quick drive down Sunset Boulevard, see the Hollywood sign, do some 'star' watching. You're always saying what a city girl at heart you are, so you'd love this. I'm sure of it. Will you come?"

That divide between her brows grows deeper. I hold my breath. Finally, she looks up. "Sorry." Her voice has an uncharacteristic crack in it. "I've got my dreams too, and I guess it's time to follow them. Anyway. I'm glad you'll be watching over Camille. She needs your . . ."

Go ahead, say it. Mel thinks I'm bossy and has never let any opportunity to tell me so pass her by.

"Guidance."

Disappointed, I let go of my hair and crash onto the bed.

WE TOUCH DOWN AT LAX at precisely 9:02 a.m. California time, our pilot earning another point in his on-time record. I release my grip on the armrest, and glance over at Camille who had been reading old text messages on and off for hours. When not fiddling with her cell phone, she spent the duration of our airtime flirting with an attendant named Blaise, tapping her ergonomic crochet hook, and tearing cute clothing ads out of the in-flight magazine.

Now that we're landing, her head bobs against the seat rest as we taxi along the runway, while one ear bud dangles against her forearm. Her snores are masked by the rush of rubber against pavement.

Claire, the woman I've sat next to for the past three and a half hours, stares out the window at the haze. I'd booked the two end seats, hoping that no one would occupy the middle chair, but the plan backfired when the airline began taking standbys. Instead of making Claire, a writer from the Midwest, sit between Camille and me, I offered her the window. Not sure why I bothered since she seemed fixated on me for most of the flight. My life story will probably show up in one of her novels.

She turns to me as we sit on the runway, waiting for clearance to our gate. "Are you excited? Quite an adventure you are about to embark on."

I lean back, resigned to the wait, an unexpected thrill rippling through my chest. We're finally here. Well, almost. I didn't want to fly on a small plane, so we'll be renting a car in Los Angeles and heading north. But really, we're almost, nearly, finally here. "I'm more excited than I realized I would ever be."

"I will be praying for you and your cousin, dear. I hope it's everything you've dreamed."

Her tone causes me to sit and question her with a look. "Oh, it will be. I've no doubt."

"And what if it isn't?" She pauses. "What then?"

"Well, for one thing, I don't let that thought enter my mind. I believe that thinking positively really can affect the outcome of our situations." Hence, the reason I've blocked every pain-filled thought of Trent from my head and heart.

She's quiet, so I continue. "It's like Eliza always says . . ."

Claire frowns. "Eliza?"

"Carlton. Eliza Carlton. You know, from the soap *Quartz Point?*" I smile at the confused look on her face. "Okay, I admit it. I'm slightly addicted to *Soaps Weekly Digest* on the Internet, but everybody has some vice. I don't drink much, and I've never lit up any kind of smoke, but I catch up on my favorite soaps every night. Don't judge me."

My seatmate laughs, the hearty sound doing what the noise of wheels landing on tarmac could not seem to manage: wake Camille. Claire and I look over at my groggy cousin, and Claire has the grace not to mention the trail of drool staining Camille's chin.

"I wouldn't think of judging you! That would invite all sorts of trouble, now wouldn't it?" She laughs again. "Jesus says I'd have to take the plank out of my own eye first!"

I shrug. "If you say so."

The voice of our pilot alerting the flight attendants that we're about to taxi to our gate slices the air above us. Silence settles over us as the plane's belly rumbles beneath our feet. Soon that familiar bell rings to let us know that we've arrived, setting off a cacophony of sounds: clicking metal, the crank of overhead bins being opened, children asking a myriad questions, a lone baby's cry.

As I roust Camille, Claire touches my arm. "I've enjoyed your company, Tara. Very much. Have a blessed trip together, you and that precious cousin of yours."

Camille stifles a burp as she yawns. She hunches her shoulders and gives me a guilty grimace.

"Thanks, Claire." I smile at her, as she gathers up a stack of books she never had a chance to read. "I've enjoyed talking to you too."

Outside I breathe in the smoggy LA air, its smoky haze a sign that we're just a few short hours from our destination. I settle my sights on the concrete garages stacked like government housing. They hold cars for thousands of people just like me, people traveling to far-off places in search of something better or a long ago memory, or just something *else*. Like I imagine them to feel, I can't wait to see what lies at the end of this road.

Chapter Four

Nothing has changed. Well, almost nothing. More inns than I remember line the meandering road that abuts the beach, and I don't recall ever seeing that sculpture of frolicking otters nestled in among the pines as we entered Otter Bay—you'd think that as a six-year-old I would have taken note of such a thing—and the area appears much smaller than I had envisioned it . . .

But otherwise, nothing has changed.

It's Sunday morning, and the ocean beyond me rolls and stretches as if it slept in late too. Camille still slumbers beneath a pile of blankets in our cozy room at the inn, but I couldn't wait and headed out for a walk at the first burst of light. The air surprises me with its sharp chill, and yet mingled scents of pine and scrub and ocean wrap themselves around me like a welcome-back hug, comforting me. I stop and rest against a wooden railing, the only thing standing between me and a rocky cliff hanging over the sea.

My cell vibrates against my bum, where I've stored it in my pocket, and a quiver of guilt creeps in. I realized on my walk this morning that I should've been straight with Camille about this trip. She may act young and seemingly directionless, but she deserves to know that while we always have Missouri to fall back on, now that I'm finally here, well, I don't want to leave.

Being here again after so much time away, immersed in the familiar smells and the warmth of the town of my birth, makes me want to pull out the yellow pages and find someone, somewhere, who remembers the Sweet family. Mother was vague about that prospect—too many years had passed, she said—but I suppose that a woman in love who is about to embark on the adventure of her life with a man as vigorous as Derrick might have other things on her mind.

Don't go there. I open my phone. "Good morning, Camille."

"Hey," she says, her voice groggy. "I'm kinda hungry. You coming back soon?"

"I could."

"Okay. Hurry, 'cuz I'm starved."

I slide the phone into the pocket of my windbreaker. She went from hungry to starving awfully fast. She can eat six square meals a day and not gain an ounce. Definitely unfair.

Julie Carobini

After one last look at the water, I head back along the narrow boardwalk to the old inn we checked into last evening. Betty, the elderly clerk at the Bayside, as the lodge is known, couldn't hand us the key fast enough. We should have been here by afternoon, but Camille had wanted to "star" watch in Malibu, then splurge in some of the shops and grab some Chai on the famed State Street in Santa Barbara. By the time we made it this far north, we had eaten our way through much of Southern California, and I for one had little energy left for anything but sleep. I awoke this morning, tucked into crisp sheets wearing nothing but my undies, proving once again that I'm doing all sorts of new things these days.

Camille stops me at the door of our room. "Yippee! You're here. Let's eat." We walk back outside and around the corner to a small diner attached to the inn. Inside, the Red Abalone Grill gleams.

As I glance around for the hostess, Camille grabs my wrist, her eyes wide and dramatic. "Do you smell that or what! This place is my new best friend, Tara. C'mon, let's find a seat."

We slide into a padded booth, and a waitress with strawberry blonde spirals flits by carrying a coffee pot and a contented smile. She pauses just long enough to drop off two menus before sliding from table to table in our row, pouring coffee and refilling creamer bowls with stash from the front pocket of her apron.

Camille shuts her menu. "So I'll have the large stack with the Texas scramble . . . and two crêpes with the silky cherry sauce."

"Really?"

"Yeah, the crêpes aren't on the menu, but I saw them on the board when we came in. Over there."

She points at a white board situated above a counter that's one part retro, one part country, and one part diner dive: Formica top with aluminum trim, oak-trimmed stools, and the customary red and yellow condiment bottles for accent. The eclectic décor hasn't done a thing to dissuade customers, as nearly every stool is filled. A portly woman moves fast, like an overstuffed hummingbird, delivering meals and shouting orders to the cooking crew behind another taller counter.

Our waitress appears with pad in hand, and Camille's ready. While she rattles off her man-sized order of carbs, I glance out the window in time to see a spray of surf ricochet off a collection of boulders. Some of the droplets land in spots on the flat dirt pad at the edge of the street and some on a jogger running by, who tries without success to dodge them. He's about the same height and build as Trent and, for just a moment, I think I'm homesick.

A silence-shattering crash of dishware, followed by a string of words fit for cable TV startles us. Our waitress yelps, shoves her order pad into a pocket, and quickly excuses herself.

Camille grunts. "That didn't sound good."

I nod, distracted by the noise, and it's then that I notice him. Has he been in here all along? Just as our waitress flies kitchenward, the man springs from his stool and in one leap lands behind the counter, his black T-shirt molded to his back and pulled taut between his shoulder blades. When he squats below the counter, a few wavy tufts of golden hair peek out over the top.

Camille leans across the table until I can smell the citrus fragrance of her shampoo. "Hot guy alert. Is he some kind of superhero, or what?"

I shake my head, still aware of the growing commotion going on behind that counter. "Maybe someone's really hurt back there."

When I move to stand, Camille places a hand on mine. "C'mon, don't, Tara. We're on vacation. Let someone else help out for awhile." She glances toward the kitchen where a group has gathered, their faces focused downward. "Looks like they've got plenty of help over there anyway. We'd just be in the way."

I chew the inside of my lip. Camille still thinks we're just visiting. Enjoying a long respite. This is not *my* intent, of course, and I do want her to take part in the decision to make Otter Bay our new home. Eventually. Anyway, until we decide this for certain together, she's right, we *are* just on vacation. Still, what could it hurt to walk over and just make sure that whoever's on that floor right now will be able to get back up?

"Be back in just a second, Cam."

She blows out a stream of air. "All right, but while you're over there, at least grab the coffee pot for me, 'kay?"

There, sprawled out behind the counter in her comfortable shoes, is the dear little old lady I'd seen bustling about earlier. Poor thing.

Superhero man's face hovers over hers. "Stay still, Peg. The guys are on their way with the ambulance."

She reaches upward, and I think she's about to whisper that she's in pain, or maybe cough out a thank-you. Instead, her voice surges from the chaos. "You tell those lamebrains not to track sand all over my restaurant. And Jorge? Jor-*ge!*"

Our waitress leans across the taller counter and calls to a stocky cook, who scurries toward the woman on the ground. "Yes, ma'am?"

"What are you waiting for? A tsunami? This isn't the entertainment hour! Get those orders out—and don't let Holly mess with my recipes!"

He salutes. "Yes, ma'am."

Our waitress, whose tag announces she's the Holly with a penchant for dabbling with recipes, dabs her eyes with a napkin.

"Can I help with anything?" I ask.

"Oh, would you? Here." Holly hands me the coffee carafe, and I think I can hear Camille whooping it up from across the diner. "Would you refill customers' cups?"

I blink and glance around. "You want me to . . . ?" I've never worked in a restaurant, or any other service-oriented business. Ever. Not that the idea hadn't ever appealed to me. I've been told that like other little girls I once owned a plastic cash register and regularly borrowed cereal boxes and canned goods from my mother's cupboards, all to supply the store set up in the living room on school-free days. Yet whenever I applied for a job, even as a teenager, management would point me toward a desk and phone, or an inventory sheet, or toward empty shelves that needed stocking. They told me I was reliable, hardworking, sturdy. Always wanted to question that last one, but figured it was a compliment so I never did say anything.

The waitress smiles at me, hope in her eyes, so I take the pot from her hand. "Sure, I can do that."

She sniffles. "Thanks."

I'm not even two steps along before finding a plain white mug thrust toward my face. "Oh, okay, here you are." I pour and manage not to splash on the man's hairy hand.

"You new here?" Several days of uneven gray stubble blanket the man's face.

Is he kidding? I hesitate, and glance over my shoulder. "Did you see . . . ? Are you aware of what's going on back . . . ?"

His tiny, colorless eyes have not left my face and it occurs to me that he's single-minded. From behind him, among the booths, a hand raises. I glance over at a rambunctious family of six squished around a table for four. The father of the group gives me a weary smile and raises his cup, and I move to give him the refill he so obviously needs.

"Whoa now"—the old man stops me again—"don't be gone long now, you hear? You just keep that hot pot comin' . . . along with that smile o' yours." He bares teeth that are yellow and uneven as a homemade haircut.

Oh, brother. It's not that I can't handle him or this pot of coffee in my hand, unfamiliar as the sensation may be. I've dealt with plenty of blustering customers in my job—in my *old* job—as the accounts receivable rep for Hudson's Auto Parts back in Dexton. By the time I have to give them a call, their accounts are more than forty-five days past due and they're in no mood to talk with me.

So why does my face feel as hot as a sizzling fry pan at the moment?

Camille appears at my elbow. "What are you *doing?*" she hisses in my ear. I smile and nod at an elderly man in a felt beret who's playing solitaire in a corner booth. Camille skips along to keep up with me as I slosh coffee into waiting cups as if I've been doing this my entire life. "Just helping. Go sit until . . . oh look, the ambulance is here."

Camille's eyes perk as two boyish paramedics enter the restaurant. "Gotta go . . . help."

Right.

Curiosity has placed its grip on me too, so I follow her toward the chaotic scene behind the counter. Besides, the coffee pot I'm carrying needs to be refilled. Before I can get there, though, a tug on the back of my blouse nearly pulls me over and when I spin around, the stainless steel pot smacks into the superhero who'd leaped over the counter to help the woman who had fallen.

I gasp.

He holds up both palms and releases a subtle "oomph."

I find his eyes, and they seem to question me, traveling from my face, down to the carafe in my hand, and back up until they meet my eyes.

I force words from a mouth suddenly gone dry. "S-sorry. Didn't mean to bump you."

He opens his mouth as if to say something when we're interrupted by an irritable voice—and another tug at the back of my shirt. "Wait your turn, slugger. I had her first."

I break eye contact with superhero guy and turn to see the grizzled man with his yellow teeth giving me a disconcerting mixture of scowl and smirk.

"Excuse me, sir, but did you just grab my clothes?"

"Like that, did you?"

I grip the coffee pot tighter. Otherwise I might brain the guy with it. That's when Eliza Carlton's fully made-up face appears in my mind, along with her admonishment to do as she would do. *Go ahead, unleash your inner kick butt girl . . . but do it with confidence. Instill healthy fear.*

Easier said than carried out. Kicking butt is not my problem. I had the highest rate of paid bills over at Hudson's. One call from me and most payments came in within a day, or most certainly within the week. But fear me? Highly unlikely. What *is* likely is that customers grew tired of me. I could hear it in their voices, or worse, see it on the faces of those unlucky souls whose bosses would rather send their gopher to drop off past-due payments than spring for a stamp.

My irascible customer dangles his mug from three fingers, and I realize that I'm the one who's tired. Tired of men who tell me what to do, who believe that one call from them, or one summons—or one grab of my clothes—will have me spinning.

"Refill, gorgeous?" he growls.

Slowly, as if Eliza is my acting coach, I feel myself bend at the waist. I lean one elbow on the counter, rest my chin in my hand, and set the carafe down with the other. The man's eyes are mere inches from mine. When a waft of his stale coffee-breath assaults my nose, I nearly lose character, but then quickly shake it off. "You know something, fella?"

His yellow smile broadens. "What's that?"

"I wouldn't lift a finger for you if I hadn't a dime in my purse and you were the only customer left on this big ol' earth."

His icky smile fades, and in its place I see acquiescence. And a flash of respect.

I straighten, both stunned by my behavior and awed by the results of Eliza's advice. When I turn around, resident superhero still stands behind me, only his head leans to one side, like I'm an algebraic equation he just can't figure out. He sends me a lopsided smirk, one thick brow cocked upward, and that's when something else that Eliza always says pops into my head:

Confidence rocks, baby.

Chapter Five

Camille's tinkling laughter punctuates the din, and my sanity returns.

"What was *that*? What happened to my sane and, sorry to say this but, *boring* cousin?" She's rocking forward and back, her hands in a praying position in front of her merry little lips. "This is huge."

I twist toward her in an effort to make this a private conversation. "Shush. More coffee?"

Camille snorts just as Holly bustles over smoothing a cascade of curls, which promptly flop forward as she pulls her hand away. She rests both hands on narrow hips and says, "Well. Things'll be a changin' around here." She raises her chin toward the superhero, whose eyesight is fixed out the window following the ambulance as it ambles out of the drive. "Thanks so much, Josh, for handlin' her. Not sure what I would've done without you to soothe that woman's nerves."

He moves his gaze from the window. "Only did what I'm trained for. And you would have done fine without me. Peg's like a mother to you."

"Eh. I love her, you know, but she can be such a pill."

He touches her shoulder. "I know, and I know." He makes eye contact with me, his acknowledgment sending a startling quake through my belly. I've always been drawn to dark-haired men, religiously so, and my reaction to him and his golden locks startles me.

That rumble in my stomach slows but he doesn't linger after nodding at Camille and me, saying, "Ladies," before heading away.

Holly turns to us. "You girls were lifesavers too. I don't even know you, but there you were. How about I have Jorge fix you a nice breakfast, on the house?"

"That's not necessary," I begin, but Camille grabs my elbow.

Holly smiles. "Go on now and sit down. I'll be right over."

Much of the diner has cleared out, all except for the few customers who have wandered in pleasantly unaware of the drama that recently unfolded. Thankfully, the letch at the counter hobbled out before I had the chance to do something even more rash. The beret-wearing gentleman still sits in a corner booth, and as our old table is now occupied, we slide into a spot next to him. He's staring at a hand of cards spread before him.

Camille's gaze follows Josh as he hops into his truck just outside our window. The corner of her mouth quirks. "I think I'm gonna like this place."

"He's too old for you."

"But not for you, Tara." She winks. "Although he's kind of tortured . . . like an artist. Do you think he paints or something?"

"Such imagination."

Our elderly neighbor cuts in. "A fireman."

"Excuse me?"

"The man you were speaking of is a fireman. One of the bravest there is."

Camille falls back against the padded booth. "Perfect! You, Miss Careful herself, with the likes of a super-hot fireman. They run into burning buildings, you know."

I fix a scowl on my face, the same kind of expression my mother should have put on when Camille would drink straight from the jug of iced tea. I hated that it was somehow my job to deal with that. Anyway, it doesn't work. Her cackling reminds me of Mel's whenever Trent and I would arrive home from the bowling alley, flush with victory. I shake my head.

The man wears a contented smile and cups his coffee mug. "May I ask you something . . . Tara, is it?

Camille, whose back is to him, wiggles her eyebrows. I ignore her. "Of course, what can I do for you?"

"I have this hand here"—he points to the cards, that until now I hadn't paid close attention to, and I see that he's midway through a game of solitaire—"and I'm perplexed about which move to make at this juncture."

Camille and I exchange the briefest of glances before I slide out of the booth. "May I?"

He nods, and I sit across from him. The cards are, of course, upside down to me, but somehow this is not a problem.

"I have this spot open here." He taps the table where a card is supposed to be. "I can move one of my kings there, but I have two available to me and it is not quite clear which one is better suited for that spot."

He has a point. He's involved in a basic game of Klondike, like Dad and I used to play when the weather became too cold to do anything but sit in front of the fire and entertain ourselves with cards. He should have seven piles of cards across, but he's already down to six and needs to fill in a spot.

Camille pipes up. "Just play eeny-meeny to figure out which one to move."

"You'll have to excuse her"—I offer a slight shake of my head—"she hasn't had her breakfast yet."

My cousin snorts, but it comes out like a dainty breath. "Mom always plays it that way."

The old gentleman's eyes sparkle and he bows his head. "The name's Nigel. Forgive my impropriety."

"I'm Tara, and this is my sister, Camille." No sense giving a thorough explanation of our relationship to a stranger.

"Your sister? Yes, yes. I see the resemblance. A pleasure to meet you both."

"And you as well. As far as which choice to make, you could go either way, but if it were me, I'd move this king here." I tap one of the cards.

"I see." With slow, deliberate momentum, Nigel sits upright and pushes himself back from the table. He watches me, his eyes gently creased at the corners. Except for those slight folds, his face is smooth as a baby's. "So you think that would be the better choice? The safer one?"

Camille laughs. "Yeah, that's Tara. We can always rely on her to take the safe way."

I laugh like I've been slapped on the back. Hard. "Well, you *could* move the other king, but if there's no usable card beneath it, you'll be stuck. Whereas if you take the king from this smaller stack," I rest my hand across the cards, "then you'll have a better chance of keeping this game going."

Nigel chuckles. "I believe you," as he moves his king. I begin to slide from the booth when he stops me with a show of his palm. "I wonder if you two will join me. I would like to—"

Holly appears with plates of crêpes, eggs for me, a Texas scramble for Camille, and bacon for both of us. "Here you

go, ladies. Fresh from the kitchen. I'll just put these at
Nigel's table." Camille slides into the booth next to me.
"I hope you like it, 'cuz Jorge was pretty rushed back there.
He wanted to make you some of his Belgian waffles, too,
but I told him, 'Jorge, those girls are skinny like rails!
There's no place for them to put all that food!' But if I'm
wrong, you just go on and tell me and I'll have him whip
some up for you."

Camille stops our waitress before she goes. "Did you
make that on a hairpin lace loom?"

Holly touches the fabric tied around her waist. "Sure did.
You like it? It's really just a scarf, but I'm usin' it like a belt.
Tryin' to dress things up around here."

Camille's eyes light up. "I love it."

Holly turns to go. "Well, too bad you girls are just passin'
through or I'd show you how to make one for yourself."

As Holly heads for the kitchen, I reach for the salt. "You
were going to say something, Nigel?"

His gaze follows Holly, as if still contemplating her use of
a scarf for a belt. He snaps out of his trance. "It was nothing
important."

Camille digs in, and an all-too familiar uneasiness settles
over me that I just can't process. What in the world am
I doing here? Wasn't it just yesterday that Camille and I rolled
into this familiar old town? And now here we sit, having a
free breakfast with a stranger. I suppress a twitter. This very
situation reminds me of the time that Eliza Carlton's Harley

broke down in the sultry desert. She managed to find a kindly shopkeeper who offered her an iced coffee and a soft place to lay her head.

Of course, the drink had been drugged and she soon found herself groggy and locked in the shop's pantry. She might have died there had she not concocted a way to jimmy the lock with a rusty can opener.

Nigel stirs his tea. "I've got a proposition for you, Tara."

I blink twice.

"I'd like to hire you."

Camille's fork stops.

I mentally erase my daydream. Of all the things this gentle, beret-wearing man might say to me, offering employment never came to mind. And despite the touch of unease I'd experienced only moments ago, the idea of finding a nice quiet job here in my birth town sends a wave of calm right through me. I shrug off the sensation, though, because Camille and I've been in this tiny coastal town less than twenty-four hours. How would it look, my setting down roots? We should at least give the extended vacation idea a try.

Then again, maybe Nigel runs an Internet business and needs someone to work behind a computer. I can do that from anywhere.

He folds his hands on the table in front of him like a polite young man asking for a favor. "An employee of mine is about to go out on maternity leave, and I believe you would quite competently handle her job at my inn."

His declaration hits me like a splash of sea water. "Your inn? I've never met anyone who owns an inn before."

He nods. "It has been in my mother's family for many years. I am the last, I'm afraid. My sister Judy operated it until just a few years ago when she took ill and passed on. I returned to Otter Bay after many years away to become the proprietor. I can only hope to continue running it for many years to come."

"No children, then?"

"I'm afraid not."

"Where is your inn, Nigel?"

"It's the one you and your sister are staying in— The Bayside."

"Really? It's lovely." *And cheap.*

"It's old."

I laugh lightly. "Well, it's weathered, and there's something poetic about that."

Camille quirks a brow. Her lips are coated with shiny syrup. Silently I beg her not to open her crêpe-filled mouth, but I've little hope that my soundless warning will reach her. Old habits are the hardest to break.

"What are you talking about, Tara?"

I glance at my cousin. Is she ready to hear about some of my long-held, hidden desires? Am I ready to let them out of their box? I exhale.

"I've always been drawn to the idea of staying along the coast in a time-worn inn that holds a secret past, you know

that." *At least, I think she knows that.* I laugh at the daft look
on Camille's face, and it feels good to let my emotions ride
high. It's been a long time. "Not that the Bayside has any
secrets, mind you. But the idea of it feels very romantic and
otherworldly. So many people have come and stayed and gone
again, and you have to wonder what some of their stories
might have been. What kind of baggage did they come with,
that disappeared with the waves? Does that make sense? Do
you know what I mean?"

Camille sets down her fork. "What I think is that you
needed this vacation more than we all thought."

My face heats and I avoid Nigel's stare. "What do you
mean, 'more than we all thought'? Who's *we*?"

She shrugs. "Mel and me. And Trent."

I stand. "Trent? You've been talking to him behind . . .
behind my back? Why would you do that?"

Her eyes widen, and her gaze escapes toward the window. "He says he broke up with you for your own good. He
says he really cares about you, but that you needed some,
um, shaking up." Camille's eyes come back to mine. "I told
him I thought that was mean—if that helps any. Don't be
mad, Tare-tare."

A thick ball of emotion lodges in my throat, and even
Camille's term of endearment for me won't dissolve it.
"I can't believe my family betrayed me. You all did, talking
with him. He's been promising me a ring for how many years
now? I believed in him and . . ." I glance over at Nigel, and

drop down again next to Camille. "I'm so sorry to be talking about this in front of you, Nigel. So much for secrets. My sister and I will finish this conversation later, but I do want to thank you for your offer of employment. I'm flattered."

He nods again. "Well then, I hope you will consider it."

"Well, no, I'm sorry, but that won't be possible. We're just on vacation." I say the word through gritted teeth, because this is hardly the respite I'd planned. What else have my sisters said about me? And do I really want to know? "Besides, I've never done the books for an inn."

"Oh, I hadn't planned to ask you to work with my accounting."

"No? Of course not. How could you have known what kind of work I'm qualified for? I suppose perhaps you wanted me to clean rooms then, but I've no exper—"

Camille squeaks. "A maid?"

I turn to growl at her. "It's honest work. And I put a high price on honesty."

"Ladies." We both look at Nigel. "Tara, I think you'd be a welcome addition to my front desk staff. I watched you serving the customers here just a half hour ago, and you have a marvelous way with people."

He stuns me with his gracious assessment. I've been in the background longer than the backup singers on *American Idol*. Like them, I've known that this was my place, and I've held that knowledge as my own badge of honor. There's nothing wrong with working behind the scenes. Somebody has to do it, or else those at the front will suffer, and then the entire production will fall apart. Not that working the front desk of an inn is any great triumph. I've just never had anyone pluck me out of a crowd and put me in a spot where customers could see me first. Doesn't he know the danger in that?

He continues. "I noticed that your reservation was open-ended, causing me to wonder if perhaps you and your sister might be in town for an extended time. I do hope you will reconsider."

I open my mouth to end this conversation, when Camille reaches for my hand. "Take the job." Something fierce forms in her expression, as if any resistance from me will be pushed back. She suddenly looks very much the adult she is becoming.

This, however, won't keep me from trying. "Oh, Camille, I'm not in the market for a new job." *Yet.*

Her brows arch. "I know you think I'm flighty, but I'm not stupid, Tara. I know how much you want to stay here."

"You mean how much you and Mel and *Trent* think I need to stay here."

She rustles her curls with a quick shake of her head. "None of 'em think you need more than a vacation. Trent'll be the most surprised, because he even figured you'd come running back after seeing that there really wasn't anything all that special here." She glances out the window to watch as the two paramedics who came in earlier—one with a particularly deep tan—stroll in, probably on break. Camille glances back at me with a curvy smile. "I don't agree with them."

Had I not been so self-absorbed, I might have smiled back at my flirty cousin, but all I could think of was that Trent expected me to come home a changed woman. As if planning my life around his for the past five years hadn't convinced him that he should love me as I am.

I straighten my shoulders and meet Nigel's gaze. "When would you need me to start?"

Chapter Six

Nigel very kindly allowed me a week to kick around Otter Bay before I'd need to report for my new part-time duties as front-desk clerk for his inn. In that time, we picked up an old red Mustang cheap, solely because Camille campaigned for something cute and colorful—in this case, apple red—and a far cry from the four-door gray Nissan I sold to our former neighbor's mother before moving out here. What I've noticed most about our new ride is the way it boisterously announces our presence even before we reach our destination.

Also this week we found plenty of time to wet our toes in our new, old hometown. Camille and I wandered along the foot-worn paths that led to cliffs so battered by waves that natural stairways have been created in the rock. I missed

Mel more than I let on to Camille, but I knew how much she'd hate all this frolicking in the great outdoors.

Until today. Today we came upon a cove protected by overhanging rock and shallow tides, and so brimming with vibrant purple urchins and golden sea stars that goose bumps alighted across my skin. I have the unmistakable sense that I've been here before. And if so, then Mel has surely been here too.

I check my watch. Her first interview is in an hour. The sure sound of a door slamming pulls my attention to the top of the cliff, and I glance up. Will the deserted spot I covet soon be invaded? No one appears, although it is tough to tell from beneath the bill of my baseball cap. All this sun is a new phenomenon, so I've been careful all week to shield my light skin from its assault.

Camille has removed her flip-flops, and now wades in a tide pool one rock formation over from me where rolling waves lap. I try, again, to remember this place, but all I can conjure are vague images, as if the pictures in my mind are veiled by sheens of running water. The briny smell of the ocean fills my senses, and I allow my eyes to flop shut in an effort to pull memories from my subconscious.

"The tide's rolling in, ladies."

My eyes jerk open, and I tip my head up just as a man lands not two feet from me in the thick sand. *So much for using the nature-made stairs.* From beneath my cap I can see that he appears to be ready for a hike in the nearby redwood forest with his battered hiking boots, scarred denims, and long-sleeved tee. His eyes crinkle as he narrows them, staring out after Camille. "Can she swim?"

There's a familiar smoothness to his voice. It's the firefighter who hopped the counter at the Red Abalone Grill last week to rescue the fallen owner.

"Y-yes, of course." *Why* am I stammering? "We all learned how when we were very young."

He doesn't look at me but stands with arms crossed and feet apart, much like a security guard might if he was, say, protecting the stage door for one Eliza Carlton. I almost expect him to turn his head to one side and whisper into a mic.

"It's a good thing," he says. "Although this isn't the kiddie pool at the Y. That water may look calm, but it can be unforgiving. You might want to tell . . ."

"My sister."

"You might want to caution your sister about the tides. They can be dangerous if you're not used to them."

Do we look like country bumpkins? "She's good. I know, because I taught her myself."

He's unimpressed, still standing there like he's keeping watch. The only thing missing is a pair of red lifeguard trunks. His presence has set my relaxed beach walk on edge and resentment settles in my back, its rigid tension crawling up my spine. Trent always seemed to know what was best for me too.

"Watch for algae that spreads over the rocks. Green, slippery stuff. She wouldn't be the first young woman to need stitches after a fall off the rocks."

"Mm-hm. Okay, thanks, but she'll be fine." *You can go now.* "When we lived in Missouri, we swam in the Lake of the Ozarks often. More miles of shoreline at the lake than the entire state of California—and I'm not kidding."

"And does the lake have swells like that?" He flicks his well-defined chin upward and out toward an east-facing wave that's gaining height and speed as it moves toward us.

I pry my lips apart. "Camille! Tide's coming in!"

She swishes her face in my direction and in a flash, her expression changes from annoyance to open delight. Apparently she's noticed who has joined us on the sand. I only wish I could express the same emotion about Josh's looming presence. We watch her stepping gingerly across the uneven surface, and I try to say something to break the silence. However, the annoying sensation of butterflies careening inside my stomach forces me to keep my mouth closed, lest one escape in the form of an awkward moment.

Camille hops down from the rock in front of us, her bare legs encrusted with wet sand. "Hey there, Mr. Fireman," she says, casual as a long time friend. "Thank you for saving my life."

Oh, Camille.

A dark shadow flows over Josh's face, his smile thin

and strained. "Enjoy your day, ladies." He turns to go, but Camille stops him.

"Leaving so soon?" She gives me a smile filled with innocence, though I know better. "My sister and I could really use a tour guide. We've seen just about all we could of this dinky town on our own. Isn't that right, Tare-Tare?"

He takes up his security guard stance again. "Have you been up to the castle yet?"

He's talking about the famed Hearst Castle, built by newspaper magnate William Randolph Hearst. My only brush with the tourist attraction is the tattered stack of cards my father and I once played with. Cards that have stayed cold, on my dresser back in Missouri, since his death.

Camille wrinkles her nose. "Boring." She looks to me, wide-eyed. "But Tara loves that kind of stuff. Hey, why don't you two go together?"

A tightrope of silence tugs between us until I'm able to draw in a breath. "She's kidding. Leave the man alone. I'm sure he didn't come here to be recruited for anything."

Camille ignores me but watches Josh. "So why are you here? Is this a hangout for firemen or something?" She cranes her neck in order to take a peek up the cliff. "Ya got anyone else up there with you?"

His cool expression falters but recovers. His gaze flicks off into the translucent horizon. "Don't come here all that much. It's just a place I know. I'm on my own today."

The sparseness of his words tells me that he'd rather be alone in this tranquil spot than subject to Camille's flirtatious whim. Does he comes here often to shake off the day's grime, to refill after life has drained him? I can't blame him. And yet, as I take in the gentle crush of water against the rocks, something inside me hopes that his visit to this cove is rare.

I'd like to claim this place as my own.

Josh turns and gives us a succinct bow of his head. "Ladies." With that, he takes the uneven stair-like ledges up the cliff, several at a time.

"Wait!" Camille calls out after him. "You haven't been at the Red Abalone Grill in a while. Will we see you over there sometime soon?"

He pauses, and I have to squint into the sun to make out the quizzical expression that forms on his face before eventually breaking into a slight grin, a sight that should annoy me further and yet, much to my surprise, thrills me.

I just realized that, until this moment, he had no idea who we were.

EVERY MORNING FOR THE past week, before Camille and I set out to rediscover this hamlet of our youth, we first stopped into the Red Abalone Grill for breakfast. And no morning was the same. For one thing, each table has now been topped with a narrow vase stuffed with fresh wild-flowers of blue or lavender or yellow—and sometimes all three. For another, the once plain whiteboard has been replaced with an oak-framed chalk board that rests on an easel just outside the Grill's front doors. Holly's crêpes are listed on it, as are a plethora of new items not found on the menu, such as mango muffins, peach fritters, and my new favorite—peanut-butter smoothies. I've begun asking for this even when it's not listed.

Holly bustles around the place, her pouf curls pulled into a loose ponytail. While her aunt's been recovering from that nasty fall we all witnessed, the poor thing's been running the place herself. Well, she hasn't been completely alone. That's another thing that changes by day: the help. Apparently Holly has lots of friends, because each day a new coffee-pouring teen appears at our table to rattle off the specials, refill our mugs, and slip the bill under a plate. It's disconcerting not to be recognized when you've sat in the same spot for a week, and yet, sadly for me, not all that uncommon.

Holly rockets past, her sneakers slapping the linoleum, a flowing knit scarf flapping behind her before she halts and spins back toward us. She flops down beside Camille, tosses her ponytail off her shoulder, and exhales. "Can I join you two ladies?" she asks after the fact.

"Pretty wild day for you," I say.

"Yeah, you got that right. And it'll only get worse, 'cuz when Auntie finds out what I've done with her diner, I might just have to find me another job."

I start to chuckle, but quiet myself when no humor appears on her face. "I can't imagine anyone getting upset about the way you've run this place. Camille and I have been here every day—"

"I noticed."

Camille pipes up. "I don't even look at the menu anymore. Just play eeny-meeny with your specials, and I think those pumpkin-bourbon muffins are my favorite. This place should be in a magazine."

Holly exhales again. "Auntie's old-school 'bout that. Says if people want to hear about us, they'll listen to their friends. Problem is, most of those old battle-axes she cooks for want the same old thing: eggs with toast and some kind of meat."

Both girls stare at me. "*What?* My eggs are poached, and I bet most of your customers order them scrambled."

Holly glances off into nowhere. "Yeah, that and sunny-side-up. Every old one of 'em."

Camille's gaze meets mine. I open my mouth to speak when Josh strolls up to the counter. Before he takes a seat on a stool, he nods in my direction. I look away and clear my throat. "So, how's your aunt's recovery going?"

"Eh, she's fine. She carried on so much that they thought she broke her hip, but she's just sore. She's home now and in bed, trying to get over the sciatica from the fall."

Peg's fall. That day will be forever etched in my mind as *the* event that sent one sure-footed and forgetful fireman careening over the counter. *And into my mind.* I try to concentrate on my eggs, but realize that Camille looks bummed.

"So she'll be back soon?" my sister asks, no doubt foreseeing the loss of her beloved daily specials.

"Yeah. Don't think I'm ungrateful. My aunt raised me. I've been hangin' out in this diner since I was a tot, and lovin' nearly every minute of it. I just . . . I just would like to try new dishes sometimes. Jorge and I have had too much fun this week." She lowers her voice. "Don't tell my aunt. Wouldn't want her to think I'm glad for her pains—which I'm not."

Camille slaps the table. "That's it then! We'll vouch for you. I'd die if I had to eat the same ol', plain ol' every day." She darts me a stare. "And my sister starts her new job at the inn today, so she'll tell every one of those guests to get their behinds into this grill, and ask for the specials!"

Holly's face lights. "That's right. I heard Nigel went and hired you on. I thought you girls were just tourists, and then the next thing I know you're moving into town. Did you plan that? Oh, what am I saying, *of course* you planned it."

I rub my cheek. "Actually, we were both born here. I always wanted to come back to Otter Bay, but this is the first chance we could find to really do it." I don't tell her about our father's last wish, nor that I let my devotion to Trent, among other things, keep me from fulfilling it until now. "We planned for a long vacation with the hopes that—"

Camille rolls her eyes. "Don't fib, Tara. She wanted to move here from the minute our mother's new husband took

Mom away to Europe. And I was bored, so I figured why not? Always wanted to meet surfers anyway."

"Hah! You came to the right place then, girls. You do know they hang out right down the hill from here at surfer's ridge . . ." Holly proceeds to give Camille detailed directions on how to get there, who she knows, and where the best viewing spot is for taking in both the waves and the guys who master them. I, on the other hand, poke at my eggs with the tines of my fork, willing my gaze to stay away from the counter.

Last night I logged on to *Soaps Weekly Digest* and caught up on a week's worth of Eliza Carlton doings. If I were she, I wouldn't be chained to this table, listening needlessly to Holly and Camille carry on about boys who spend more time in water than at work. I wouldn't be convincing myself that poached eggs are mesmerizing enough to stare at for long lengths of time. I'd put my fork down, get up, and walk over to one handsome firefighter. I'd say hello and ask if the stool next to him was taken. And then I'd . . . I'd . . .

Hm. I just can't put myself into Eliza's "come hither" stilettos.

Both girls stare at me. "What? The eggs again?"

Camille snorts. "You had the stupidest grin on your face, Tara." She wags her head, then looks to Holly. "She's not been the same since we got here, I swear it."

"Please." Even without turning my head, I notice Josh dart out of the diner, like he was headed to a fire.

Holly raises her chin, her smile wide, but her laughter turns choked and garbled. Abruptly she rises from her seat in the booth and bangs her hip on the table, which jostles enough to send the bud vase tumbling over and its liquid contents spilling down through the seam in the center.

A powerful voice cuts through the diner's din. *"Hol-ly!"*

Ah. Apparently Holly's Aunt Peg, who's standing in the doorway waving a cane in the air, feels just fine.

Chapter Seven

 I didn't have much time to stick around this morning and watch drama unfold over at the RAG—that's the acronym the locals use for the Red Abalone Grill, though if you asked me, something a little more pleasing-sounding, like The Grill or The Red Abalone, might have drawn more business. But then, no one asked me.

I left Camille at breakfast and dashed off to dress for my afternoon of learning how to run the front desk of Nigel's quaint, though slightly worn, inn. After living in one of the inn's cheapest rooms—a viewless studio bordering the back parking lot—its flaws have become more apparent than I'd like to admit. This same thought might also apply to my relationship with Trent, but that too was something I'd prefer not to own up to at the moment.

I smooth back my hair, making sure the bun looks straight, and glance at the mirror. "What are you doing here, Tara May Sweet?" I ask myself for the umpteenth time before settling myself with a drawn-out breath and slipping out the door. Although our room hasn't many amenities, my stroll across the parking lot has plenty with its view of the vast blue sea. I take another quick peek, then enter the inn's lobby—and my new life.

"There you are!"

Tina, the uberpregnant front-desk clerk, the one I'm here to temporarily replace, stops me with her sharpness. I open my mouth, but she continues, eyes affixed just beyond my left shoulder. "Forget what you had on your agenda today, Mary. We need you here."

An egg-shaped woman, her snug housekeeping uniform damp and soiled, pushes past me with a groan. I take one look into her bag-laden eyes and fear that the housekeeper just may go AWOL today. I'd seen her bustling in and out of here throughout the week, but other than an occasional request for extra soap, we had yet to formally meet. The stout woman stops. Her cheek twitches, and her eyes narrow, but she keeps her glare on Tina's face.

Tina rubs her stomach and glowers at Mary. I start to speak just as Tina turns to me. "This town is full of loafers!"

A vision of slip-on shoes lined up in tidy rows pops into my head. "Can I help out with something?"

Tina's lower lip quivers. When she starts to speak, her eyes well up and she sniffles twice. *Wasn't she just angry?* If I didn't know better, it appeared she'd be sobbing in seconds. "I know that it's your granddaughter's birthday today, Mary, but—"

"It's my *daughter's* birthday today! And I have already been here since dawn."

"But Alicia quit yesterday, and we still need more clean rooms today, and there is no one else. No one."

Mary jerks her head in my direction. "How 'bout her?"

"Me?" I press a hand to my chest. "I'm just here to work at the front desk. Nigel hired me to take over for Tina."

Mary harrumphs. "Oh, you must think you are too good to clean bedrooms." She starts to remove her apron.

The threatening force behind Tina's tears wins out, and she begins to cry. "So Nigel hired you to 'take over' for me, huh? What's wrong with everybody? People have babies all the time . . . it's not like I'm . . . I'm *disabled* or something!"

My eyes could not widen another inch, especially as I watch her yank her coat from the hat rack in the corner and wrestle it over her body. "Let Nigel know I'm taking my leave early."

I move after her, following her to the door like a scorned woman. "When? When will you start your leave?"

"Today!"

Mary fiddles with the apron in her hands, a grim set to her mouth. She drops it into a laundry cart behind the counter. "I'm so sorry, but I have to go."

"No, wait!" Too late. She shakes her head and slips through the doorway. When she hesitates in the parking lot, and swivels in my direction, I think that maybe she has changed her mind about leaving. But then she says, "You will do just fine, dear," and resumes her quick step to her car.

I continue to watch her go, my mind not quite accepting this sudden change in my plans. Threadlike clouds stretch out over the parking lot and appear to stop at the edge of the inn's property, threatening to suffocate me. Would it be too unbecoming if I were to quit even before I started? Instinctively, I know the answer to that, so I slink behind the front desk. My first day as a clerk at the Bayside has officially begun.

And I don't have a clue what to do next.

THE REGISTRATION CARDS HAVE been alphabetized, and keys to ready rooms attached. My attempts to reach Camille have failed, and I've accepted my fate, knowing she most probably is surfer watching for most of the afternoon. Thankfully, though, I'd seen Eliza Carlton do this over and over when her first husband, Charles, died and left her that tattered Bed & Breakfast in the Sierras to run. She had to deal with frozen pipes, wayward wolves, and unwelcome guests. So surely, I'd decided, I could handle a few hours alone in Nigel's inn.

Check-in time is still two hours off, and so I wait, thankful for the nearly constant cries from overflying gulls. They can be a nuisance, and yet their sound stands as a reminder of the nearby sand and swells. Between the birds and the waves, my mind falls into a relaxing lull, a surprise considering the circumstances.

The squeal of tires across the asphalt lot, followed by two door slams, pulls me out of my daze. I slide a hand over my ear to touch my upswept hair when Josh and a scrawny teenager with big eyes step into the lobby, each carrying a bucket of tools.

Josh stares at me.

I stare back.

He sets his bucket down, and extends his hand. "I'm Josh, and this is Mikey."

I say hello, all the while taking in the green of his eyes and thickness of his brows. The lower half of his angular face wears an even layer of stubble, and yet it does nothing to hide the long, smooth dimples that sink into his cheeks even without a smile.

He drops his hand to his side, but still eyes me. "We haven't formally met until now. I didn't realize you were working here."

"Well, that's . . . it's kind of a long story. I just started today."

"Today? Oh so, is Tina around? Mikey and I are here to redo the wiring in a couple of the rooms."

I thought you were a fireman. "Hm, no, no Tina here today."

He picks up the bucket. "That's okay, we can find Mary to show us what needs to be done."

"Well, not exactly. Mary's gone too. And it's Betty's day off so I'm on my own today."

Josh's forehead creases. "You don't happen to know which rooms need the work done, I suppose? We're part of a volunteer crew from our church, but unfortunately, I'm only around today to do this."

Ah, a good Samaritan. I think that maybe our parents took us to church when we were young. All I remember is a lot of singing and Play-Doh and seeing the hem of my mother's skirt up close as she talked with other ladies while I ate sticky doughnuts. Funny how the simplest thing can spark a memory.

Behind the desk again, I begin rifling through the registration cards, losing a couple of keys in the process. Instead of a modern locking card system, dear Nigel's inn still lives in the 80s. The hotel keys bounce across the desk, making a metallic racket that draws even more attention to my novice status. I start to shake my head, and in my peripheral notice Mikey shift uncomfortably next to Josh. My fingers catch on a note.

"Here it is! Room 4 has an outlet on the west wall that doesn't work, and the bathroom outlet in room 6 needs a GF . . . hm."

Josh looks over at Mikey. "Needs a GFCI socket." He looks back to me. "Thanks. I'll need to get the keys from you and then we'll take care of it."

I find the keys and hand them to him, our fingers touching in the exchange. His hand lingers over mine for a beat, and then he turns to leave. I begin fiddling with the key drawer when he stops, and turns back to me. "By the way, did you and your sister ever tour the castle?"

"No, actually, we haven't made it that far away yet. We had . . . well, we spent our time exploring Otter Bay instead."

Mikey nudges Josh with his shoulder and starts to head down the hall. Josh hesitates before offering me a nod, his eyes warming me to my toes. "You should try to fit it in when you can. I might have some other ideas for you, if you need some." He glances down the hall. "Better get going before Mikey tears into the wrong wall."

I watch him go, mindful that I haven't looked at a man like this since early on with Trent. Probably not even then. Alone again with nothing but the hammer of my heart and a disheveled mess of registration cards, I think about Josh and how often we've run into each other in the past week. He caught my attention that first time at the diner—who wouldn't notice him with his effortless leap over the counter to rescue Peg? Not to mention that tangle of golden hair and rugged day-old beard. That day he eyed me with a mixture of curiosity and what might have been suspicion. After he showed up at the beach and doled out all that unasked-for advice, I started to wonder if any suspicion might be better aimed at *him*. But now he's here today, doing another good deed, and causing me to think about things I never thought I'd be considering any time soon.

Dreamy thoughts.

Romantic notions.

Unrealistic expectations.

Trent is the only man I've loved for five years. Even when he criticized me for my less-than-sophisticated looks—my lack of makeup and fine jewelry and haute couture—eventually he'd scoop me into his arms and profess his forever love for plain old me.

Sometimes I still can't believe he walked away. After all the promises, and the talks about our future, everything I'd made myself believe—that even ugly ducklings could live happily ever after—turned out to be an aberration in the end.

Yet something about that fireman in room 4 has revived a spark of hope among the ashes. The thought so catches me that I don't notice Nigel shuffling into the lobby until he stands directly in front of his own counter.

"I see you have made yourself quite comfortable, and this is how it should be."

"Nigel! Hello—I'm so glad to see you! I called your room but missed you." I fill him in on all that's transpired since I arrived, and he just smiles as if this were any other day.

"Thank you for a job well done, Tara. Somehow I knew that you could handle whatever might come your way. However, since you have no hotel experience per se, allow me to join you behind the desk where I will teach you our system."

Relief fills my chest, and I let out a held breath. "I'm so glad you're here, Nigel."

He nods then, his beret staying securely on his head. Nigel's eyes are some of the kindest I've ever looked into, and a pang of sadness fills me as I realize how often I thought the same of my father's.

Our first guest of the afternoon arrives windblown, with lines etching the skin around her eyes. And yet she wears a telltale peaceful expression, the same kind I felt spread across my own face when I drove into Otter Bay for the first time in many years. The dramatic coastline and soft dunes will do that for a person. Of course, for me there's something more.

She takes the key to her room from me. "I just left the job from you-know-where, and boy, this feels like paradise. I may never want to leave!"

Who could know how she feels better than I?

After Nigel and I work side by side for over an hour, I notice him leaning more than ever on his cane. I smile at him. "Phew. Nothing like learning on your feet. Why don't you take a rest now. You've taught me enough that I think I can handle things for a little while."

"You can handle more than you know." So saying, he hobbles toward one of the floral couches in the lobby. He's barely had time to rest, when in walks trouble.

"Nigel Thornton! How could you let Holly desecrate my restaurant in this way!"

Holly's Aunt Peg may have been out of commission for a week, but if it's true what they say—that body parts strengthen after being broken and healed—she's become one powerful lady. Her nostrils flare as air flows in and out of them, and she stands over poor Nigel, wagging a rigid finger at him. If it weren't so demeaning, I'd drop to my knees and pretend to look for a lost contact lens.

Unfortunately, in my haste my toes kick up against the trash bin. Distracted by the noise, Peg looks upward and sniffs the air like a dog. She spins toward me, that finger still stuck straight out in front of her. "You're new here."

Nigel jabs his cane into the floor and pulls himself up to lean on it. "Peg, I'd like you to meet my new desk clerk, Tara. She'll be working in Tina's place, and perhaps even longer, if I can convince her of it." A satisfied smile rests on his face.

"Hello, Peg. I just love your diner. My sister and I have breakfast there just about every morning."

She narrows her eyes at me, not in a mean way, but in a way that says, "I'm assessing you." Her flat, creased lips push into a pucker.

I continue. "I hope you're feeling better. I was there the day you, uh, the day you had your fall. I'm so sorry, but oh, Holly has done a terrific job keeping things going. You should be proud of her."

"I've never seen you."

"Well, that's because we're new here, my sister and I."
I reach out my hand. "Tara Sweet. I'm pleased to make your
acquaintance."

Her lips droop into a frown. They seem to fit naturally
into that position, as if an upside down crescent had long
been carved into her face. Before her fall I remember the
way she pinned on a winning smile only to let it fall into that
same frown as she passed by. I remember it because it stood
in direct contrast to what I'd been feeling.

My hand dangles in front of her, but she doesn't take it.
Instead, Peg turns her head slowly toward Nigel, who has
lowered himself back onto the couch. She walks to him,
her thickset body towering over his seated one, which looks
small, frail.

"You"—she says, through clenched teeth—"will be the
death of me."

Chapter Eight

 Whatever new me had surfaced over the past few weeks as I prepared to live this adventure, I cast it all aside at the sight of this cranky woman rebuking Nigel. Out from behind the desk now, I'm standing close enough to hear Peg's angry, labored breathing.

"You'd better go." I make little attempt to disguise the command in my tone. I did not come here to make enemies, but I also cannot stand to see such unworthy treatment of such a lovely man.

Peg swings around and, by the way she hunches her body, I expect to see daggers coming from her eyes. Instead, they are open wide, her pupils dilated, almost abnormally so. She swallows and backs away from me, like I'm a criminal who's jumped bail.

Sweet Waters

A distinct rattle grows in volume behind me. Josh's voice rolls over my shoulder. "So you're back to the grind already, Peg? Hope this doesn't mean the disappearance of Holly's crêpes again."

Mikey snorts next to him. "Good one."

Josh's sudden presence is like a glass of cool, mountain spring water on a blistering summer day. He sets down his bucket, leans comfortably against the rounded corner of the archway, and surprises me with a wink.

Apparently Peg has had a similar reaction to Josh, because she draws up straighter, and if I'm not mistaken, her deep frown has become more of a tiny dip. "I leave and that girl thinks she owns the place. But I'm back now and I'll be straightening that child out."

"Let her be, Peg. She's still a kid, and who knows, you might just be raising an executive chef. Better give her some freedom."

Peg harrumphs. "Or else some rope!"

Josh laughs, a hearty, from-the-gut sound, and I marvel at how he's changed the room's temperature from bitter cold to balmy warm. When a family of harried-looking parents and two young kids bounce into the lobby, I move behind the front desk to check them in. Still new at this, I fumble around looking for their registration, and swiping their credit card, and trying to remember everything I need to tell them about the inn and Otter Bay. Of course, I might not be so antsy if I weren't straining to hear the conversation playing

★ 76 ★

out between Josh, Nigel, and Peg. What I do know is that, occasionally, Josh glances at me and each time, a cool wave rolls over my ribs.

Mikey, who's been hanging back and watching me work, looks like he has a question on his mind. "So that was kind of you to fix up a couple of rooms like that," I say to him. "Do you volunteer regularly?"

He shifts. "Yeah. A whole bunch of us from church try to do stuff like this. Josh does the most, though."

"Really? I wonder how he finds the time."

"Can't always. When he's staying at the firehouse he can't come, so most of us just wait around until he's back home."

"Well, you sound like a great group of people."

"Yeah. Hey, you could come to church. It's pretty awesome. You know where it is?"

Back behind River Lane . . . I shake away the random thought. "Hm, no, I don't think I do."

"It's over on Pines Way. You take Stone Creek to Willows, then you'll make the next left and you'll see it back behind River Lane."

I look up. "What?"

He searches the counter, finds a pen and a brochure. "Here, let me write it down for you." He doesn't see that my hands have begun to shake so much that I've clasped them behind my back. *How did I know his church was back behind River Lane?* My mind churns, trying to spit out the source of that memory, but all it comes up with is a jumble of meaningless words.

". . . so it's real easy once you get the hang of the turns up there near the ridge." Mikey holds his notes out to me.

"Thanks. I'm not sure when I'll have the chance to stop in, but now I'll be able to find it." I pause. Maybe I should tell him that I have a random memory of the address. Then again, I don't want him thinking I'm one of those people with mental powers, like Eliza seems to have at times. Instead I accept the brochure, and glance over to see that Josh has just given Peg a hug, and she is turning to leave—but not before assessing me one more time. Her mouth is a thin line, and yet her brows knit together, making her eyes look afraid. *Did I sound that intimidating?* I cringe. Someday I'd like to learn how to get my point across without drawing blood.

Surprisingly, though, Nigel wears his same benign expression, and I'm beginning to wonder how and why he does that so well. I turn back to Mikey. "What's the name of your church, by the way?"

"Coastal Christian."

Somehow, I knew he'd say that.

THAT NIGHT CAMILLE AND I take a walk along the boardwalk that snakes its way along the edge of the coast. While I keep gnawing on difficult-to-recall memories of us as a churchgoing family, Camille chatters on about the drama at the diner this morning. Peg's sudden reentry into the place had sent both crew and customers scattering, according to Camille, who stayed put to eat her pumpkin-bourbon muffin.

"You should've seen her, Tara. She was barking and banging pans and shouting out words like 'muesli!' and 'brie cheese!' Oh it was the funniest thing of my life. One guy came in the door, heard the racket, and turned right back around. But poor Holly kept on twisting her hands together and glancing at Jorge and then at me. I was glad to be there for her this morning." She stops. "Look!"

My gaze searches the darkness for what she's found. "I don't see anything."

"Two surfers out there in the dark. Can you believe they night surf?"

A month ago my mother was still in the United States, I was waiting for an elusive engagement ring, and traveling to California was still in my "someday" mental file. Now . . . I'd believe anything. I nod, and we continue walking along the wooden planks. "Someone invited me to church today," I finally say, not sure why it seems this statement will create a pause along our walk.

"Really? What kind of church meets on Monday?"

I stop and look at Camille. "I mean that he invited me to come on Sunday. He would've invited you too of course, but he doesn't know you exist."

"Gee, nice. So who is this 'he'? Is he the type of 'he' worthy of attending church for?" She giggles.

"Actually, he seems like a sweet kid—a teenager. He and Josh fixed some electrical problems at the inn today."

"Okay, so now we're getting to it. You saw Josh today. Working at the inn? How convenient is this? Ha-ha . . . Tara's going to snag herself a hunky firefighter."

"Stop it. Mikey—the kid who was working with Josh—he's the one who invited me to the church. The weird thing is, even before he said it, I knew where it was located. I think we must've gone there as kids."

"To church? I don't think so. Daddy was always so down on church people." She laughs lightly. "Remember that time he complained so much about Anne's wedding being held in a church? He kept mumbling under his breath, and carrying on. I could just see Mom's bare shoulders blushing in that strapless bridesmaid gown. Ooh, she was so mad."

"You were just a baby, Camille, but I remember running around on a blacktop with other kids, singing songs and eating snacks. A distinct memory popped into my mind today."

Camille giggles again. "You mean like preschool?"

I pause. Maybe I am thinking of preschool? But why would there be so many women around wearing heels and skirts, and so many men in slacks? "No, I really think it was some kind of church. It's weird because I haven't thought about that in all these years, but when I learned that Josh and Mikey were members, the memory popped into my head."

"You're not thinking of going, though."

"Maybe somebody there would remember us . . . or it might spark another memory. I just think it might help us connect with Dad again, somehow." I'm struck by how many things I never asked him, so many new questions now that we're back in our old hometown.

Camille groans. "Well, don't wake me when you leave."

We make it to a lookout that juts over low, flat rocks where tide pools gather during daylight. Narrow lines of foam sparkle in the soft moonlight as the water recedes from the shore. Camille shows no interest in this conversation, so I move us in another direction. "Speaking of leaving, I think it's time we find a place of our own."

As if doused in fresh sea spray, Camille comes alive. "I was thinking the same thing! No offense, Tara, but your snoring's driving me crazy—it's the saddest thing of my life."

"Guess you'll be wanting to get a job so you can have your own room, then." I refuse to let her get to me. Snoring. Right.

"I want to go back to school."

I snap a look her way, wondering if she's serious. "Do you really? Because I'd let you slide on the job thing for awhile if you did."

She sighs softly, like she's musing. So unlike her. "I'm serious. There's a junior college down the road that has a fashion-design program. I'd like to check it out, at least."

"How did you hear about it?"

"A guy I met told me about it. Says it's where a lot of the surfers go 'cuz they have night classes." She giggles then. "Not that they're all into fashion design. That's just one of the programs they have there. Anyway, surfers like it because night school doesn't mess up their wave action."

Of course.

She continues. "Oh, I meant to tell you. I saw a cute place for rent today. After a lot of the surfers left, I was bored and went for a walk past the pines over there." She points in the air, her finger enveloped by the darkening night. "Anyway, there's a pretty nice neighborhood, all except for a creepy house that's boarded up. Looks like a fire got it. Other than that, though, the houses are small but really, really cute. And one of them had a For Rent sign on it. It's blue—I knew you'd like that."

I'm both surprised and gratified by how quickly she's taken to Otter Bay. I'd worried that maybe one of her friends would talk her into leaving me here and flying back home. I actually expected that to happen soon, yet now she talks of cute cottages and getting a degree in fashion design. More and more, it seems, we're finding our place here.

"Let's run by tomorrow and take a look. Sound good?"

I can hear the smile in her tone. "Yeah—wait. What time . . . ? I'm meeting Shane at 9."

"Shane? Who's he . . . and isn't that a little early for a date?"

She turns to me, a thick curly lock over one eye, and even in the dark I see the twist of a smile on her face. "Not when he's giving me my first surfing lesson."

Chapter Nine

The din at the Red Abalone Grill has taken on a sour note. It wasn't so much a sound, though, but a sense that the funky vibe we'd come to expect over the past week has been chased away and replaced with a surliness that makes me want to try out the Coffee Cart up in the village. True, word is they only serve coffee and rolls of questionable freshness over there, but at least they provide a stress-free dining experience.

Camille leans across the table, her eyes imploring mine. "Check out the battle-ax at three o'clock," she hisses.

Peg plunks a plate in front of a woman, the porcelain making a harsh rattle upon landing. The solitary diner flinches—not exactly the stance a paying customer should take when served.

What happens next, however, makes my stomach roil. I want to turn away, but my eyes stay fixed on Peg as she grabs Holly by the cap-sleeve and begins to gesture at Camille and me. Let's just say she doesn't appear pleased.

Camille plops back against her seat. "What'd we ever do to her?"

I stare at the scene, answering Camille without looking at her. "I'm not sure, but it probably has something to do with me."

"You?"

I glance at Camille. "I barked at her yesterday, over at the inn."

Camille presses both palms to the table and leans in again. "Ta-ra. No. Holly and I were just beginning to be friends. She was going to teach me more crochet tricks! You better make up with her."

Guilt finds me as I watch the desperation in Camille's eyes. I've every right to defend myself, considering how ornery Peg behaved toward Nigel, but this is not the point. Friendships are everything to Camille, and apparently I'm responsible for the growing wedge between her and her newest one.

Speaking of friends, Holly appears, her skin flushed. She fills our water glasses, her eyes cloudy and downcast. "Sorry, ladies, but no special requests today. I know how much you like your peanut-butter smoothie, Tara. We do have a regular ol' vanilla milk shake that you can try." She peeps over one shoulder. "I might be able to sneak a scoop of peanut butter in that."

I shake my head. "Forget it. Your aunt's pretty upset today . . . about something."

"Yeah, she's in a snit all right. Barking at the cook and at me. Says she took her pain pills, but I'm not buyin' it. Somethin's got to change around here or there won't be any customers or staff left!"

I shut my eyes and draw in a breath, then slide out of the booth, intent on making this right. No matter how much it hurts. I ease up to Peg, ignoring how she stiffens. "Excuse me, Peg? I think I owe you an apology."

That fear I noticed yesterday flashes in the old woman's eyes again, but she holds her mouth in that constant frown.

I continue. "I'm sorry for asking you to leave the inn yesterday." *Even though you were horrible to my boss.* "And I hope we can start over."

Her nostrils flare, but she swallows before speaking. "You're Robert's child."

Her proclamation causes me to take a step backward. I recover, a lift in my heart. "Yes. Yes, we are Robert's daughters. That's my sister, Camille, over there with me. You knew our father?"

Peg flicks a look over at Camille, who's still talking with Holly. "Your . . . sister."

"Well, really, she's my cousin. Her father was my mother's brother, Grant. Maybe you knew him too? He died—"

"In a motorcycle crash. That man was trouble."

Her bluntness deflates me. "Please don't say anything negative to Camille about her father. It would really hurt her. She's been with us since she was a baby, so she's always been like a sister to me."

The lines around Peg's mouth soften and, for just a moment, I believe I'm about to see someone other than the huffy diner Nazi. Holly rushes past, calling out an order of Belgian waffles to the cook before picking up two plates from under the heat lamps. She winks at me as she darts past, and I smile. Unfortunately Peg glares at me now and my newly formed smile fades.

"What are you doing here?"

I shrug. "I've always wanted to come back home, and finally the time was right. My father passed away, and Mom remarried and left the country. This was our father's wish . . . for us to come back to Otter Bay."

"Robert's dead?"

It's been years, and yet the coarse delivery of her words stings. When I don't answer right away, Peg takes a towel from a bucket and begins to wipe down the counter in sloppy, agitated circles.

"Yes, my father died six years ago. Did you know him well?"

She shrugs one shoulder, concentrating on the counter beneath her hand. "I knew him. And Marilee too. You say she's out of the country now?"

"On a long honeymoon." It still seems unbelievable. "She and her husband are spending a year touring Europe, so I figured this would be the perfect time to come home to Otter Bay."

She stops. "Home?"

"At least for a while. That's why I agreed to take a temporary position at the inn . . . so I could see if this move should be permanent."

Peg sucks in a breath and tosses the wet rag under the counter. "I see." She stares off toward our table, where Camille fidgets with her food. "Your food's getting cold over there."

I nod. "Yes, right. Can I just ask you though . . . did you know our parents well?"

Peg's eyes study me before she answers. "As I remember it, your mother was a beautiful woman, but your father—" her lips thin even more, if that's possible.

"That man was no friend of mine."

"AND THAT'S REALLY ALL she said?"

Camille continues to question me as we walk the three long blocks to view the rental house she spotted yesterday. Peg's pronouncement about our father knocked the sea air from me and I've been down ever since. Thankfully I'm not due back to work at the inn until tomorrow morning.

"When I asked her to explain, she blustered something about having to get back to work, so I limped back to the table."

"I think we should just forget about her, Tara," Camille says, a pout in her voice. "She's obviously deranged, and if it weren't for Holly—and Jorge's cooking—I'd never even want to go back there."

"I guess. Besides, if we rent this cottage, we can start making our own meals anyway." I kick a pebble with the toe of my flip-flop. "Just can't imagine how anyone could dislike our father. It irks me."

"There it is."

We've turned onto Fogcatcher Lane, where single-story beach bungalows line up, each with a small porch for storing sand buckets and surfboards. Most of the redwoods and pines that would normally thrive around here have been cut down, probably to provide views to the water. The cottages, painted the muted colors of the sea—blues and greens and sandy grays—look so well maintained you'd think we were strolling through a Hollywood movie set. All except for one forlorn house, its windows covered by clean plywood, sitting across the street and just two houses past the one we've come to see. Black soot lies in uneven spots across its front and down its side.

We walk up to the sad place in silence. Camille speaks first. "Wonder whatever happened here."

"I don't know. Look. Weeds are growing up the sides, so the fire must've happened awhile ago. Wonder when this place will be fixed up."

Camille sighs. "Yeah, kind of depressing to live near it."

A purple VW Beetle cruises down the street and pulls into the driveway of the rental cottage. The driver, a tall woman with short, sandy-colored hair and a quick step, climbs out and swirls herself around, her gaze switching from the available property to us and then to the paper in her hand. She looks over at us again and calls out, "How-dy! If you're looking for the rental unit, then I'm your gal."

We glance at each other, before making our way toward her. Camille's eyes can't hide her giddiness.

The woman holds out her hand. "Cheryl Draughon here, retired teacher turned realtor at your service. Which one of you ladies is Tara?" She shakes my outstretched hand. "Then you must be Camille," she says, turning to my cousin. "Well. So you gals are new in town then. Come in, come in . . . let me show you around." She slips the key into the lock, then turns to us. "I think you're going to love-love-love it here!"

Any worry over the burned-out house up the street dissipates the second we slip off our flip-flops and pad around the small cottage, with its marred wooden floors and beadboard-covered walls. From the front picture window there's an ocean view over the rooftops, and that's almost enough to get me to sign on the dotted line right now.

"Oh my stars, would you look at this! Come see, gals."

We wander to the kitchen, where French doors open to a wide patio. Our realtor sits in a generous Adirondack chair, one of three situated beneath the overhead sun, its beam illuminating her like a celebrity. "Because it's on the side, this view is better than that one out front. I could sit here all day with a cup of tea and a square of chocolate and just watch the bunnies in the garden and that glorious ocean down the street."

Sure enough, as if on cue, a bunny scurries across the scrubby grass and hides behind an overgrown bush. Camille steps onto the deck behind me, her eyes riveted on the view. "Tara, this is perfect. And there's even an extra bedroom back there."

Cheryl pipes in. "And it's furnished too."

I sit next to Cheryl, reveling in the surprising comfort that hard wood offers. I breathe in the salt air, attempting to calm my racing heart. "How long of a lease do the owners expect?"

"We're looking at a year, although I might be able to sweet-talk them into something shorter, if you're not sure of your plans."

I release that breath. Things are moving fast—faster than I'm able to process. Dreaming about doing something is one thing. Actually putting money and effort behind it can be daunting. What if Mom and Derrick come back from Europe early? Or if Camille hates it here, or we miss Mel too much? And what if the rest of the town turns out to be curmudgeons, like Peg?

Cheryl sits there, just nodding her head. "That's right. You take your time. This is a big decision for you gals."

Camille's popping up and down on her toes, a fallback to

her high school ways. "Come on, Tara. Just this once, let's do something crazy. This place is perfect for us."

I laugh. "You don't think flying out here in the first place classifies as crazy?" My cell buzzes, and I excuse myself to take it inside. Most people would just slide it open and take the call right there, but I've been in enough lines at the grocery store where I've overheard things that strangers should never learn. So, out of respect, I take the call in the living room.

"Tara? It's me, Mel." I listen to my sister while watching a V-shaped formation of pelicans flying out toward the sea. Like our realtor, who sits enchanted out on that wooden deck, I too can see myself sitting in that spot, sipping coffee and watching waves engulf the rocks. I finish my conversation with Mel, and head back to see Cheryl and Camille who, though they've only just met, chatting like old friends. They stop when I rush through the doors.

"We'll take the house," I say, unable to stop the singsong in my voice. "Mel will be here next week!"

Chapter Ten

The tide lays flat, at its lowest level since Camille and I have been here. That hasn't been all that long, of course, still it's comforting to see these waters again and all that lies beneath their refuge. I'm wearing water shoes today so I can climb across exposed rock and hunt for a peek at what lives in its many crevices.

Camille and I got up this morning, put our suitcases in the car, and drove into the village for stale pastry and strong coffee. Afterward, we picked up our new house key from Cheryl, then moved in to our rental cottage. All we have left to do is give Anne a call, and she'll ship just a few things we'll need from storage. Just like that.

It's Holly's day off (another reason to skip the diner today), so she and Camille drove into the next town over to check on that fashion-design program at the college. And since Betty's on duty at the inn this morning, I'm free to explore these tide pools until late afternoon.

On my haunches, I dangle my fingers into a swirl of water containing several shell-packed sea anemones as the ocean's spray dances across my face. Gulls cry in the distance. A familiar tangle of waves and air fills my senses, and my mind steps back in time. Daddy's sad, and Mother's been crying again. We sit, Daddy and I, our legs dangling over the edge of a precipice, the waters rolling rhythmically beneath our feet, each wave climbing higher than the last. I'm tossing tiny spiral shells into the sea, trying to make them skip like Daddy does, only they sink on impact each and every time.

Unlike most days, Daddy's not happy. He's just staring into the water, wide-eyed and distressed, mumbling something. I strain to recall it. "She lied," he's saying. "If only she hadn't lied."

I yank my hand out of the water, the suddenly vivid memory stunning me. A noise from behind causes me to spin and I nearly lose my footing. A man's voice calls to me, and I hear his steps bouncing across the rocks.

"Did you get stung?"

I squint up in the sun to see Josh towering over me. He bends down and takes my hand. "Did something sting your hand?"

I pull it away, still reeling from the memory of my father and me, my mind fuzzy. "Not at all. I'm fine."

Josh's crinkled eyes inspect me. "I was watching and saw you jerk your hand out of the water. Figured something tried to take a bite out of you."

I want to be annoyed by his presumption. I half expect him to act like Trent and begin reciting deadly facts about the dangers of sea water, showing off how much more he thinks he knows than I do. Instead, though, he reaches for my hand again, a gentle *May I?* in his eyes, and his protectiveness has a calming effect.

I'm quite sorry I pulled my hand from his so quickly. "No. I–I was just thinking of something, and the move was completely involuntary." I roll back onto my rump, and hug my knees with my hands. Eliza would know the right things to do and say at this moment, how to dazzle and delight, but all I can do is tighten the grip on my legs and hope Josh says something soon.

He settles back too—right into a puddle—then rolls back onto his feet. "Ahh!"

I cover my mouth with one hand. "Cold?" *Eliza would be proud.*

He grunts, his face twisted into a mock grimace. "I meant to do that."

It feels good to laugh, and he's wearing a smile too—although maybe a bit restrained—the fresh stubble on his face shining golden in the sun. "So. All I know about you is your first name."

"Sweet. My name is Tara Sweet."

"Hm. It fits you."

A hot blush fills my cheeks. "Um, you're smooth, aren't you?"

A laugh erupts from him, as if I've caught him by surprise. It reminds me of the other day at the inn when the sound of his voice dissipated the tension in the air. It's doing the same for me now. "Now why would you go and say something like that?"

I shrug. "Tell me about you, Josh . . ."

"Adams."

"Okay, Josh Adams, the firefighter. Have you lived in Otter Bay a long time?"

He rubs a hand over his stubbly cheek, eyes guarded again. "We moved here from Los Angeles when I was a kid. I went to SLO—that's San Luis Obispo—for college, then decided to settle back here. It's a good town."

I nod. "I see that."

He searches my face, and I glance away. "What brought you here?"

Just how do I answer that, exactly? My life has always been about stability. Working hard, saving money, getting married, raising a family . . . But now? The longer I'm here, the more I sense the need to fill in the long-forgotten pieces of my family's past. Do I tell this to Josh, a near stranger? Certainly I can't tell him Mel's prediction—that I've come to run away from a broken heart.

I let out a soft breath. "My family lived here until I was six, and I've always wanted to come back and visit."

"You're just passing through then." He frowns.

I press my lips together into a smile and shrug. "Well, secretly, I've always wanted to move back. My father died a number of years ago, and this place reminds me of him. He loved water, and I always wondered why he let this town slip away from us. He never would say. Anyway, my mother remarried, and the company I worked for was sold so . . ."

"So you took the leap. That's courageous."

Simple words, yet they touch me within. No one has ever called me courageous before. Headstrong, strong-willed, bossy . . . I've heard those monikers, but never anything as noteworthy as *courageous*. "Thank you for saying so," I tell him, meaning it. "Although, you're a firefighter, and that's got to be one of the most courageous jobs out there."

Josh's eyes, which look out to sea now, take on a dark cast again. He's quiet for several seconds—have I somehow said exactly the wrong thing? Wouldn't be the first time. He glances down to where one of his hands toys with a stone. "It can be, if it's done right."

"Nigel says you're the best."

He cocks his chin toward me and smiles, although his eyes still carry a certain sadness. "There aren't enough people like Nigel in the world, but I guess you know that, working for him, I mean."

"Yes, I—"

A sharp ring tears into the peaceful morning. Josh looks to his side. "That's me." He stands and reads a text on his phone. "My shift doesn't officially start until tomorrow, but when duty calls, it calls." He snaps his phone back onto his belt, and pulls me up before I realize what's happening. "Got to run. Be careful out here . . ."

"I'll watch for the tide. No worries."

He sends me a wave, and I watch him dash back to his truck.

I RIDE INTO WORK on a wave of mixed emotion. On the upside, we've found an affordable place to live near the beach—quite the feat—and Mel will be here soon. And, I can't deny, running into Joshua Adams, firefighter, hasn't put a damper on my time here one bit.

Still, questions remain about Peg's hostility toward my father, not to mention the cryptic memory that bored its way into my mind earlier today at the tide pool.

Betty's behind the desk when I arrive, her gray-haired head drooping to one side. When I approach, she bursts awake and calls out, "Checking in? . . . oh, good, it's you."

It's good to be needed.

"Long day, Betty?"

She chortles. "I'll say, but oh my dear, having you here to get us organized has already been so helpful. Imagine, after only one day!" She removes her black vinyl purse from the coat rack, and pulls it gingerly over one shoulder. "You have a blessed night, dear. Don't work too hard."

After handling a rush of check-ins in the late afternoon, a lull settles in and I spend some time reading through the piles of tourist brochures Nigel has available for guests. I'm studying one that gives directions and information about a nearby sanctuary for elephant seals when a hostile wind blows in through the front door.

Peg stands there in her grease-splattered apron, looking angry as a bull. "You didn't show for breakfast."

All sorts of responses zip through my head. "I didn't realize we had an appointment."

She stares in silence, and the admonishment to be kind to your elders pummels me with guilt. I sigh. "Hello, Peg. What can I do for you?"

"Where were you this morning? Because I had something to say."

I measure my response. "Well, Camille and I moved into our rental this morning, and then she took off with Holly to visit the college."

Color drains from her face. "Holly is with your . . . with Camille?"

"They should be back anytime now, but yes, they drove down together. I'm surprised Holly didn't mention it."

"She's over eighteen. And what do you mean your rental? I thought you lived in this inn?"

I run a hand over my smoothed-back hair, figuratively pushing away the thought of telling her to mind her own business. "And now we've found a place more . . . permanent. It's lovely, even if it's not the house I once lived in."

She harrumphs. "Oh, well that place—that place had to be condemned. It was derelict from all the neglect."

I shrug, masking the pain. "Must have happened after we left."

Peg's eyes relax, exhibiting a rare flash of compassion. "Let me make this easy for you, Tara." She moves closer, her chin raised into the air, as if it makes her feel more brave. "Your father—you may not know or understand this now—but I will hand it to you straight. The man was one smooth character. He could cheat a man out of his lunch, then get the chump to buy him dinner."

I step out from behind the desk, panic rising it my throat. "Stop it."

"Get your deposit back. Or just cut your losses and go back home."

"This *is* our home now."

Peg grunts. "Trust me. It's better if you go, before you learn more about Robert Sweet than he ever wanted you to hear."

Panic has turned to anger unleashed. "You're nuts! My father was an honorable man . . . a beloved man. Everyone who knows him will attest to it. So take your gossip and your advice, and get . . . out!" I grind my teeth, top row into bottom, yet I can't stay quiet. "My sister, Mel, will be here next week, and let me tell you, Peg, if you think *I'm* tough, you won't want to mess with her."

Her eyes turn dull, like she's given up. "Then you give me no choice but to tell you the truth. Your father, God rest that man's soul, took nearly eight thousand dollars from me."

"Take it back."

Peg's eyes catch on something behind me, but she can't make an accusation like that, and then just turn away. My jaw tightens. "Take . . . back . . . what you said about my father."

Nigel's soothing voice glides into the room. "Good evening, ladies."

My hands begin to shake. This woman is nothing but a stranger—I've never even heard of her before. My fingers curl into a ball until nails dig into palms as I try to draw air back into my tightening lungs. The last thing I want, though, is for Nigel to hear Peg's accusation. Daddy's reputation cannot be sullied this way. Gathering myself together, I adjust my claw clip, its tines scraping against my scalp. I take a slow, even breath. "Hello, Nigel. Nearly a full house this evening, I see."

Nigel's eyes carry a flicker of unease, his usually smooth face showing lines of concern. I let my eyes plead: *Don't. Don't ask me what's wrong.*

"Then you've done a marvelous job caring for our guests. You were in no need of me to assist." He nods at Peg. "Getting acquainted with my new desk host, I see."

Peg wipes her hands on an apron that should've been thrown into the wash hours ago. "Just telling her all she needs to know. Got to get back to the diner now before Jorge starts making tamales again. I'll see you at breakfast, you know how I always keep your table cleared for you." She makes eye contact with me again, but this time I see no hint of compassion.

Only the cold, stone glare of a desperate woman.

Chapter Eleven

Even before my feet hit the floorboards this morning, I attempt to dial Mom. She had promised to sign up for international calling, and all I can think of as that blasted recording starts again is, why did I not insist on handling that for her?

Camille's asleep, but I can't stay in bed another second. Instead, I'm thinking about my parents as I sit out on the deck, watching the churning ocean spit waves across the rocks, often engulfing them. The light of morning has done little to cheer me after last evening's confrontation with Peg.

My father took care of the financial records of various businesses in Dexton, his work always bringing in enough for us to have a decent life. If we needed money, we never knew it. And people absolutely loved him. He donated his time by

volunteering to help so many charities set up their accounting systems that anything doubtful on his part . . . well, it's
impossible to fathom!

The coffee mug keeps my hands warm. I'm grateful.
Grateful that my father scrimped and saved and worked hard
enough that I can be sitting here in this Adirondack chair,
not overly worried about money. We're no trust-fund babies,
not in the traditional sense, but he left the girls and me with
enough to make this new start.

In the midst of sorrow, a fissure of hope startles me. *What
was that little prayer Dad taught us when we were little, the one
about Jesus being as close as our hearts?* He always said that when
we felt sad, we should remember the prayer and how it meant
we'd one day live forever. Hadn't thought of that in years.

With resolve, I drain my coffee cup, head back inside,
and grab my purse from its hook. No way will Peg's accusation be allowed to stand.

The RAG bustles with early morning diners, something
I'd not seen to this extent. Holly propels by, a pot of coffee
in one hand and two mugs in the other. "Mornin', Tara. My,
you're here early today."

I slide into a two-person booth that appears to have been
an afterthought in the planning of this place. Kitty-corner
to my table, a young woman with perfectly angled hair the
color of dark chocolate coos at a child perched in the high
chair next to her. I steal glances at her while waiting for
Holly to fill me up on more coffee.

So far, the royal pain in my you-know-what has failed to appear.

"Phwee. Camille and I had a good time yesterday." Holly plunks down a mug in front of me and sloshes coffee into it, dropping two hazelnut creamers nearby. "My aunt's AWOL so far, though, so I can't stop and chat. Be back in a minute."

As she swivels away, Nigel appears at my side. I smile at him. "Good morning, Nigel. Have you had breakfast? Please, join me."

He leans on his cane. "My dear, I thank you, but I have had my fill for the morning. I need to stand for a moment now, to get my bearings."

"Of course." Josh, imposing in his head-to-toe blues, walks from the other end of the diner with another blue-uniformed man. *Was he here when I arrived?* He doesn't notice me, but instead makes a beeline for the young mother feeding her baby. I watch as he bends down to tickle the child's chin, his wide smile producing deep creases in his cheek. Still bent over, he turns to say something to the woman, and she grins into his face. The other man stands just off to the side, his smile shy.

Josh seems to be the only one on an intimate footing with this woman.

Holly reappears. "Hey, Nigel. You didn't sit at my station today." She holds out her order pad and looks to me. "I almost put your order in myself, but thought maybe you'd like to try something different today."

"Um—" I glance at the menu like I haven't already memorized the thing—"I'll take . . . hm, you know what, I'll just have the eggs, with bacon and—"

"Wheat toast. Yeah, I know." She sticks the order pad in her pocket and takes my menu, offering me a playful smirk before turning away.

I try to focus on Nigel, but my gaze flits past him to Josh, who has taken several glances at me. When Nigel turns to see where my attention has gone, Josh waves bye-bye to the baby, says something to the woman and the other firefighter, and then approaches us.

Nigel smiles at Josh and takes a step to one side. "Mornin', Nigel." Josh tips his head first to Nigel, then to me.

"And a grand morning to you, Joshua." He lifts his cane in the direction of the open seat in my booth. "I believe this space is open for you."

Nigel's invitation jerks me up straight, and the back of my hand connects with my coffee cup. It shimmies and gives up a slosh of coffee, smack onto the table.

Josh stalls. He glances at me, as if for permission.

"Please." I motion toward the empty seat.

"All right. Thanks."

A tingle runs through me when our knees graze each other.

"We meet again."

It isn't difficult to smile as long as I focus on his model-worthy face and not on my reason for coming here this morning. "Yes, we do. You're becoming a habit." *Did I just say that?*

He smiles. Even his white teeth, which I'm seeing up close for the first time, are gorgeous. "A good one, I hope."

Nigel cuts in to our nervous banter. "Well, I must be taking my leave now. Much to do this day." He turns to go, then stops short. "Say, Joshua. I believe this would be the proper time to ask the lady for a dinner date."

I swallow my gasp and watch in silence as Nigel makes his way to the exit, acknowledging various diners as he moves along.

"I'm not sure that crossing Nigel would be a very good idea." There's underlying laughter in Josh's low voice.

I wave my hand. "Please. No. He's quite the matchmaker, but shotgun dates are out of vogue these days."

Josh's laughter bursts through, and my heart leaps. For the first time since we met, Josh seems to have dropped the inhibitions.

"I know this is one of your favorite places," he says, "but what would you think about fresh seafood?"

"Actually, I prefer it to be fresh."

"All right then, it's a date."

I groan. "Really, Josh. Don't feel obligated by Nigel's coercion . . ."

His grin flattens and a brow arches. "Do I look like someone who is easily swayed?"

I've been struck mute. *Wow, he's handsome when he's being forceful.* I shake my head, trying not to laugh at his earnest expression.

"Okay then."

"Okay."

He slides out of the booth, never taking his eyes off mine. "So, I'll see you next Saturday. Where can I pick you up at say, 7:00?"

"5225 Fogcatcher Lane. You know it?"

His smile dims, but he nods. "Sure, I know where that is . . ."

"Josh!" His friend approaches. "Fire on Elm."

Josh breaks eye contact with me and flips his attention to the other firefighter. "I'm on it. Let's go." He says a hurried good-bye as he and the other man streak out of the diner, and I'm beginning to have déjà vu.

I'm still watching the door when my breakfast arrives at my table. "Didn't think I'd be seeing you around here anymore." Peg plops my plate in front of me. "Need ketchup?"

I try to center myself, still stuck in the daydream that just tore out of here. A breath escapes me before focusing on Peg. "I came to talk to you."

Peg glances over shoulder, her flat lips pursed. "I said plenty last night. As it is, I could hardly sleep."

"What makes you think my father took money from you?" My voice is a whisper.

She pauses. "That's easy, because it's true. Your father

worked for me when you were just a kid, and he figured out a way to siphon cash right out from under me. It was terrible and bitter, but he left town and that was that. If this were my father we were talkin' about, I couldn't bear to stay in a place with so much bad karma."

"Do you have proof?"

Peg flinches. "Are you calling me a liar?"

"Because if you don't have some sort of proof, I will expect a retraction."

"This isn't some newspaper article. I don't have to retract a darned thing." She collects my empty coffee cup, signaling that my breakfast is nearly over. "And another thing. I'd suggest you stay away from Josh Adams. I've known that boy since he was a pup, and he's fixin' to be the next fire chief in this town. Wouldn't be right for you to stand in his way."

"Me? Stand in his way? I don't know how I could be any worse for him than someone else in this town who's obviously full of stories."

Peg slams my empty coffee cup onto the table and leans in so close I can see soft breading squished between her teeth. "I've tried to keep this under my hat, but you are a stubborn girl. You want proof, I'll get you your proof. Just heed my advice, young lady. There are some things best not remembered, and that's all I have to say on the matter."

Holly zips by, slowing only long enough to toss me a troubled glance. "Everythin' all right here, ladies?"

I nod, and Peg waves her on before leaning toward me again. "No need to worry Holly over this. I don't want her to know that her Aunt Peg once almost lost her inheritance. In fact, why don't you girls steer clear of my niece. That way none of us will have to lie about our past."

I take a sip of coffee, which unfortunately is imaginary considering my cup's empty. "I've got nothing to hide. In fact, I plan to stick around, at least long enough to prove you crazy, Peg."

She backs away while I, with forced cheerfulness, accept a refill from Holly.

SUNDAY MORNING HAS ARRIVED, and with it, my need to attend church. Not for any religious reason, of course. Though if you count the desire to defend one's father's honor as a spiritual thing, then I'd accept that definition. What draws me most, however, is pure curiosity.

The building itself is only vaguely familiar, but then again, it stands much like any other nondescript church found along the road in Anywhere, USA. Plain, beige building, two tall entry doors, and a green lawn with little else sprouting up around it. I lock the door of my vibrant Mustang, reminding myself once again that without Camille's enthusiasm I'd have been just as happy with a less showy model, and stroll up the church steps.

A pleasant looking woman with pearlescent hair swept

up into a halo-sized bun holds out her hand. "Good morning. Welcome."

"Thank you. Do I need to be a member to go inside?"

Her eyes flutter. "Sorry?"

"I-I was just wondering if I can just go in."

Her eyebrows knit toward one another. "Why of course! Please, come in, come in."

She directs me into a wide-open room with a bright white ceiling and rows of light-pine pew benches, enough to seat a small town. Surprisingly large considering the building's modest appearance from the outside. A teenager in jeans and a button-down shirt hands me a flyer and shows me to a seat, like I'm here to see a production of *Cats*.

"Tara!"

I turn my chin toward my shoulder, and see Mikey, whom I recognize immediately by his enthusiastic greeting. He crosses the aisle and squats beside me. "That's cool you came. Find it okay?"

I nod.

"There's room with me and my mom, if you want to come sit with us." He points toward his family. "My sister's in her class, and my dad's home sick."

Relief at not having to sit alone in the place that may or may not hold a piece of our family's past floods me. A woman with a smile that matches Mikey's slides down the pew to make room for me to join them. "Hi." My voice is a whisper among many.

She leans to speak in my ear. "Mikey told us that you are new to town. Welcome."

"Thank you. But I was born here, and I think my family may have attended this church when I was a child."

Her brows lift. "Really? What is your last name?"

When I tell her, she smiles, but shakes her head. "Sorry. It's a lovely name but doesn't ring a bell. You might want to try the early service. Lots of old-timers attend then."

The band begins to play, signaling the start of service. I fiddle with the flyer handed to me when I walked in, alternately reading it and letting my eyes dart around the room filled with people. Most of whom, by their smiles and hugs and laughter, appear to genuinely care for one another. I should feel out of place, and partly, I do. But that's mostly because I'm unfamiliar with the traditions and ways of the people here, not because of how I've been treated. And perhaps the most startling thing of all is that once the band begins the refrain, I seem to be able to recall the words.

An hour and a half later, I'm standing on what a carved-wooden sign refers to as the Promised Lawn, talking with Mikey's mother, Norma, and watching his little sister, Emi, do round-offs with two other young girls.

Norma nods at Emi, even while talking with me. "How do you like working at the Bayside? Pretty nice view from there, isn't it."

"I like it more than I thought."

"And the church? How do we compare to your church back home?"

"Well, it looks much like the others around my hometown." Eliza's voice cuts into my thoughts: *Why don't you just tell her that you've hardly set foot in church in your life?* I clear my throat. "I often worked on Sundays." *Coward.* Okay, so I didn't actually have to, but I liked working in the quiet office on the weekends, when no one was around to interrupt me.

Norma seems unfazed by my newbie status, if she noticed at all. "You have such a beautiful voice. I thought maybe you sang on a worship team or in the choir." She glances to the right. "Beth! Come and meet Mikey's new friend."

It's the woman from the diner, the one with the to-die-for hair, and she's carrying her son on one hip. She tiptoes across the lawn in her pointy-toed heels, attempting not to sink.

Norma's bubbly voice continues. "Beth, this is Tara. She's new here and just took a job at the Bayside."

I grin. "Hi there, cutie." At Beth's startled expression, I laugh. "I meant the baby . . . he was smiling at me."

Her smile curves gently, even as her chin stays lowered when she greets me. Does her lack of eye contact mean she's shy? She's wispy, almost frail somehow, like a new bird, and on this warm summer morning, her long, slender arms are covered with thick woolen sleeves. She whispers a "hello," then focuses her attention back on her child, bouncing him softly on her hip.

"I sat near you yesterday at the Red Abalone Grill." Thankfully she left prior to Peg's invasion. "I just love your hairstyle and was noticing it when my friend stopped by your table."

Her saucer-shaped eyes flash, catching mine for an instant before landing back on her son. "Josh. He's a good man."

Norma nods. "Yes, he is. I didn't realize you knew Josh, but that's right. Mikey was with him the other day at the inn. Is that how you met?"

Beth stills.

"We officially met then, but we had run into each other a couple of times before." The way Beth acts—as if she's focused on her son, and yet leans in as if to hear my response—makes me wonder about her relationship with Josh. "He's becoming a . . . friend."

Beth's cloaked eyes find Norma's, and an unspoken thought seems to pass between the two women. I flit my gaze around as if I don't notice, but I do. Norma pats Beth on the shoulder, and the younger woman turns quickly away with only a whispered good-bye.

Something, it seems, happened between Josh and Beth, and curiosity wedges its way into my mind. Really, though, how much do I need—or want—to know?

Chapter Twelve

 *Meet me at Surfer's Ridge.*

So much for Camille sleeping in on this fine Sunday. Other than the syrup-coated plate and fork she left in the sink, and her rumpled bed, our cottage stands quiet, giving me more than enough space to ruminate on all that's happened this week. I consider slipping into flip-flops and heading out to meet Camille, but opt instead to find answers.

With a click of a button, I switch on my laptop, and log in to Camille's Facebook. If I can't reach her by phone, then it's time to find other means. Mother's been spotty in her reply to my e-mails, but I notice that she's better about updating her status on Facebook. Her posts always sound so cheery.

Saw the royal family . . .

Ate at a Paris café . . .

Toured chapels in Belgium . . .

Sigh. Hopefully she's not off on some mountain peak now, and unable to check her computer. I send a note to her inbox asking if we'd ever attended Coastal Christian and telling her I *really* need to ask her something, then click shut the lid and hope for the best. Glancing around the living room, I wrinkle my nose. While this oft-rented cottage with its vintage furniture suits laid-back Camille and busy me just fine, it'll never do for Mel. And wait till she finds out that there's no major department store for miles.

My cell phone buzzes. It's a text from Camille: *Where r u?*

I text her back that I'm on my way, and with a cluttered mind, head back out the door. Ten minutes later I'm standing behind her.

"You're so amazing, Shane!"

Camille's fawning over a bleach-blond surfer with a Cheshire-cat grin. He's about to make his move when he sees me, stops for a brief second, then goes back in for the kiss before I have a chance to say hello.

I cross my arms, and Camille spins around, laughing. "Hey, Tara. Shane, this is my sister."

He jerks up his chin, eyeing me. "'Sup?" His speech is drawn out, lazy.

Rolling my eyes is a bad habit, but one I can't avoid at the moment. I look at Camille. "I've got to work this afternoon."

"First church, and now this! You're such a fuddy-duddy, Tara. Sundays are for lying on the beach!"

Shane cuts in. "Among other things."

I don't even want to know. "Mel will be here tomorrow. Maybe we could run into town and see if we can find anything to decorate her room."

Camille grabs my hand and pulls me down beside her. "Would you relax already? The waves are perfect today, and I want you to hang with me, okay?"

I glance around. She's right, the waves curl long and slow, making a perfect ride for surf maniacs. I stretch my legs out in front of me, and stick my fingers deep into the pebbled sand, reveling in the sensation. Unlike those famous Caribbean beaches, the sand's not fine around here, but grainy and interspersed with flat, smooth rocks called moonstones. I pick one up and rub it with my thumb, the motion easing away the tension that's been with me for the past two days.

"There, see? You look more relaxed already."

Shane's on Camille's blanket with her. "Mmm. I like relaxed."

Camille giggles while I try not to gag.

He turns to me. "So, Tara, you up at Coastal Christian today?"

I turn to him, my gaze questioning.

"Been there. Lots of dudes go there early before climbing into the waves. The pastor surfs."

Really. "So have you been attending there long?"

"Nah. I don't go on Sundays or anything. Just when they have their Friday night barbecues."

"Ah."

Camille playfully shoves Shane and he feigns hurt. "He's in a band. He plays the guitar, Tara."

Of course.

She flips one long curl over her shoulder. "We should go see them. Oh, and Shane's cousin Jo-Jo plays too—you'll like her, she keeps the group organized."

Why is Missouri suddenly sounding so good? "So, Shane, you live around here?"

"Yeah. My buddies and I share an apartment in the village."

"And what do you do for work?"

Now Camille's rolling her eyes at me.

"I'm a painter."

Great. An artist.

"Yeah, I get work from contractors around here all the time, but all of 'em know I'm not available until after eleven most days. I tell 'em I'm at a board meeting."

Camille giggles. "Get it? A 'board' meeting? As in 'surf' board? You're so funny, Shane."

Oh, brother. But at least he's got a real job and isn't some hungry artist making his living off oils and a tin cup.

Shane watches the waves, his arms resting on bent knees. "You two over on Fogcatcher Lane, right?" He shakes his head, still gazing seaward. "Man, that's sweet. I might have a job up there if the Horton house ever gets opened up."

My hands continue to fiddle with the coarse sand. "Which one is that?"

He cocks his head toward the cliffs. "The burned-up one on your street. Thought they'd tear it down, but nope, plan is to fix her up and get the owner back in there. Don't know when it's gonna happen though, but when it does, I'll be takin' my lunch breaks right here."

As if the surf has suddenly called out his name, Shane stands, pulls Camille to her feet, and I watch them take off into the tide, my cousin squealing like a teen. For a moment a tinge of jealousy threatens to overtake me. If Eliza were here, she'd strip off her sweats to expose a Porsche red bikini fitted over her tanned and toned body. She'd laugh gaily as she romped in the water, easily shrugging off the burdens of the week.

Maybe someday I'll be that girl. Not now, but someday.

I allow my fingers to take one long lunge back into the pebbled sand before hoisting myself up and smoothing the earth from my bum. While a part of me longs to enjoy the beach longer, I'm still too keyed up over meeting Beth this morning. Something about her timid demeanor coupled with her obvious interest in Josh has my mind spinning. That and Peg's accusations, which I've no intention of accepting, but must deal with nonetheless.

"YOU THE SWEET GIRL?"

I've been at the inn for two hours, watching relaxed travelers leave, and the harried arrive. The old man towering above me sounds ornery, but there's a twinkle in his eye.

"Yes, sir. What can I do for you?"

"If I were forty years younger, I'd tell you."

Well.

He taps his fist on the counter. "Heard you were asking around about your family this morning at the church."

"You attend Coastal Christian, then?"

"Darn tootin'! Been there through the last eight presidents, although some of them were repeats. Served on the church council in the seventies, the elder board in the eighties, the compassion ministries in the nineties, and now I'm an usher. During first service."

"So . . . you remember us?"

His gaze runs down one long, narrow nose. "Might. Burton Sims." He shakes my hand. "Thought you folks moved east after the scuttlebutt."

My hope sinks. "You know about that then? Can you tell me more?"

"Maybe. Could use a cup of coffee first. You have cream and sugar, I hope."

I pour him a cup, thankful I'd had time to brew another pot between check-ins. When I turn back, he's already grabbed two of the welcome cookies from the tray on the desk.

I hand him his coffee. "Would you like to sit down?"

He mumbles that he would. As he takes a seat on the couch in the lobby, a dripping wet boy in swim trunks traipses in. "I need a towel."

I hand him two and follow him out, mopping the entire way.

"Your dad still an accountant?" Burton has downed both cookies.

I straighten. "My father passed away, but he worked almost until he died."

"My condolences then. He was good with numbers. Helped us out on the church council sometimes."

"Really?"

"Your mom still a looker?"

I smile. "She is."

"Never knew why those two had so many problems . . . a good-looking couple like that should be immune in my book."

I'm back behind the counter now. "Oh, they didn't have any more than most couples do, I think. They took good care of us, and, well, they'd still be together if Daddy hadn't gotten so sick."

"I'm sorry to hear that Robert got sick. After the wringer that ol' Peg put him through, he deserved better, I thought."

His words land a crushing blow. "So . . . it's true. Everything Peg said about my father . . . is true?" I inhale a jagged breath. How could this be?

"It's true, but he who is without sin, let him first cast a stone. Or something like that. I remember that one from Sunday school when I was a kid."

I make my way into the lobby, hoping that no guests will choose this moment to arrive, their faces cheery and hopeful, and find a chair to lower myself into. "What do you mean by that?"

Burton swigs another sip, his gaze flickering off into the distance. "So he's a man who made some mistakes? Don't we all. But that one"—he points through the window, toward the diner next door—"that one was like a burr in his saddle, and I've always believed he had no choice but to pack up his young family and head out of Dodge." He sets his cup down and shakes his head. "Too bad too. He was one fine choir member."

I sink deeper into the chair, like a feather turned to stone. Weighted. Almost breathless. And yet, unlike a stone, a hint of life prevails within me. It makes itself known by the straining twist that wrenches my heart.

My mind searches for any recall, for any memory of what I'm learning about my father. And there is none. Yet, from some deep place that I cannot fully grasp as I sink further into this loathsome chair, an itch, like a gnat on the skin, unsettles me.

If only scratching at it would make the sensation stop.

Chapter Thirteen

I'm unprepared for what awaits me back at the cottage. Nine suitcases—all shapes and sizes—and three large moving boxes lie haphazardly on the front porch, leaving only enough room for one person to stand. If that. A yellow moving truck idles at the curb and, as I stare gape-mouthed at the mess on the porch, a heavy man with moppish hair hops out.

He takes a pen from atop his ear. "You Mel?"

No, me Tara. "No—is this all for Mel? Mel Sweet?"

"Yup. Sign here."

I take the pen. "Can you help me move them indoors?"

"Nope." He rips off a yellow copy of what I've just signed and hands it to me. "Company policy says we drop off at the door. No exceptions."

Alone, I squeeze through the screen door's narrow opening and enter the cottage. Why isn't Camille home yet? We'd talked earlier and she had planned to buy pierogies and sauté them up for dinner. With my work schedule and all her free time, we'd decided to divvy up the duties more. The screen door slams shut behind me, sending the smell of dampened wood into the room. I fumble for the light, my mind and heart a cloudy mess.

The old lightbulb from the table lamp sends a sallow cast throughout, doing nothing for my state of mind. After Burton Sims corroborated Peg's story, I moved through the rest of the afternoon and evening just a shell of myself. My hands may have handed out room keys, but my heartbeat felt more like a thud in my chest—a steady, but labored thump.

Although there's no sign of buttery onions or sautéed pierogies in the kitchen, the room has been cleared of the morning's mess. All except for a stash of Camille's magazines and an explosion of yarn that litters the cozy booth at the end of the room. I shove her things aside and sit down. Just then, laughter perks my attention. Three doors slam simultaneously, followed by Camille's giggles mixed in with other voices.

"Mel is here!" Camille leads the way into the house, Mel behind her, followed by one spit-and-polished Shane. "She called from the airport in SLO, so Shane drove me down to get her—and we got burgers!" She holds up two grease-stained sacks.

Mel's hair falls in cascades on and around her shoulders. I've always been a bit envious of its lushness, and tonight is no exception. She looks prettier—and happier—than ever. She hugs me, and I squeeze her back, wishing this reunion wasn't filled with so much uncertainty.

"You made it here a day early," I say.

Mel glances around, her eyes stopping randomly, staring at the kitschy beach décor that came with our cottage. Her attention turns to me. "It works. And close to the beach too. You didn't have to fight it out with someone else, did you? There's no little old lady crying in her soup over losing this one, I hope."

I shake my head. "Being on your own hasn't changed you one bit."

"In other words, I'm still as nasty as always."

"Hey, admitting it is the first step."

Shane's already helping himself to a burger as Camille pulls plates from the cabinets and sets them on the table. "Would you two quit it? Here you haven't seen each other in weeks and you've started bickering already." She tosses forks and napkins onto the table, surprising me with a rarely seen take-charge attitude. "You're both stubborn, if you ask me."

We answer in unison. "Am not!"

We scooch ourselves into the built-in booth, and I snag a fry, thankful for the lightness of the moment. Mel takes a whammy of a bite from her burger. "Ahm. Stahved."

"Don't talk with your mouth full," I scold.

Camille wags her head, curls flopping all around her. "Nothing's changed here." She turns to Shane. "Of the three of us, Tara's always been like the mom . . ."

Mel swallows her bite. "Yeah, like the mean, old mom."

Camille laughs. "And Mel is her bratty child. I, on the other hand, am the angelic baby of the bunch." She bats her eyes, which looks quite adorable until Shane wiggles his eyebrows at her and I have to resist the urge to slap him.

I clear my throat until all eyes look my way. "Mel, you have more stuff on the porch than Camille and I have together. Almost looks like you're planning to move here indefinitely." I laugh, as if that's absurd.

Mel shrugs, but then her shoulders deflate and she glances away.

Camille looks to me, then to Mel. She sets down her hamburger and wipes her fingers on a paper towel. "Shane, honey. Help me drag in Mel's things, will you?"

The screen door bounces against the frame, and I reach across to touch Mel's wrist. "I am sorry, you know."

"About what?"

A sigh escapes me, and I'm not sure if it's for her—or for me. "I just meant that although the interviews didn't go well, there's something better out there for you. I know it, Mel."

"Who says they didn't work out?"

Through the open doorway, I can see Shane tottering through the living room carrying more bags than any rational person would. *Probably didn't want to make two trips*. Camille's behind him, pulling a single case on wheels. "Well, they obviously didn't, because why else would you be here?"

"Both companies wanted me, but I . . ." She shrugs, her gaze landing nowhere. "I turned them both down."

"Oh. Oh? Then there must have been something wrong with the working conditions."

"Not really."

"The money. They were offering you a pittance. In this day and age, that is just . . ."

Mel sits back, her arms crossed. "The money was pretty fabulous actually."

I stand, and walk over to the garbage can, filling it with the paper that had held our meal, confused. Turning back to her, I flip my palms upward. "Then what in the world was wrong?"

She studies the fingernails on one hand, as if checking for dirt. Her eyes flash briefly, before her gaze catches with mine. "I missed my family. You have a problem with that?"

Despite everything I've learned in the last few days about my parents' past in this supposed Shangri-la, I find myself further surprised. Ever since she was a teenager, Mel has been planning her escape from our family. I always thought she'd make her move during college, but instead she attended school nearby—although we rarely saw her face around home before 11:00 p.m. When she finally earned that degree last year, I thought, *She's out of here.* But then she helped her friend Mary Jane set up and run her own line of organic baby clothing. And now, after setting out on her own and finding terrific work in marketing, she's come back across the country . . . because she missed us?

I slide into a seat across from her. "We missed you too, Mel-Mel."

"Don't get all sloppy on me. I'm not staying forever. Just thought I'd, you know, come check the place out. See what's the big deal."

"I'm so glad to hear you say that." I gesture to the side deck with my head, and Mel follows me out. We settle into the Adirondacks, the night enfolding us. I sigh. "Frankly, Mel, things really aren't working out here, and I want to head back to Missouri."

I hadn't realized that Camille stood just behind the French doors. She charges onto the deck. "You *what?*"

Mel's arms stay crossed across her body. She shakes her head. "You're going to have a tough time with this one, big sister."

Camille tosses her curls to one side. "You dragged me all the way here and now you want to leave? I don't think so."

Tension wraps itself around my forehead and temples like a thick leather strap. "Camille, I've thought this—"

Her eyes grow big and round and angry, and her normally bouncy voices cuts into the night quiet. "You never give anything a chance!"

My fingers clench. "I give *everything* a chance." I try hard to control the emotion in my voice. "I worked at the same auto parts store for five years—that's chance. I believed Trent when he said he wanted to marry me, and I asked Mom many times to take us back to Otter Bay—all chances. *And* I came all the way out here only to find out that, hey, it's not the happy place I remembered. At least I *gave* it a chance!"

Camille scrunches her round face until her cheeks turn red. "That old woman said one thing—one mean thing about Dad. You didn't have to be so snarky with her. Why does what she has to say matter anyhow?"

Mel stands and walks back into the kitchen. I hear the fridge door open and her steps back out to the deck. She holds a bottle of water, opens the cap, and takes a long, lingering drink. "So much is clear to me now, Tara." She recaps the bottle, sets it on the large, flat arm of her chair, and sits back down next to me. "You want everything to be easy. Controllable. And when it's not? You run."

"Oh brother, that's just not true."

"Oh no? What about your old job? I couldn't have stood being in that drab office all day, but you withstood it mainly, I think, because it was easy. You knew the job, they paid you well, and you didn't have to spend anything extra on a new wardrobe to work there. So why leave? And Trent. I couldn't have made it more than a year of that boy's half-hearted commitment, but you—you lasted five."

I'm incensed. "You're the one who said he was the best thing that ever happened to me!"

She shrugs. "I always figured that's the way you wanted it, but now I see that it was just easy. You knew him and his family and didn't have to stretch yourself at any time. If it weren't for a little thing called a marriage license, you'd still be there with him in a relationship that had less passion than two pieces of fruit."

Camille giggles, then sobers. "Sorry. That was funny."

I smooth my hair back in place, gathering my temper with it. "I told you from the start that this was a long vacation, that we'd see how it went. Look around you, Mel. Camille and I are still living mostly on the paltry supplies we brought with us. *You're* the only one with more luggage than the Queen of England. Okay, sure, I admit that I'd hoped we'd love it here—I even rented this cottage, for goodness sakes!"

A throat clears, and all three of us turn to see Shane standing in the doorway looking as uncomfortable as a pre-teen boy seeing his mom in a bikini. "Uh, thanks for the burger. Cam, I gotta go." He steps out onto the patio and slips down the stairs and almost out of sight to the street. Camille follows him and catches him by the corner of the house. She does nothing to hide the drawn-out kiss they share.

When she returns, her face remains flushed, probably not from our conversation. "You're not fooling me, Tara. You planned on staying here all along—just like I said that day at the diner, when we first met Nigel. But I've been thinking, and Mel is right. It would take a burning bush for you to do anything new. I think you've been wanting to come out here ever since Dad died, but you were too scared. When Mom left, you somehow found the courage—"

Mel cuts in. "And now that it's not going the way you planned, you're giving up and crawling back to your old, dull, *predictable* life."

Camille flops into the empty Adirondack, her eyes on me. "I'm not going anywhere."

Mel joins her. "And neither am I."

WHAT WOULD ELIZA DO?

The girls are in bed, but once again I'm up into the night because no sleep will come. The laptop whirs against the quiet. My sisters are against me, and other than a brief, vague "yes" about Coastal Christian from Mom via Facebook, and a promise to call me "just as soon as I sign up for international calling," I'm alone. Thankfully, the plucky Eliza Carlton has kept me company with her philosophies on life and all its idiosyncrasies.

From the daily digest I learned how Eliza handled a similar situation when her older brother, Emil, was accused of plagiarism. So he was guilty? He'd always been her protector, the one who took care of her and another brother when their parents died in that Guatemalan plane crash. Because of his devotion and care of her, and because she knew his heart had been spun from gold, she'd decided to defend his honor, no matter what he may or may not have done.

I sigh. Part of me still wants to pick up and move back to Missouri, to forget about this crazy thing I've done and go back to the comfort of familiarity. Mel and Camille accuse me of running, but who doesn't wrap themselves in their favorite wool sweater when they're cold? Or take a sip of their mother's chamomile tea remedy when they're sick? No, the girls have me all wrong.

And yet, I have to admit, another part of my heart longs to be here, despite what appears to be a mistake my father once made. Whatever my father actually did, well, it happened many years ago. His life is a testament to something so much more, so much better, than old sins. Like Eliza, I long for the world to know the real man.

And so they shall. My mind is made up. I will defend my father's honor, no matter what. Peg, and anyone else who questions our family's right to be here, better get used to the idea.

Fast.

Chapter Fourteen

 "Well, well, big sister. You've been holding out on me." Mel peers over the menu at a parade of surfers strolling through the Red Abalone Grill, their bodies carved lean, and tan. "Not bad. Not bad at all."

Camille giggles. "Tara's not interested in them. She's got her eye on a fireman." She stretches out *man* like she's some flirty country singer.

I smirk. "Can I help it if he knows hotness when he sees it?"

Mel and Camille scream, their volume cutting through the diner's din and drawing all eyes on us. Mel slaps me on the head with her menu, and Camille flops back against the booth, her curls falling all over her face, peals of giggles refusing to stop.

I lean forward. "For heaven's sake, it's not that funny."

Camille lays one delicate hand across her middle, still laughing. "I'm telling you, Mel, Otter Bay's been so good for our Tara."

Mel's smile flattens out, her face watchful. "I see that. But I wonder why just yesterday she seemed to want to leave." Mel and Camille speak to each other as if I'm invisible.

A waitress named Mimi comes by, swinging a coffee pot and whistling. It's late morning, later than we usually show up for breakfast. Camille and I place our orders, and wait while Mel mulls over the menu. After taking Mel's order, Mimi zips on, and I look back to the girls. "I've decided to give it another chance—something you, dear Camille, say I never do." Camille swallows her smile, probably feeling the aftermath of last night's conflict. "I'm still not convinced this move was my best decision ever, but . . ." I steal a glance at Peg who's barking at Jorge in between glaring at me. "I've decided to be proactive about our new adventure. To examine it from all sides, if you will, and be ready to intervene when necessary. Most of all, to stay positive."

Mel cocks her chin. "Why Tara May, you're becoming downright daring. Next thing you know you'll be wearing real red on your toes . . ."

Camille sticks out her tongue. "Instead of baby pink. Blech."

I shrug. "If that's what it takes."

Holly flounces over to our table and sits down beside

me. "Scoot," she says, a lavish scent of vanilla enveloping the space as she slides closer. "Aunt Peg changed my station for some reason just about the time you girls walked in. Hi, I'm Holly, and you must be Mel-Mel."

Mel's eyes narrow slightly. Her pet name is usually reserved for those times when one of us senses her deep need for buttering-up.

"I'm Holly, and your sisters have just been missin' you so. Welcome to our little Otter Bay."

Mel cocks her head. "I've heard about you. Cam says you're in charge of the specials menu. I can appreciate that."

Holly's eyes open wide. "You call her Cam too? So do I! Camille's a nice name, but kinda old-fashioned if you ask me. Cam is more fun, like she is."

Mel's poker face breaks into a grin, an amused and slightly sarcastic one, but a grin just the same. "I agree. And I guess you know by now that when Cam needs to be on Tara's good side, she calls her 'Tare-Tare.'"

Holly slaps back against the seat, one of her curls slipping out from her ponytail. "Ahhh—I love it. You girls are so much fun, I don't know what I've done without you to make me laugh each mornin'."

"Tell me something else, Holly." Any sign of judgment on Mel's face has vanished. "Where can I get myself some cooler clothes, something more . . . more stylish than a foofy skirt and flip-flops?"

I straighten. "Hey! I think I'm offended."

Holly waves me on. "She didn't mean anythin' by it. You look good in your clothes, Tara, although if we're goin' to be critiquin', I'd say more color would make those big brown eyes of yours just stand right out. But anyway, I've got the perfect place for Mel to go." Holly turns to me again. "You can go there too, if you want."

Should I feel insulted?

Camille pipes in. "SLO! There's lots of shopping in San Luis Obispo, Mel. Holly and I went down there to check out the college and we saw the neatest stuff in downtown."

Holly shifts her shoulders side to side, her face animated as she leans folded arms onto our table. "Yeah, yeah, you could go all the way down there, but try my friend Simka's store first. It's kinda hard to find, but I could take you there after my shift. She's got stuff like nobody's business, but folks around here just aren't buying. I don't understand it. Anyways, I took one look at you and just knew you'd like Simka's. With that hair—oh, to have straight hair like that!—you could be on TV. Now all you need are more tapered jackets, cotton ones, so you don't roast."

Beth walks in wearing sleek sweats and a knit jacket. Her baby's not with her, so she takes the small table in the corner—the one I snagged last week. Peg greets her almost immediately, the sour woman's face wearing a rare smile, and I'm beginning to wonder what this young woman with the perfect haircut has that everyone else does not. Especially me.

"So what do you say about that, Tara?" Camille's watching me, her expression hopeful.

I give her a weak smile. "Sorry. Missed it. What were you saying?"

Holly slides out of the booth, just as Mimi delivers our food. "I'm about to get myself fired for the fourteenth time if I don't get goin', but we thought . . ." She looks around for support. "We thought you might be open to letting Simka help you with your colors."

"My colors?"

"Yeah. Something to liven you up some. You're so beautiful, and all, that maybe you could learn to show it off more. And a better foundation will go far, Tara."

"Foundation?"

"You know, bra-*zier*. Everybody knows the proper foundation will make you feel younger, and look perkier!" She glances up. "Oh-oh. Gotta go."

Holly takes off into the kitchen with Peg nipping at her heels. Mel stares after her for a long while, her face a recipe of confusion and laughter. "She's perfect. You know you've arrived in a small town when someone like *that* joins you for breakfast." She's cracking herself up. "Basically, Tara, you've exchanged one quirky small town for another. At least the people around here know how to get a great tan."

Camille gives Mel a punch. "Aw, she's really nice."

Mel winks at Camille, then clears her throat. "Who's she?"

I raise my eyebrows, but Mel doesn't back down. "The chick with the good hair that you were gaping at. Another friend of yours? Is she going to come over here and tell me about her stylist 'Franck,' and how much he'd love to stick his fingers in my hair?"

I put one hand over my mouth, stifling a laugh, and realizing just how much I missed Mel's wit—strange as that may seem. Fortunately she has the good sense to lean forward and whisper this time. "You were staring at her like she stole your dolly. What gives?"

Quickly I sober. "I was not. We met at church the other day, and I was just trying to catch her attention so I could say hi."

"Okay, now I've heard it. You. In church."

"Yes. Stop staring, you'll pinch a nerve. And I don't understand why all the surprise. You went to Mary Jane's church a few times."

"And you rolled your eyes each time I went."

"Eat your biscuits," I scold, sneaking another glance at Beth. She's no longer alone, but talking with the man who was with Josh here in the diner the other morning. He's tall like Josh, but thicker around the middle, and softer looking than your typical firefighter. As if sensing my gaze, Beth turns and recognition registers on her face. She waves demurely, and I offer her a wave of my own.

Camille sets down her fork with a clank. "Are you ever going to tell us about your date with a burning hot fireman?"

Mel's mouth curls upward. "I'm so glad I flew out here. Okay, dish."

My mind's been too muddied to think much about my upcoming date with Josh. I considered telling Camille about it, but then I had that confrontation with Peg, and then I saw Beth's reaction to my friendship status with Josh, not to mention Mel's early arrival home . . . I'm starting to wonder if it's even a good idea to date anyone at this point in my life. I open my mouth to speak, when Holly shows up and once again scoots me over with one flick of her hip.

"What'd I miss?"

Mel flips a lengthy strand of hair behind her shoulder. "My sister's about to tell us why she's been keeping her new man under wraps."

Holly sighs a baby sigh. "Josh. He's just the nicest guy. You could do a lot worse."

I begin to speak, then sputter. Breathe in. "How do you all know about . . . Josh?"

Holly's eyes pop open wide. "Well, I saw him just sit right down with you the other day, acting all goofy eyed, and then I read his lips when he asked you to dinner next Saturday night. Wasn't I supposed to say anythin'?"

Horrified, I watch as she turns to Beth and the man who's now sitting across from her and calls out, "Don't you be tellin' Josh we're talking about him now."

My hands fly to my face. Mel's laughter makes me part two fingers so I can attempt to still her with my steely gaze. I fail.

Holly goes on, as if she hadn't just embarrassed me beyond recognition, but at least she has enough mercy to lower her voice. "That's Billy over there. If you asked me, those two shoulda gotten together before all this mess."

My laughter stops. Mess? Is she talking about Beth and . . . Josh?

Camille rests her elbows on the table. "We haven't been here long enough to know anything about it. Is he the father of her baby or something?"

Mel cuts in. "Not you too, Cam. One soap addict in the family is enough."

I open my mouth to protest, but Camille shakes her mane and squeezes her nose and mouth into a pucker as if Mel suggested she eat a slab of liver. Holly's nonplussed. "What're you girls goin' on about? Beth's husband ran off with their babysitter. It was the biggest mess ever. Billy really liked her a long time ago, and everyone thought they might work out, but then she off and married Gordon. He was a piece of work, that one."

Mel wags her head. "Jerk."

Camille nods. "I'll say."

Holly continues, her eyes squarely on mine. "Are they lookin' this way?"

I glance over. "No, you're safe."

"Good. Okay, so she married Gordon, and then had a baby—well, you know everyone was countin' the months—

and the next thing you know, he's walkin' the sitter home and not comin' back!"

Is no one immune from pain? Certainly Beth's countenance had been a tip-off to hard things but, and I'm ashamed to admit this even to myself, I'd been jealous of her. A young mom with a petite body, an adorable baby, and an obvious friendship with a man I'm drawn to. How could I see the meaning behind her downcast eyes when I refused to look beyond the obvious? I smooth my updo and stroke my ear. "So no wonder Josh was so tender with the baby."

"Well, it's more than that. That baby doesn't have a father to look after it, and if it weren't for Josh, he wouldn't have a mother either."

I stare at Holly, more confused than ever.

"Don't you know? Beth's house caught on fire, and Josh saved her life!"

Chapter Fifteen

 It's one thing to discover that you misjudged a person, and quite another to find out that they almost *died*. After Holly drops this bit of Beth's and Josh's history into our laps, Peg shoos her away from our table and we never get to discuss it with her further. We almost pay the bill and leave, but much to Peg's obvious chagrin, dear Nigel hobbles in and asks to share our table.

He lowers himself into the booth, leaning carefully on his cane until he makes contact with the seat. A brief sigh escapes him, and we wait while he unfolds his hanky, mops his brow, then neatly folds it back up and slides it into his pocket.

"Now," he says, his face serene, "who is this beautiful child with whom I've yet to become acquainted?"

"Nigel. I'd like you to meet our sister, Mel."

Mel reaches out a hand across the table. "A pleasure, sir."

"It's Nigel." He smiles at her, then glances around the table at each one of us, never altering his expression. Mimi attempts to whiz by when Nigel quite slowly but deftly lifts his cane. "Mimi, dear, I'd like a cup of . . ."

". . . half-caf coffee."

He gives her a nod and a slight wave. "You remember." She pours his coffee and offers him cream and sugar. "Thank you, dear. Also, I'll have the oatmeal, no raisins, please." She takes his menu and spins away as Peg calls her name.

"Mel, I work for Nigel at the inn next door. We met right here in the diner, when he was playing a game of solitaire."

Camille cuts in. "Nigel asked Tara for some advice, and the next thing I know, she's working for him." She giggles.

Nigel's nodding. "And doing a mighty fine job, I must say. Betty says you've made her job easy. We have other systems that are in need of a makeover, so when you come in tomorrow, perhaps we can discuss them."

Mel leans her head to the side. "Tara's efficient all right."

Camille takes a sip of her water, as all the rest of her dishes have been cleared away. "It was Nigel who first told Tara and me that Josh was a fireman. You even said he was one of the bravest, didn't you?"

Nigel stirs his coffee. "That I did."

Mel twiddles with her napkin. "He must be if he saved a woman from a burning building."

Nigel savors his coffee, his bland expression masking his thoughts. "The bravest souls understand the fears that drive them, and they attack those fears. Relentlessly."

Mel stills. "So you're saying that Josh is actually afraid of fire, but that he faced that fear when he ran into a burning house. Am I reading you right?"

I frown. "I don't think that's what Nigel meant. Maybe he just meant that Josh—that all firefighters—are afraid of losing what—or who—they are supposed to protect."

Mel's forehead wrinkles. "And so . . . ?"

Camille takes her twelfth sip of water, her eyes constantly darting between the window to the outside and back to us. "And so his fear of letting someone die inside a house is bigger than his own fear of fires!"

We all got quiet, and look to Camille. Nigel continues to nod. "Lovely. Each of you has a very good head on your shoulders. Such a rare treasure to find, especially with television and computers taking up so much of young peoples' attention in these times."

Oh, no, you don't. No dodging the issue. "So which one of us is right about what you said?"

Nigel creases his brow. "That's not for me to say. I will say that you girls all appear to be quite brave, quite brave indeed."

"Or stupid." Mel gives me the bug eye, but Nigel's unfazed.

"On the contrary. Not many young women would pack up and move across the country to a strange place, such as you have done. It's charming that you all want to see the land your family once knew, and to experience it fully. I do hope you enjoy Otter Bay."

Mel and I exchange a look, but neither says anything. Camille, on the other hand, is swooning over the beach life. "Never had views like this in Missouri," she's saying, her eyes riveted on a surfer who's standing next to his old square-back VW and peeling a wet suit from his skin.

Mimi appears with Nigel's oatmeal and the check. Nigel furrows his brows. "Are you in need of this table?"

Our waitress keeps her eyes down while wiping our table with a rag. She applies so much elbow grease that beads of sweat appear on her cheeks and forehead. "Peg says she's expecting a crowd." Mimi straightens up, then bends backward to stretch, and several joints pop. "But I'm not so sure."

Mel crosses her arms. "A crowd? In Otter Bay?"

"Oh yes." Nigel offers affirmation with a lifted coffee cup. "We have had our share of traffic, especially on art-show weekends. Wine tasting festivals often bring out the crowds as well. I'm not aware of any particular event this week, however."

Holly careens toward us. "That's it!" She unwraps the

apron from around her waist and tosses it onto our newly shined table. "She's more ornery today than a squirrel at feeding time. I'm supposed to be off now, but Peg thinks we're suddenly gettin' a crowd. She wanted me to work overtime—and it's only Monday! I just don't know what's gotten into her lately, but I'm not stayin' to find out. You ladies ready?"

Camille brightens. "For shopping?"

Holly nods. "Naturally."

The girls say good-bye to Nigel, and file out. I linger a moment, and thank him for joining us. "You don't mind us leaving you here alone, I hope."

"Not at all, my dear. Enjoy every minute with your sisters."

I turn to leave, and just as I reach the front door an inkling draws me to take one more look at my new friend and boss. He doesn't notice me, though, because Peg stands over him, one crooked arm on her recently healed hip, her lips moving faster than one of those hammer-head rides at the county fair.

To dear Nigel's credit, his face shows as placid as ever.

I've got to ask him to teach me how to do that.

SIMKA'S SHOP RESIDES IN a pink-stucco cottage off Main Street on Alabaster Lane. Unfortunately, and despite its eye-drawing color, it's difficult to see because the road bends so that if you're standing at one end and looking up, her shop's tucked into the curve.

Inside, I immediately notice the smell. Oranges, cinnamon, and nutmeg permeate the place, as if we'd just walked into an out-of-the-oven winter pie. The second thing to stand out—and why I missed this I'll never know—is color. Everywhere. Come to think of it, the colors remind me of an array of desserts of berry and citrus, pumpkin even. So maybe the whole aroma thing was not by accident.

"Hey, girl!" Holly waves at a woman whose deep-purple dress contrasts stunningly against her porcelain skin. "I brought you some fresh customers."

"Hello, ladies. Welcome to Simka's. How may I assist you today?"

Three index fingers turn my way. I twist my chin left, then right. "What? I don't really need anything . . . I'm really just window shopping today. Camille's the one who likes to shop."

Holly puts both hands on my shoulders, and nudges me forward. "Tara needs some color. She has a date with Josh-u-a." She draws out his name, her voice sounding both sultry and teasing.

Simka claps her hands together. "Oh how I love a mission! Let me see, let me see. Turn around now."

I feel silly as I twirl.

Simka walks around me counterclockwise, one finger on her chin as all eyes in the room examine me like I'm an art project gone bad. "Why do you dress like a winter when you are clearly a summer?"

Camille rocks on her toes, obviously thrilled by the direction of this conversation. "Darn, I wish I had a pencil. I should take notes."

Mel grabs a pad and pen from her purse and hands them to her. "Go crazy." She turns to Simka. "Now I've always thought that with Tara's fair coloring she should go with brighter colors. She always wears such—"she fingers my sleeve—"such blah clothing."

"Ironically, if the palette she wears is too bright she will appear horribly dull."

Mel laughs, and I glare at her.

Simka cuts back in. "I was referring to her skin tones. Tara needs colors to complement her beautiful but pale tones. Mellow, but not blah—like beige or ecru, which hardly anyone wears anymore anyway—and definitely not black."

Both Mel and Simka run their gazes along the lines of my black pedal pushers, which until now I thought slimmed me down. Camille's scribbling notes like I'm some sort of science experiment. She stops, rests the eraser end on her chin, then returns to her pencil scratching.

Simka roams the main showroom of the store gathering blouses, while the telltale sound of hanger metal chirps against display rods, then settles with a clink in her arms. Camille shadows her, and Holly trickles off to a scarf-laden room that probably once held a dining room set. Mel strolls around near me, her arms folded neatly.

She speaks quietly. "Funny. After your little announcement last night about going back, I'd never have guessed that you had a date set up with Mr. Wow. Maybe you're not all that into him."

I browse through a rack of camisoles too sheer for comfort. So much for the proper foundation Holly went on about. "Guess I've had a change of heart."

"What's he look like?"

I pause. "He's strong. And tall. His hair's usually messy, not like it's uncombed, but like he's just been out at the beach and only had time to give it a quick shake. Um, and he's got eyes that I can't explain exactly. Lots of color in them instead of just one. They're flecked in fall colors, like a kaleidoscope."

Mel stares at me, her shoulders taut and her arms still tightly crossed. "You make him sound positively perfect. You're really into him, then."

I shrug, unable to hide the hint of a smile. "Nobody's perfect, Mel. There's just something special about him, and he's easy to talk to so that's a plus. Please don't make more of this than it is, though, okay? I'm kind of nervous."

She softens her stance, her arms now loosely folded. "You'll do fine. Dating takes practice, and you just haven't had much of that. Might as well practice on this guy."

I stare after her. *What's that supposed to mean?*

"Here we go!" Simka's arms hold a mountain of clothing. "I've chosen a plethora of outfits in hues to complement your skin, Tara. Simply a plethora! Lavenders and yellows, crisp whites and powder blues. And do not underestimate pink. Dusty pink, especially, would look marvelous on you."

"There! You see?" I lift up one pinkly manicured foot and wave it for the whole room to see.

Camille's nodding and writing. "Score one for Tara. When you're right you're right, big sis."

I'm ushered to a dressing room that's nothing more than a couple of curtains hung from the vaulted ceiling. But inside there's a narrow upholstered chair that oozes elegance and comfort, and calls to me for a respite, reminding me just how much I detest trying on clothes. Is there anything worse than being forced to examine your body as strangers watch your feet from beneath a swath of fabric?

I puff out a long breath, and remind myself this is all for a good cause: my date with Josh. Eliza Carlton never passes up the chance to go on a good power shop, so I rally, and dig into the pile finding denim. Unfortunately I don't share the world's enthusiasm for jeans. Oh, I love the way they look on other people, but me? They sag or hang or don't button. And the process of trying them on could put an otherwise positive soul into a deep, dark depression.

Instead I opt for a knee-length dress in silk, its fabric sliding over me like it's butter and I'm toast. Shoving the curtain aside, I step out in my bare feet.

Simka's nodding, Holly's cooing, Camille's bouncing on her toes, and Mel, dear Mel, wears an actual smile.

"Well?"

"That sunflower yellow is divine on you, simply divine!" Simka's clapping her hands, encircling me. "Those braided straps, that high waist . . . it's you."

"Oh, it's super feminine, Tara," Camille says. "I love it on you."

Holly steps closer. "You would look so good in jeans with a pretty top, Tara. Try on the jeans and maybe that lavender one."

She's so hopeful to find me in denim that I can't let her down. Back behind the curtain, I rehang the dress, silently giddy to find something that looks that good on me. Never would have chosen that for myself. Never, ever. Still skeptical, I tug on the jeans, surprised by how easily they wear. With a shrug, I slip the lavender blouse on over my head, thankful that it doesn't get stuck somewhere between my elbows and my head. Been there before, and let's just say, it wasn't pretty.

"Okay"—I step into the room—"this wouldn't be my choice but—"

"Tara has a butt!" Camille's giggling and bouncing again, declaring to the whole shop (thankfully we're the only ones in it at the moment) that, yes, I can claim ownership of at least one curve.

Even Mel appears surprised. "Tara's got her groove on all right. And look at your legs—they're so long and lean."

"It's a miracle!" Camille is almost dancing. "I hope they teach me how to do that in school."

I hold up both palms. "Okay, all right already. You've had your fun, let's move on, shall we?"

Holly and Simka laugh, their heads together as they watch us. "Now try the blue blouse with those denims, Tara. It's less billowy than the lavender, and I want your sisters to see how spectacular you'll look with a little more skin and a lot more cling!" She shimmies her chest when she says that, and I hope she didn't hurt herself. "And here." She hands me a skin-colored lacey bra with underwire and padded cups. "You'll want to give the fabric something divine to cling to!"

I step back into the makeshift dressing area, a strange mixture of hope and trepidation filling my mind. While the girls continue to hoot and chatter from just beyond the thin curtain, I can't help but wonder who has higher expectations for my date with Josh. Me . . . or them?

Chapter Sixteen

Wind with an agenda greets the night, its gusts tossing the loose shutters over and over against our cottage's outer walls. The racket unnerves me, rattling my already shaky emotions. It's just a dinner date, and yet I'm drawn to this man whom I hardly know in a way that's so very different from with Trent. Trent and I, well, we were compatible and comfortable, everything I'd always thought a good relationship should be. We'd come to expect certain things about each other, and those things—like Friday night dinners at the Dexton Café and Sunday afternoon bowling—were my weekly lifeline. Now as I think about the stirrings of anticipation over my date with Josh, I wonder if that old lifeline was actually a crutch.

I roll my shoulders and take another peek into the mirror. After much debate, the girls talked me into wearing the shapely and ubercomfortable denims I'd bought, despite the fact that I nearly fainted at the price. Suddenly it all became very clear: my bum never had a chance in bargain jeans. Although the girls rooted for the clingy blue halter, I opted instead for the sleeveless in lavender sateen. Hey, a girl's got to know when to be decisive. That's what Eliza always says. Besides, depending on how things go, that halter just may find its way out of my closet one day.

The bell rings and Mel answers the door. Josh's tall frame fills the doorway as she backs up to let him in, and I step across the room, not quite used to the heels I borrowed from my younger sister. When Josh's eyes light up, I'm won over—although truly, it would have taken much less than that.

"Hi. I'd like you to meet my sister, Mel."

He offers her a hello, and she looks him over thoroughly. "You kids behave yourselves."

He winks. "I'm not making any promises." Both his mouth and eyes greet me with a smile. He leans close, as if intending to greet me with a kiss. My eyes flutter.

His voice is low, deep. "You look . . . you look incredible. Ready to go?"

I nod as he offers me his arm, and whisks me past the girls, down the steps, and quickly into his truck. In that brief moment, the wind undoes every bit of effort I'd given to my hair. The relaxed bun slides down the side of my head and hangs there in an unforgiving knot. As Josh slides into the driver's seat, I work quickly to repair the damage.

He turns to me, his eyes watchful. Nerves have taken hold of my breath, and I can't speak. "Here, let me help you." With a quick and deft hand, he reaches past me, gently brushing my cheek with a warm touch. In one motion, he removes my clip, then carefully loosens the bound strands until they rest on my shoulders. The moment's suspended, and Josh's gaze travels over my face until he finds my eyes. "There."

I lean against the seat, soaking in the newness of this sensation. Palm trees bow in the wind, and a swath of fuchsia jets across the evening sky. Josh's voice folds into the silence.

"I haven't seen you in over a week. Tell me what I've missed. Have you had a chance to tour the area much?"

"No, not really. Between my job at the inn and Mel's arrival, there hasn't been as much extra time as I'd thought. Oh, but I went to church on Sunday."

He turns to me, his eyes finding mine before looking back to the road. "Coastal Christian?"

"Yes. Mikey introduced me to his mother and sister."

Josh exhales. "His father wasn't there?"

"No, he was sick, Mikey said."

"Poor guy's been battling an immune disorder. He's been really sick lately."

"He said it so nonchalantly. I had no idea his father was *that* ill."

"It's tough on the family, but they're faithful."

"That's so good. He's their husband and father, so of course they should stay faithful to him, no matter what."

Josh rubs his chin with one hand, his other still securely on the steering wheel. He glances at me. "Loyalty has its place, but I just meant that they're faithful to God, despite how bleak things have been for them."

The truck slows as we turn into a parking lot just off the road that borders the sea. Josh's comment about Mikey's family stays with me, as we pull into a spot and he switches the engine off. *Was Josh implying that going to church is a sure sign of someone's faithfulness to God?* Because if that were true, no one in the Sweet family would be considered faithful. I've never thought all that much about church or religion, but I've believed, ever since Daddy died, that he's looking after all of us . . . from somewhere. I couldn't stand to think otherwise.

Josh opens his door and holds it there while leaning toward me. "I'll come around and get you." As he makes a dash through the barreling wind for my side of the truck, I resolve to push aside anything that would dampen an otherwise enchanting evening.

Once inside Moonstones, I fluff my hair while we wait to be seated. Josh watches me, his gaze taking in my newly relaxed hairstyle. I haven't worn my hair down in public in . . . well, I can't recall the last time. Josh's hand finds the small of my back as we follow the hostess to a row of booths on a raised platform for better views of the ocean. She seats us in the one farthest from the open walkway, and I make a mental note to thank her on the way out.

"Ah. Finally." Josh rests against the seat back.

Despite the setting sun, we're close enough to see white-caps on the water. "What a beautiful view. You picked the perfect place—thank you."

Josh takes a quick glance at the stunning sea and wrinkles his nose before turning his attention back to me. "It's all right."

"All right? It's amazing! More beautiful than I imagined, and certainly more than I ever remembered."

His wide grin gives him away.

"You're teasing."

He leans forward, leaning on crossed arms. When he looks up again at me, those eyes dancing, I think I might just melt into the booth. "So, tell me. What do you remember about Otter Bay, Miss Sweet?"

A busboy serves us water, and I take a sip, along with a cool breath. "So much, yet so little really. I remember my dad taking me to the tide pools, and my mom standing on the cliff—probably corralling Mel." My laughter is light. "I'd hoped to find our old house, but it's long gone. It looks like someone razed it, bought the lot next door, then built a mansion across both properties. Progress, I guess. But I still remember the feel of the street—that's one of the reasons I was so excited by the location of our rental. We lived over on Pelican Place, and it's got a similar incline to the one on Fogcatcher."

"No family out here?"

I shake my head.

"Or old friends?"

I begin to shake my head again, but slow myself when I remember Burton, and unfortunately, Peg. Our waiter appears, ready to recite the heady list of specials of the night. "May I get you started with something from the bar?"

Josh gestures to me. "I'm happy with water for now. Thank you."

Josh orders himself a Coke, and after our waiter leaves, it's my turn for questions, and I opt to shift subjects. "Do you like fighting fires?"

"No one's ever really asked me about it that way. People usually either treat me like a saint—or a pyromaniac." One corner of his mouth quirks when he smiles. "I'm kidding, but to answer your question, it's a rush—facing fires head on. I don't like the fact that danger happens, but I wouldn't be doing this kind of work if I didn't love it. Besides"—he gives me a teasing wink—"the uniform works for me."

A picture forces its way into my mind. He's bare-chested except for those thick-strapped fireman suspenders, grinning and camera-ready like he's Mr. August. I laugh nervously. "I'd have to agree."

"I like a woman who's not afraid to be honest."

"Are you ready to order?" Our waiter reappears, serves Josh his soda, and listens to our orders without writing down a thing, just like on *Quartz Point*. Who knew that in real life, waiters memorize orders? I'm beginning to think I've lived a sheltered life.

Menus gone, I lean forward. "I met Beth at your church last week."

Josh glances away, ultimately making eye contact with his water glass, his mouth suddenly grim.

When he doesn't respond, I continue. "It's okay. Holly told me about the fire at Beth's house and how you . . . saved her. I've never met a true hero before."

Josh looks up. "I'm *not* a hero. I just followed my instincts, and thankfully, she got out."

"Holly says you were the only one around, and if you hadn't dashed into that house then . . . oh, the thought terrifies me. That baby could've lost his mother, but you—" I shake my head—"you changed the course."

"I just did my job. Nothing heroic about it, just excellent timing. You're right, though, that it could've been more tragic. Terribly. Not something any of us likes to think about."

I straighten. "Sorry . . . I didn't mean to bring up bad memories."

His lips curl into a smile. "Getting back to you, there's got to be someone around who lived here back when your family did. One of these days you'll run into them, although chances are you've changed some."

"I've heard I was somehow more adventurous. Hard to believe." I laugh, but it bothers me not to tell him that there are at least two people in town who knew my family. I haven't even talked much about it to the girls, but I've wanted to protect them from the ugliness. Nor do I tell him that, if Mel hadn't showed up when she did, I may have packed up Camille and myself and headed home.

Josh sits across from me, his collared shirt open several buttons below his neck. I look away. Missouri would be one lonely place right now. Josh's words cut through my wayward thoughts. *I like a woman who's not afraid to be honest.* Maybe he's the one objective person I can share my secret with, the one who's able to help me figure out how to restore my father's name.

"You know when you asked if we had any old friends still here? There are a couple of people who've, um, told me they remember us."

"Really? Who? Maybe I know them."

"Well, one is a man from church. Burton Sims? He stopped by the inn the other day and introduced himself."

Josh grins. "Burton's a good guy. I bet he guzzled a load of that free coffee, didn't he?"

I smile through my trepidation. "As a matter of fact, yes. He did."

Josh nods. "He's one for the coffee and donut room at church. When service is over—or even before it begins some days—you'll find him there. That's great. I bet he can fill your head with stories."

I feel a squirm coming on. "Well, actually . . ."

A woman who's about as tall as she is wide appears at our table, her cheeks flushed red, like a jar of cranberries. Her neat ponytail brings out my envy. "Let's see, you're the

Caeser," she says to me. "And you would be the soup . . . oh, hey there, Josh. I didn't realize I'd be serving your order."

"Hi, Therese. This is Tara Sweet. She's new to town."

Therese shoves a chubby hand toward me, nearly knocking me in the chin. She giggles, then offers me a hello. "You two look amazing together, like one of those tourist postcards that says 'Come to Otter Bay and you'll look as good as these two.'"

Josh groans. "More likely it says, 'How'd this beautiful woman get stuck with the likes of this guy?'"

I blush.

Therese swipes a hand at him. "Aw, Joshua. You're much too hard on yourself. You're not *that* ugly."

This time I crack up.

Josh shakes his head and gives her a mock evil eye. "Therese's a friend of the family—or actually, she *was* a friend."

Therese tosses a napkin at him. "Speaking of them, how *is* your family? They all well? The mayor enjoying his retirement?"

I perk. "Mayor?"

"*Former* mayor," Josh says.

Therese ignores him. "Josh's dad was the longest running mayor Otter Bay ever saw. We all love that man. The whole town's honoring him, you know." She scolds Josh with her eyes. "Didn't you tell your new girl about your family? Really, Josh. The strong-silent type is *so* yesterday."

Josh shrugs. "I'd have gotten to it eventually. Yes, Dad's fine, the family's fine, we're all good. Some of us, better than others." Josh winks at me, but the gleam that had sprung to his eyes earlier now appears dim. Like he was keeping up a front somehow.

"Well, I'll leave you two kids to enjoy each other." Therese clears away the other two place settings. "Any pepper before I go?"

We both decline, and she leaves us, as promised.

"So protecting the good citizens of Otter Bay runs in the family?" I take a bite of my salad, reveling in the fresh shaving of Parmesan.

"You could say that."

"Why do I have the feeling you don't like talking about your personal life?"

"You're beautiful *and* perceptive. It's not that exactly, but I'd rather hear about you. Tell me about your parents. I remember that your father passed away, and your mother?"

His question jolts me, and I draw in a breath too quickly, inhaling a vinegar-laden lettuce leaf. It catches in my windpipe, and that, along with the saltiness of the food, makes my eyes water. I begin to cough, and then lunge for my glass of water, holding up my index finger to let him know I'll be out of this ridiculous situation in seconds. Hopefully.

Josh quirks a brow. "You okay there?"

I offer him a halted smile as I recover. That fleeting thought I'd had earlier, the one about sharing my newfound secret with Josh, seems reckless now. How would a man whose own father has such a stellar reputation accept my uncomfortable news?

An awkward silence drops between us, until I hear my heart pounding in my chest. It's as if I am standing high on a precipice, contemplating the distance to the ground. Should I stay where it's safe? Or jump into the unknown?

The waiter appears then to refill our water glasses—and to buy me more time.

Chapter Seventeen

 Along with the obvious need to get out of small town Dexton, and to search out the area where my family once lived, I realize my other reason for making this move. I sit here across from Josh, that realization so emblazoned across my mind that I wonder why I've not considered it before. At least not openly. I want to be liked.

More to the point, I want to be loved.

I don't know what causes me so boldly to admit this now, at least in my head, but I do. It's not that I have felt unloved by any member of my family, except for perhaps Mel, who sometimes acts as if it takes great pain on her part to consider me fondly at all. I've always felt, though, like an outsider, like wherever a party's going on, I'm more like the forgettable neighbor instead of an honored guest.

I take another bite of my salad, careful not to talk and chew at the same time—the very thing that makes me cringe about Camille's eating habits. Piano music fills the room, along with muted gusts from the blowing wind outside, and I'm wondering how my muse, Eliza, might handle similar feelings. And just how would she respond to Josh's statement about the wall that seems to rise every time the conversation turns personal?

I set my fork down, knowing I should save room for the rest of my dinner. Eliza's an open book; the woman has no secrets—or at least she makes it *look* like she has no secrets. True, she's been keeping her pregnancy a secret for months—just gathering enough time to make sure Maurice, the father, has truly fallen in love with her. Can't say that I blame her completely. Maybe those around her will be peeved, but she has handled everything with such grace and style, and with a boldness that would certainly backfire in less capable hands.

I'm still not ready to divulge what I've heard about Daddy to the girls—why spoil things for them now? I do know that, somehow, I have to make things right. Even if it means paying back every penny to Peg myself, a thought that weakens both my appetite *and* my pulse.

Josh gazes at me. "You seem preoccupied."

How long have those mesmerizing eyes of his been focused on me? "Just thinking about my parents, and why they left Otter Bay."

"Why did they?"

I shrug. "Well, I don't exactly know. My mother has a friend in Dexton, Anne, and my father worked for her many years, so I always thought they were following the work."

"With three girls to raise, that's understandable."

"There's something else, though. Please don't mention this to the girls, because I'm still working through some things here."

He sits straighter. "Sounds serious."

"It is." I take a breath, then push it back out. "Apparently, my father once worked for Peg."

"Peg—from the diner?"

I nod. "According to her, he, well, she says my father took a large amount of money from her."

Josh's eyes widen, and a steady breath escapes. He leans his elbows on the table and observes me, as if contemplating how to phrase what's on his mind.

A busboy removes our salad plates, and I lay my clasped hands in the empty spot. "I'm sure there's more to the story, though. Burton says something like that happened . . . but he also said that my parents were great people with, unfortunately, many troubles."

"And your mother? What does she say about it?"

"If I could get her to respond to e-mail, I'd tell you. Mom's always been kind of carefree, I guess you'd say. She's really good at answering deep, dark questions—like why is the sky blue?—with some kind of fairy-tale answer that has nothing to do with anything. It made us laugh as kids, but . . ."

"But now you're not laughing."

"Right."

Therese sidles up to our table with our dinners, and we put on polite smiles and wait as she places them in front of each of us. She opens her mouth, but shuts it quickly, and bustles off.

Josh clears his throat. "It's tough finding out the sins of our fathers, isn't it?"

"What do you mean?"

He gives me a wry smile. "Just a phrase. I just meant that it's not easy when a parent lets us down."

"Mom's still in la-la land, on her honeymoon and all. I'm sure she'll eventually come down to earth and talk to me." *I hope she will.*

"I was talking about your dad."

My fork stops. "Daddy? He just made a mistake, I'm sure that's all it was."

"But didn't you say that he stole from Peg?"

"I never used the word *stole*. I've been told that he took some money, yes, but no one seems to want to fill me in on the details. Or the reason he would supposedly do such a thing. Since he's not here to defend himself, I will. My job is to make sure he's remembered for all the good things he did. I wish you could've known him as I did."

"I didn't mean to put you on the defensive."

I cross my arms. "You didn't."

"Listen, my father's a popular guy. You heard Therese—everybody loves him. But there are things . . . things I've had to come to terms with so that I don't fall into the same traps he has."

My salmon filet has lost all flavor. Joshua Adams had seemed so different from Trent, but now? Not so much. Maybe definitive judgment is hard-wired into most men these days. I shake my head, my eyes focused on my partially eaten fish. "For some reason, I thought I could share all this with you. What was I thinking?"

He reaches across the table. "Tara."

I withdraw my hand. "Listen, maybe it's best we stop this conversation now." *Before I say something that'll send us to the point of no return.* "I've run across a hitch in my plans, but I've been there before, and I can handle it."

"Are you sure? Maybe you should tell your sisters about the allegations."

I look up. "No!" My heart races, but not in a good way. "Camille's too immature, and Mel has reservations about being here in the first place. If she heard this, she'd probably flit off forever. I like having them around."

"Mm. To mother them."

I recoil. "That's not fair. Why does everyone think that just because I'm the oldest, that I have some deep-seated need to mother my younger siblings. Well, sister and cousin anyway."

"Your cousin? Wait . . . have I met her?"

I sigh, and sit back, all traces of an appetite vanished. He can go ahead and change the subject—doesn't matter anyway. "Camille's really our cousin, but we've always been like sisters. My parents got custody of her after my mother's brother Grant died. He was her real father."

"And her mother? Is she in the picture?"

"No. She had a history of drug abuse and disappeared soon after Camille was born. After my uncle was killed—he died in an accident—my parents took her in. Daddy always hoped to adopt her, but Mom never wanted her to forget her real father, I guess."

Soberness spreads across Josh's expression. "You shouldn't be handling all this alone, Tara. They're big girls, and it sounds like they've already been through plenty of turmoil. Besides, they're bound to learn about your father's . . . indiscretion eventually."

I nod, but beneath the surface of my forced, bland expression, my blood simmers at a low and steady roll. For as long as I can remember, the burdens of our family life stopped at my door. Until now I haven't wanted to admit the number of times that Mom shared with me her disillusionment with life, then told me to keep it "just between us." I'd learned early on to keep family matters to myself . . . so why did I let myself crack with Josh?

Our waiter appears and offers to wrap up our dinners, since neither of us ate all that much. Josh gives him a succinct nod. "Two doggy bags would be perfect."

Together we wait in silence for our leftover food and the check.

THE MORNING AIR LAY cool and still, unlike my life, which has been a blur since the moment I awoke. It started last night when Josh brought me home and had to rush off to an emergency before we could come to some sort of truce satisfying to both of us. Aren't days off sacred anymore? You'd think that after working that many days in a row, the fire station could handle new business without him.

It didn't matter anyway, because for me the night ended when Josh took the stance he did about my father's past. Just why did he have to look and smell so good doing it?

I sit here in this pew, in the back of the church, watching the morning worshippers file in. They're a quieter bunch than those who attend the later service, and I don't know why I've come, but I'm here, feeling confused and more than a little battered.

The ushers arrive after me, men with smooth hair split on one side like a lopsided parting of the Red Sea, except for Burton whose shiny head reflects the dappling of stained glass. They move in unison, with vigor and spirit, and a whole lot of eye contact. I slink down against the wooden seat back. Hopefully, no one will point out how I've disrupted the symmetry of their art of packing them in.

"May I sit?" Norma grins, and I slide over, still hoping not to attract attention. She follows my line of vision, notices a compact man stuffed into a powder gray suit scrutinizing us, and waves him away.

A boom resonates, drawing our attention to a thick, open door. Twelve men and women dressed in flowing green and burgundy robes enter through what resembles a secret passageway from beneath a choir loft I'd not noticed on my first visit here.

"We sing hymns at the early service," Norma whispers.

I nod as if to say, *of course,* when really, this is news to me.

Norma removes a fat, blue book from a rack, flips through the pages, and cracks it open wider while holding it in front of both of us. A wafting of incense mixed with the scent of old wood overtakes me. From some hidden place, a resounding organ begins to fill the church like something out of an old movie, or maybe a major league baseball game.

I'm beginning to wonder whether coming here this morning was such a good idea.

The congregation stands to their feet and I follow, albeit with a two-second delay. This seems to light extra energy beneath Norma, who thrusts the book out in front of us as if it were a treasured photograph. Her voice fills the space between us . . . and it's magnificent.

All the frustration, disappointment, and worry that stumbled in here with me this morning has been made mute as I add my own warble to the mix. There's ease in following along, richness in the melody, and inherent strength in the textured, aged voices. I think I might cry.

Norma slips an arm around my shoulders, loosening the knot at the base of my neck, and I fight off the growing urge to let my emotions out of the safety of their locked cage. Tears prick the corners of my eyes, and a few escape down the sides of my cheeks. As if on instinct, Norma squeezes me tighter, and we stand like this until the last note of the organ is played.

My new friend hands me a tissue as the entire congregation is seated, and the pastor, this time wearing a robe of his own, approaches the podium. He proceeds to welcome us, then read through a lengthy list of announcements before settling into a story . . . about food?

"The prophet Isaiah writes, 'Listen to me, listen well: Eat only the best, filling yourself with only the finest.'"

I perk. Josh and I were feasting on fine food last night, until . . . well, until the conversation changed and I found myself without an appetite.

"'Pay attention.'"

I jump a little. I'm convinced Pastor Cole can tell my thoughts strayed from his sermon to my date last night, until I realize that he's still reading. *Oh.* "'Come close now, listen carefully to my life-giving, life-nourishing words.'" He closes the Bible and steps out from behind the podium. "My friends, God is letting us know here, that the things we hunger for the most, even more than good food and drink, are the things that only God can give us."

My first reaction is to ask, like what? What can God give us that will fill that nagging hunger within me? Other than last night's doggy bag, that is. If I'm honest, though, the pastor's words have a calming effect. It's as if something deep inside tells me to listen up because the antidote to my worries is near.

"He's instructed us to seek Him, and to pray to Him while He is near. This is because He has made a covenant with us, a promise of a life of honor. He wants you and me to have a life of joy, to be whole and complete. And that starts with Him. He is the foundation on which the most fulfilled lives are built."

I press the backs of my fingers over my mouth, suppressing a smile, remembering Holly's counseling on proper foundations. Then my eyes flit around, as the pastor continues to speak. No lightning bolts have struck, so I guess I can safely assume that the man of the cloth cannot read minds.

Seriously, though, Eliza's longtime motto has always been, "It starts with me!" Her confidence and fortitude have impressed me, guided me even, as I've taken seriously my role as firstborn. Admittedly, though, I've never quite been able to follow her lead *and* find the success in life that I've longed for.

Maybe I'm missing something.

"Amen." The pastor concludes, and it's obvious that, yes, while lost in a swirl of conflicting thoughts, I must have missed something important. I want the life of joy he talked about, and to feel whole and complete. *Seek Him*, the pastor said, and *pray to Him*.

Although it feels like baby steps, I resolve to start there.

As he takes a sheet from the podium, it looks as if Pastor Cole's about to launch into more announcements. With a sudden rise of his chin, he looks up from the paper and into the crowd.

"I'd like you all to join me in praying now for our friend Josh Adams, who's in the hospital after suffering from a fall last night . . ."

I hear nothing more. Norma and I twist toward one another, mouths open, and dart quickly from the pew and out through the massive double doors.

Chapter Eighteen

 My heart races again, full-on, catch-in-your-throat racing. Norma and I made it through town fast, considering its length consists of one major street and two stop lights. But getting to the hospital took another twenty-five minutes along a winding, dirt-edged road.

We dash down the hallway of Twin-Towns Medical Center and halt just outside Josh's room. Words like *consciousness* and *pupils* and *vomiting* flow into the hall and land on us like a stifling hot blanket.

Two beautiful people emerge from Josh's room. Both tall, the woman's auburn hair rests on her shoulders and she holds the elbow of a man with deep crow's feet bordering captivating eyes. Josh's eyes.

The woman lets go of the man's elbow. "Norma! So good of you to come."

The women embrace and Norma reaches to me. "Shirley, have you met Tara?"

The lines near Shirley's eyes soften. She takes my hand in both of hers. "No, we've not yet met, but I've heard your name. I'm Josh's mother. So good to finally meet you." She hugs me like I'm her own and tears prick my eyelids for the second time this morning.

Norma guides the man my way. "And this is Pete, Josh's father."

He shakes my hand vigorously, like we're old friends. "Josh said you were beautiful and he wasn't kidding."

Okay, so now I'm blushing, but at least their son must be all right or they wouldn't be acting this happy as they greet me in this stark hall.

Shirley takes my arm. "We are thrilled to meet you. I so hope you will accompany Josh to his father's celebration next month."

I'm taken aback. "Uh, well . . . that would be lovely." She's over the moon; I clear my throat. "Can we see him?"

Pete steps back and sweeps an open arm toward Josh's room. "Yes, of course. Please."

Norma stays behind as I step into the room. The low buzz of medical machinery greets me and I grip the doorjamb. I haven't been in a hospital room since Daddy died and a familiar taste of nausea builds in my throat.

★ 182 ★

"Tara?" Josh lies in a half-sitting, half-prone position.

I release the doorjamb and approach his bed, fighting a floaty sensation. I'm not sure if it's a leftover from the days of visiting Daddy, or because of the new kind of intimacy this visit brings. "Hi."

"How'd you hear?"

"The pastor mentioned it at church—"

"You went to church this morning?"

My eyes narrow. "Why the surprise?"

Josh's mouth opens and he draws in a quick breath. "No, I mean . . ."

I lower myself to the bed and cover his hand with mine. "Stop. Sorry. You've obviously been hurt so this may not be the best time to get into another argument."

Josh's lips curl into a smirk. "So we were fighting last night, then?"

I look down at the pale blanket beneath me. "Not fighting, exactly. Maybe moving just a little too fast, though." I glance into his face. Even with fresh scratches and that yellowing bruise along one chiseled cheekbone, he makes my heart flutter. "What happened to you . . . after you left?"

Josh blows out another breath, this one hard and jagged. "I got careless. Found myself up on a roof in the middle of the night and landed on a soft spot. Tried to right myself, but couldn't."

"So you fell off a roof?"

"Onto my shoulder . . . and head. It's only a mild concussion. I'll be back at it next week, or maybe sooner."

"Is that what the doctor told you?"

He tries to shrug, but winces from the pain of a beat-up shoulder. When he sees me watching him, Josh drops the pained expression—as if I didn't already notice. "They have their policies and I have mine."

"You're getting ahead of yourself."

Josh sets his jaw. "I thought you weren't going to start any more arguments?"

"I'm the one starting all the arguments? Last night you were the one making more of my situation than even I did."

"If it's no big deal, then why not tell the rest of your family?"

I stand and cross my arms. "Apparently your memory's still intact. And I never said it wasn't a big deal, just that you made more of it than expected. I'm still trying to figure everything out and to make an intelligent decision about where to go from here." I glance out the window toward a stand of pine so thick it's a wonder birds can fly through it. "I told you about it for . . ."

"Sympathy?"

I unfold my arms and spike the air with my palms. He's made up his mind about my situation, which I find odd since even I'm unsure of all that's transpired. If only he actually knew my father, he'd be less inclined to accept the worst.

"We're doing it again." He glances out the window. "You're driving me crazy, you know."

And vice versa. "Josh, I'm glad you're okay. I know you are committed to your line of work, however dangerous it might be. And when the pastor asked everyone to pray, I just . . ."

He quirks an eyebrow. "You prayed for me?"

"Will you quit doing that?"

He turns both palms toward the ceiling. "What?"

"Finishing my sentences! All I'm saying is that I felt *bad* that you were hurt, so I came to check up on you. It's not a crime to care."

This time Josh's eyes penetrate mine and despite the budding indignation forming in response to his attitude, a generous ripple skitters through me. "You're right," he says. "It's not a crime at all."

"C'MON, LET'S GRAB A bite."

Norma wraps an arm around my shoulder and nudges me toward the hospital cafeteria, which by medical facility standards isn't all that terrible. They even have color on the walls—azure-blue and fuchsia stripes. Simka would be proud.

Norma fills up her tray while I take a salad from the ice bin and a bottle of water. I could use a cup of coffee, but the last time I'd tasted a cup at a hospital almost cured me of the addiction.

"You and Josh have a spirited relationship." Norma smiles and takes a bite of mashed potatoes drenched in dark, dense gravy.

"We have differences of opinion."

Norma wags her head, her mouth in a conceding smile. "All best love matches do."

I exhale. "Can I ask you something?"

"Of course."

"Why's he so . . . mysterious?"

Norma laughs. "Mysterious? I've never thought of Josh in that way. What makes you ask that?"

"He's got some strong opinions, but won't fully explain himself. And why does it seem like he's on-call with the fire department 24/7? Everybody needs a day off, am I right?"

"I know what you're saying there." She takes a sip of her coffee, winces and sets it right back down. "Ever since he handled a particularly tough rescue, he has seemed more focused on the station. I've seen him fly out of church even and he spreads himself pretty thin already with all the volunteer hours he puts in."

"Were you talking about the fire on Fogcatcher Lane—Beth's house? I live on that street."

"So you've heard about that. It's still very hard to think about." Water redness tinges Norma's eyes. "I'm not sure if he's really over that one."

"What happened?"

"Beth hasn't talked about it much. Not to me, anyway.

I was on the care committee that visited her in the hospital afterward and that's when our friendship really began. All I really know is that the fire got started in the kitchen." She lowers her voice. "Gordon—he's her ex-husband—he was always such a cheapskate and the rumor is he rigged a lot of the switches and outlets himself. I read in the paper that some of them may not have worked, which may be one reason a couple of the outlets were so overloaded. Just a matter of time till one of them sparked."

I shake my head, my eyes stinging.

"In any case, the fire got big real fast and Beth was asleep. Thank God the baby wasn't with her at the time!"

"So Josh was on the fire crew that got called."

Norma touches my hand. "Oh no, honey. No one had even called the fire department. He was just walking by when he saw the smoke."

I cover my mouth.

"Of course, Josh called in and by the time they arrived he'd already pulled Beth out. Poor thing was bleeding heavily . . . she got caught on some broken glass." Norma pushes her tray away. "She's private about it and I haven't wanted to pry, but her arm's very scarred."

"That must be why she always wears long sleeves."

Norma scrunches her lips, then something like light dawns on her face and she nods. "Yes, I hadn't noticed that, but yes, you're right. I don't think she wants to draw attention to herself."

"Or remember what happened." Heaviness sinks in my chest as I dwell on Beth's misfortune. "Then Josh is truly a hero, isn't he?"

Norma chuckles. "I and just about anyone around here would say so. But don't tell him that."

"I know. He'll deny it."

A shadow crosses Norma's face. "I can understand humility, but Josh has a way of almost taking offense when someone suggests he was heroic. Did you know the town wanted to give him a medal? Wouldn't hear of it." She shakes her head. "Some have said that he blames himself for her injury, but no one else would. Not ever. That man's just too hard on himself."

"Hard on himself, yes. I'd agree with that." *Maybe that's why he's also hard on his father and even on my father.* I push the lettuce around in its drippy dressing. "So the daredevil thing. You think he wants to prove something?"

Norma, whose emotions had been bordering on the edge, suddenly smiles. "Like just about every other man I know."

We laugh, lightening the mood when a familiar face arrives at our table, tray in hand.

"Can I and the missus join you?" Burton Sims stands there holding a tray with four donuts and one large cup of coffee. Beside him, a white-haired woman holds a small jar of apple juice.

"Of course, please sit." Norma slides her plate over to make some room and I follow along. "Burton, I'd like you to meet—"

"Tara Sweet. I never forget a pretty face."

I lean forward. "We actually met last week."

His wife elbows him in the side as he begins to sit, causing Burton to jolt to a stop mid-bend. "And this is m' wife, Glory."

I smile at her. "Hello, Glory."

"You're the spittin' image of your mother, Tara. The spittin' image!"

I've heard this on occasion and although it certainly is a compliment, I just don't see it. But I nod and grin anyway. "Thank you for saying so."

"When Burton told me you were back in town, I said, 'I just can't wait to see those girls again!' After all the mess your parents went through, I was just so tickled to hear that you girls came out on the better side."

Norma gapes at me and I want to bolt. "What did your parents go through? Or is it okay for me to know?"

I open my mouth, but Glory's faster than I am. "We thought they'd make it—Tara's mother was so darling— until that Gigi or Fifi, or whatever she called herself, came back into town. Oh, she had a mean thing for your father, but so hot and cold, that one. It's no wonder the man was confused."

Gigi. A thing for Daddy. Confused. The echoes ricochet through my mind and a slow, steady heat wave burns through me. I catch my breath. "I don't know what you're talking about."

Glory's mouth and eyes morph into three large circles. "Oh, dear. Burton, I thought you said you talked to the girl."

Burton swigs his coffee and slams the Styrofoam cup down so hard it dents one edge. "Darn it, Glory. It's not right to talk about the dead. Tara's had plenty of time to get past old news, so let her be."

Everything around me slows. Chatter in the cafeteria sinks into the background. Indistinct sounds of chairs sliding and dishes clinking become dim. Colors fade. Although my eyes remain open, I see nothing until a picture forms in my mind. My parents argue in the living room of our old home on Pelican Lane. Mom's crying and lurching toward the front door. Daddy's crying too and pulling on her sleeve. I turn from my vantage point just inside the archway that leads to our dreary hall and see Mel standing there, dressed in one of our mother's long gowns. She's wearing bright yellow beads, a pair of Daddy's dress shoes and a scowl that could chase babies away.

I slip my arm around her tiny shoulders and together we turn from the commotion and head down the hall to the room we both shared. The memory of leading Mel away from the awful scene constricts my breathing, like a punch to the stomach. What were my parents fighting about? And is it my imagination, or had Mel and I witnessed their arguments more than I've been willing to accept?

Chapter Nineteen

I snap out of my trance and bolt right out of that hospital cafeteria. Norma tries to stop me, but she was no match for all the breath training I'd had in high school. I may not have been the fastest runner in the pack—okay, the slowest, really—but I could discuss the story line of *Quartz Point* for the entire six-mile run without breaking a sentence.

A feat to be proud of as any.

I'm halfway down the winding hill that leads to the hospital when it dawns on me that I'm not in high school anymore. That and I have no idea how to get back. As I wonder where to turn, Glory's pronouncement settles into the deepest part of my psyche, the place that has the ability to make me either rise above, or collapse into the bitter depths.

I move slowly in the direction that instinct tells me to go, rolling rogue thoughts over in my mind.

Glory's words were blunt and biting, although by the way she delivered them she had no idea they'd hurt. In fact, they cut me in a way that even Trent's abandonment could not match—which says something about my attachment to him (or lack thereof). And yet, somehow, though it's painful to admit, there's a truth attached to them that I have yet to fully acknowledge.

Tires spinning to a stop pull me to the present. "Tara! Let me take you home." Norma's across the street, calling to me.

I cross toward her, zombie-like, and climb into her car. She takes off when I shut the door and we wind along in silence.

Finally she speaks. "Do you want to talk about it?"

I turn my chin, making myself look at her. "Sorry. No."

Norma nods, both hands still grip the steering wheel. "So I guess Glory dropped a bombshell on you back there." She looks over at me. "Hate it when that happens."

Her attempt at humor pokes a hole in the dam and I start to laugh. The absurdity of the past weeks hits me then and I laugh more. Harder. Instead of a ring, Trent gives me the boot. I lose my job. My mother marries a *boy*. I laugh until tears fill my eyes and drop onto my lap. I pack up our home—and our life, for goodness sake—only to find out that paradise stinks! The laughter that began with the flood of realization gradually turns, until I'm crying into my hands, the world as I know it flowing away with each tear. The sobs come next,

wracking me from my gut and I can't stop the emotion. Nor
do I care to try very hard at all.

At some point the car stops, and Norma's familiar hug
pulls me close. I'm gasping and spewing tears and snorting,
trying to keep snot from sullying her blouse. "First I learn that
my father took someone's money. And now this. I want to go
back home, but my sisters want to stay. I'm . . . just . . . so
. . . unhappy."

Norma pats my back. "I didn't know all that. It's been a
hard time for you, but what about Josh? Isn't he worth staying around for?"

I wipe my eyes with the back of my hand and look
out the window, as if somehow this would shield me from
Norma's gaze. "I'm not sure having Josh in my life would be
such a good idea right now."

Norma pulls back. "Why in the world not?"

"Why am I bothering you with this? You barely know
me." A staccato sigh forces its way through my lungs. "I just
ended a relationship back in Missouri. Actually, he ended it."
I drop my head forward and stare into my hands, my tears in
a hovering stage.

"So then you're free. Right?"

I lift my eyes and find Norma's. "On the contrary, I feel
more burdened than ever. Josh is an amazing man." A palpable pain runs through my chest. *He's already under my
skin.* "This . . . this in there . . . the things Glory said, along
with the angry things Peg has said . . ." I shake my head.

"I just can't comprehend it all, not in a real way. My parents had this love, this connection, you know? I've always wanted the same thing, but now? I'm so confused."

"That makes perfect sense, but what doesn't is why you won't let Josh work through this with you. I think he really cares for you, Tara."

"And what about the next time he decides to put himself in danger in the middle of the night, just for sport? What then? I need a man I can rely on, not worry over all the time."

Norma's expression falls, a frown tugging at her mouth. She looks away. "Sometimes that's not possible. But you love anyway and it doesn't matter anymore because you are loved back."

I reach out to her. "I'm sorry. Josh told me that your husband's been ill, and of course you worry about him."

Her smile's flat, but her eyes glisten. "And I would not change knowing him for one second. He's my . . . he's my life." Her voice cracks. "He's my gift from God."

Gift from God. Almost a cliché. This time, though, the sentiment sounds as real to my new friend as the tears still dripping from my chin. We sit in silence for a second, before she twists the key in the ignition and starts up the car. My mind continues to sway under the pressure of bad news. If Daddy did have an affair, why did he and Mom stay together? For us? And who is the other woman, this Gigi? Is she still in Otter Bay, ready to pounce on my sisters and me with more degrading secrets?

No, I'm not buying it yet. Not completely. I came to Otter Bay to find myself again, to find that carefree little girl lost among the watery tide pools . . .

And I'm just not ready to give up on her yet.

AFTER NORMA DROPPED ME off at my car, I wanted to go home, crawl beneath my quilt, and start this day again. Or at least head to the cove just down the block from our rental. Those calming, familiar waters draw me like nothing else ever has. Instead, I slipped into my new white cottons and went to work at the inn.

In the last two hours I've checked in a family of four visiting from India, an old woman with a very bad dye job (but who seemed happy about it, so why should I care?), and a middle-aged man with deep-set lines and a laptop computer.

So buried in paperwork that I don't notice Nigel toddling in until he lays his cane across the front desk with a resounding clunk.

"Nigel!"

"Tara, dear."

"I didn't see you come in. It's been busy today." I force lightness into my voice. "You should be proud of how popular the Bayside has become."

"A blessing from the Lord above," he says, then proceeds to lean against the counter and watch me without a sound. I force a smile in his direction, all the while wondering if

I'm doing something wrong. Finally he speaks again. "You seem troubled today."

I swallow and muster up what probably looks like one more sad attempt at smiling. "Josh is in the hospital . . . did you hear about that?"

He nods. "I thought that may have been the source of your sober expression today."

You don't know the half of it. "Yes, well, I heard about it at church this morning and went to see him. He's doing fine. Ornery, but fine."

Nigel laughs. "I'm glad you two have become friends. Tell me how you like the church. I attend myself, when I'm able to, although the mornings have been getting more difficult for me these days."

I cock my head to one side. "I'm sorry to hear that, Nigel. Anything I can do to help?"

"My dear, just your face around here has brightened the mood. No need to worry over me."

I laugh, well, for the first time all day. "You make my day, Nigel, you really do."

He slides the cane off the countertop and settles it beneath one steady hand until he's sitting on the sofa across the room. He offers a slight sigh. "Now," he says. "Tell me about church. Do you like it there?"

I glance outside to the distant horizon. *Hm, do I like it at church?* "Well, I didn't stay long this morning, but overall, I don't know. I'm drawn to it, because I attended there as a child. But I'm not all that familiar with the customs, so it remains to be seen whether I'll continue."

"You make it sound almost like a foreign country."

"In some ways, it feels like one—like a strange and wonderful place from long ago."

"Perhaps as you become more familiar with the service and step into a more active participation, then you will feel completely comfortable."

Movement through the front window catches my attention. I pull my eyes from Nigel and see Camille's surfer guy, Shane, wrestling with a woman, curvaceous and coppery-skinned, her bikini nothing more than an answer to societal rules of decency. And just barely.

"U-huh. Maybe you're right, Nigel." I take another peek and realize, they're not really wrestling, because although Shane's hands and arms grope her all over, the woman's doing nothing to fight him off.

I feel ill. He smacks her on the rear, then pulls the giggling woman down over the rocks to the sand below which, thankfully, can't be viewed from this vantage point. Gah. I shut my eyes, hoping Camille has not let him get too far with her and wondering if she'd listen to me anyway.

A soft rippling draws me back to the lobby. Nigel's hands rest on the cane in front of him and his head has dropped forward. I step closer to realize that Nigel has fallen asleep.

My cell rings from across the room. I grab it on the second ring, and Nigel rallies as I pick it up.

"Tara?"

"Camille. I'm glad it's you. Listen—"

"Can't talk long. Holly and I are going to get some dinner and then I'll be going out tonight."

"Where's Mel?"

"What? Oh, Mel. She's at Simka's. They're working on some marketing ideas she has for her. You know Mel."

"Oh, okay, good. But where are you headed tonight?"

"What?" Laughter spills through the earpiece. Camille comes back on the line. "Gotta go! Surf's up and all that . . ." She ends the call, and I'm kicking myself for not warning her about Shane. I try her back, but all I get is a message telling me she's at a "board" meeting. Sigh.

Nigel pulls himself off the couch with no mention of his ten-second snooze. "It appears you have everything under your expert care. Mary will be here until late tonight should you need any supplies. I am off to enjoy my dinner."

His gait moves unevenly, but he looks happy. "I'll see you tomorrow, Nigel."

Just after he departs, Mel blows in through the front door like a strong east wind, her face a rage of emotion. "Just when"—she says, both arms jabbed into the cinched waist of her silk jacket—"were you going to tell us about Daddy's little escapades in Otter Bay?"

Chapter Twenty

That old quote about a woman scorned comes to mind as Mel's eyes narrow, dart-like. Inside my heart jerks around like it's set upon a heap of coals, but on the outside I keep it cool. Like always.

I straighten my back. "Hello, Mel."

"Don't 'Hello Mel' me." Her voice mocks me with its high pitch. "Some kid just told me that our dad's a thief and that he . . . had an affair?"

One of my hands reaches for the low part of the counter, to steady myself. My expression, however, I keep even. "I've heard the rumors."

"Duh! And now so have I, from some zitty teenager. And so has Simka. Good grief, Tara, you could've warned me what we were walking into."

"Who told you?"

She crosses her arms. "I was at Simka's store discussing some superb marketing ideas I had for her when in crashes a bunch of teens with paint buckets. Apparently they're from some merry fix-it crew from that church you go to and they had volunteered to paint Simka's office. One thing leads to another and this kid says to me, 'Hey, I'm sorry to hear about all the stuff your dad did,' and I'm like, 'What stuff?' And he says, 'You know, like stealing and *cheating on your mother*.'"

I wince. "Was it Mikey?"

"I guess. Who cares? Some kid knows more about us than we do, or at least, than Camille and I do." She throws up her hands. "You could've warned me."

"I didn't think you'd find out. At least, not yet." Numbness enfolds me and my gaze flits around the sun-draped lobby. "Besides, I don't know too many details." *Nor do I want to know.*

"Always the big sister, controlling *everything*. What gives you the right to treat us like children?"

A car pulls up just outside and a woman hops out of the passenger seat and scrambles up to the door. She peeks her head in. "You got any rooms available?"

I paste on a smile. "Just a moment while I check." Mel stews in the corner, as I flip through our book. "For how many?"

"Two adults and a kid."

"I have one king left and can offer you a rollaway. Will that do?"

Her face lights up. "That'll do it. Be right in."

I begin prepping the paperwork, keeping my eyes on the work before me. "Let's talk about this later, okay Mel?"

"I'll wait."

Sigh. Fine. Be like that. "Could be a while."

Mel drops her arms to her sides and marches into the attached sitting room. With a huff, she plops down onto a couch from whence she can watch me work and crosses her legs. "You know where to find me."

I check in the young family of three, patiently explaining Otter Bay's finest assets and answering their many questions. Behind them a line forms, so for the next twenty minutes I work to fill up the Bayside. When the last guest trails off down the hall or back out the door, depending on where their room is located, I begin the task of straightening the desk and avoiding my sister.

She approaches the desk. "You didn't think you could get rid of me, did you?"

A thought springs to mind. *Camille.* "I almost forgot. We need to warn Camille about Shane. Before you came, I saw him getting handsy with a half-naked woman just over there." I point toward the sea.

She places the back of one hand on her forehead and looks up toward the ceiling. "Whatever will we do?"

"This is serious. Camille thinks he's really into her, but he's obviously not. I tried to call her but—"

"Who did Dad have an affair with, and is this the real reason they packed up and took us halfway across the country?"

I smooth back my messy bun. "We don't even know if this rumor is true. It may just be the figment of some old woman's imagination."

"You believe it, or else you wouldn't have cried your eyes out all morning over it."

Argh! Just how much did Mikey tell her? "Who told you about that?"

"No one, but your eyes look dry and red. They always look dry and red after you've cried."

"Oh." I close my uncomfortable eyes and let out a long breath. "Has it ever occurred to you that Mom and Dad kept this a secret for a reason? Maybe they never wanted us to find out—if it's even true."

"And what about him stealing money? Are you kidding me? Maybe our inheritance belongs to someone else! Did you ever think about that? Maybe she'll sue us for it!"

"Sshh!" I glance around. "He had to have a reason for that. He *had* to have. Have you heard from Mom? She's only sporadically answering my e-mails and when she does, she conveniently leaves out anything important."

"Well, you haven't been dropping Dad's criminal record on her over the Internet, I hope."

I roll my eyes and glare back at her. "I haven't mentioned anything about that specifically, no. But I have asked her to call me so I can ask her about Peg."

"From the diner, Peg? What about?" When I don't answer her right away, her eyes broaden. "Dad stole from Holly's aunt?" She shakes her head slowly. "Well, well. No wonder that woman wasn't all that hospitable when we met."

I open my mouth, but snap it shut when Shane and that barely-clad woman emerge from the rocky beach. Much of her chocolaty hair tumbles over her face and—ugh—she must have forgotten to retie her bikini top right because Shane's laughing and tugging one side, evidently to keep her legal.

Mel has stopped yammering about Peg, her attention also drawn to the daring duo licking face as they lean up against a pickup truck by the side of the road. "Did he just smack her rump?"

"Yup." I'm still watching the disgusting PDA, which continues even as near-naked gal climbs into her truck. She shuts the door, but in an admirably seamless maneuver, her head's now out the window while said PDA continues.

Mel grunts. "Nothing is as it seems, eh? Well, whatever. At least one of us trusts that Camille's smart enough on her own."

I duck, at least mentally, not allowing her backhanded slap to land on me. I'm quite skilled at that.

Betty steps into the lobby, patting her newly rolled hair. "My goodness, how the wind has picked up."

"Betty, hi. You're early today."

Her hand stops mid-pat. She flicks over her wrist and squints at her watch. "Oh, for heaven's sake, would you look at that. I misread my clock by more than an hour. Poor Roy. I made him rush through his barley soup so I could be here on time. Nearly burned his tongue on it."

"Well, now that you're here, I'd like you to meet my sister, Mel."

"Good to meet you. I'm not usually this daft, although I've had my moments."

To her credit Mel has erased all evidence of the day's events and smiles, warmly even, at Betty. "Haven't we all. It's a pleasure, Betty."

Betty holds her handbag in front of her. "Why don't you take off early, my dear? Go see some sights with your sister. Oh, if only my sister was still living, we'd have such fun together, she and I."

"You're sure?" I ask, already finding my purse.

She waves me on, and Mel and I head for home.

"LET'S PLAN THIS OUT." Mel meets me at the sidewalk, where I've parked my car.

I have an inkling she's referring to how we're going to deal with our newfound knowledge of Daddy, et al, but do I let on? "You mean plan what we'll have for dinner?"

Mel stomps one pointy-toed foot into the patchy lawn. "Since when do you attempt humor?"

"Daddy always said I was the funniest, you know that."

"Whatever." Mel glances around. "Let's decide right now how we're going to spill the beans to Camille."

"Oh, that. We just need to tell her that Shane's a creep. She'll listen."

"*That's* none of our business, and you *know* that's not what I was talking about. We need to tell her right away about all this business about Daddy having an affair with some mystery woman and about the money he took from Peg."

"Right. And this is going to be helpful how?"

"She and Holly are beginning to be good buds, so we need to tell Camille before Peg does it out of spite."

She has a point. I wouldn't want Camille to find out from someone else—the way Mel did. But then again, Peg specifically said we should keep this to ourselves and she seemed to mean it. We would need to talk with Norma and Mikey, not to mention Burton and Glory—oh, it's getting complicated . . .

Fueled by a sudden desire to take things into her own hands, Mel charges the front steps as I struggle to keep up. She whips open the screen door, nearly smacking me in the head and twists the antique door handle. I'm on her heels when she suddenly stops and stares into my face.

"Don't try to stop me."

I hold up, knowing that once she sets her mind, life gets complicated. Still, she knows better than to think I'll lie down like some compliant lap dog. The room's dark, yet the smells of cinnamon and nutmeg flow straight to my nostrils. No lights on in the kitchen. Instead, only a sliver of bouncing light, along with some faint laughter and music, comes from somewhere down the hall.

Mel drops her purse on a chair. "Camille?"

Together we follow the scent of thanksgiving down the hall. I'm right behind Mel. "Camille?"

Mel raps twice on Camille's bedroom door, which is ajar. "You in here, Cam?"

No answer.

A waft of smoke and perfume alarms me and I gesture to Mel to go ahead in to Camille's room. She does and hops backward, careening into my chest, but not before I get a glimpse—one sickening glimpse—at the source of her fright. Shane has just leapt from the rumpled bed, while Camille scrambles to yank up one sleeve of her cock-eyed blouse.

In a room lit only by candlelight—one wax draped and infused with cinnamon and nutmeg—Camille's annoyance shines. Her forehead scrunches so tight that her lines have had to introduce each other. "You weren't supposed to be home yet. What're you doing home?" She adjusts her clothing and glares at us. "And where's your manners? You didn't knock!"

Mel has composed herself and stands there in her standard way, a bored expression on her face and arms crossed firmly against her chest. "Actually, I did knock. And besides, your door was open."

Shane's in the corner, watching the drama unfold with a little too much pleasure. I'm inches from his face before I can stop myself, my index finger poised to injure him should he try to leave. "You. You will leave this house and never even look at my sister again."

Camille flies across the tiny room and tries to wedge herself between us. "You are so bossy, Tara. You can't just chase away my boyfriend like that!"

His taunting grin never leaves my face. "He's a sleaze."

Camille gasps. "Don't say that . . . I love him!"

My heart clenches. I loved Trent too, but look where that got me. Shane winks at Camille and takes a step toward her. I thrust out my arm to divide them, my palms smacking up against the wall.

Camille tries to push my arm away. She whips a look at Mel. "Do something!"

Mel's bored expression falters. She thinks I'm over the top again, the "sergeant," the name she often called me to her friends when we were teens. Why can't she just forget about her pride, that nasty need to prove me wrong? *Admit it, Mel,* I want to shout. *Shane's a loser only out for one thing and if he gets what he wants from Camille, he'll just leave her broken.*

Is that what she really wants?

"Just go." Mel's voice cuts through Camille's tears, and I drop my head forward. Defeated. Mel pushes me aside and gets in Shane's face. "Tara's right, Camille"—she never takes her eyes off surfer boy—"this one's a loser among losers."

Chapter Twenty-one

 Camille shed tears into her pillow until long after dark, the pitiful, uncomfortably familiar sound seeping beneath her door. I hate that she thinks my zeal for Shane's head on a platter has more to do with my own sad dating experience than with my desire to protect her. I've been trying to change my ways, to find a balance between the mothering older sister and the cool Eliza Carltonish dynamo who can make life happen as she calls it.

So far, I'm losing that battle.

Unable to let sleep claim me for the night, I hunker down on the couch, my computer on my lap, half-listening as Mel closes up the house, shutting windows and shades. She straightens the kitchen and steps into the living room, standing there until I pull my attention away from the screen and focus it on her.

"I've been hard on you."

I don't even hesitate. "Yes, you have."

Mel groans. "Don't make me want to take it back."

"Eventually you will anyway."

She crosses her arms tightly about her. "You're not off the hook with all this Daddy business, you know. You were right about Shane." She lowers her gaze and wags her head from side to side. "Thank heaven. But we still need to have a conversation about this. And to figure out what we're going to do. Good night."

She turns away and heads down the hall, and I linger on her words before allowing my attention to drift back to the computer on my lap. I log in to my soap account to see that Eliza apparently had quite the busy day on *Quartz Point*. In just one episode she used a rusty razor blade to chase away an intruder, fired two dishonest employees, carried out a lunchtime tryst with her long-time lover Maurice, and . . . hm . . . caused the breakup of her son and his fiancée.

Well, she must've had a good reason. No one would get in the way of someone's happiness just for sport. Right?

I read more of the synopsis. Huntington, Eliza's son, was about to marry Justina, who had once worked as the family's housekeeper. This did not go over well with Eliza. So she gave a call to the agency and had them send over Vicky the vixen, one blonde, bold, bombshell of a maid—and threw in a little extra to have her corner Huntington in the master bedroom closet. Unfortunately Justina witnessed the whole thing and got the wrong idea about her husband-to-be. Or the right idea, according to Eliza.

I read through it again, this time with more attention to the details, actively searching for some solid reason for Eliza's actions. In her defense, she did think Justina had quite possibly been behind the recent rash of thievery in the kitchen. Seems the silver had been disappearing, one piece at a time.

Not exactly solid evidence. I groan and rub my face with my hands. Before I can shut off the computer, a message pops onto the screen. It's from Mom.

> Having a grand time, Tara. My weight has
> dropped considerably, so much that I wonder if you
> girls will recognize me when I return.

Question is, will she recognize *us*? I shake off my weariness and resume reading her message.

> Yes, in answer to your question, your father and
> I took you and Mel to that church when you were
> young. I am surprised that it is still standing.

That's it. Weeks have gone by with little contact and that's all she wrote. Good job, Mom. Could you care any less? I hit *delete* and another message pops up.

> And Tara? Please don't forget what I said to you
> on my wedding day. Love, Mom

p.s. International calling is not cheap! But I will look into it *domani*. (That's Italian for tomorrow.)

I lean forward and press two fingers to my temples. What did she say to me on her wedding day? The day was a blur and—other than that moment when she casually mentioned that she'd be leaving the country for a year and oh, would you keep an eye on the girls for me?—I remember little else.

Nowhere closer to sleep, I wander through the house following the same path Mel took earlier, double-checking doors, tugging on windows, eyeing the burners.

I almost hear Mel's voice accuse me. *Don't you trust me, Tara?*

It's not that I don't trust Mel, or Camille for that matter. I'm just trying to do the right thing. To protect them, to . . .

Mel's imaginary voice slices through my thoughts. *"To be the hero?"*

Is that what she thinks? That I suffer from an inferiority complex and need bolstering from my alter ego? Something like nausea sinks in my stomach. Maybe I shouldn't have dragged my sisters into my dream. Maybe Mel would have found happiness in New York if I hadn't put a guilt trip on her. As for Camille always being on the young side . . . did I have anything to do with that? Was I too protective? Too . . . controlling?

Shane may have been a jerk—scratch that, he *is* a two-timing fool—but I could've interrupted them less forcefully. Maybe Mel's pronouncement of my hero-complex (okay, so it was an imagined pronouncement) was the right one. I stop in the hall and lean against the wall, replaying the evening. Each scene flows across my mind in vivid color. Each expression of pain or hurt on my sisters' faces pierces me.

I never meant to cause my family pain, so the least I can do is apologize.

"WELL. THAT WENT OVER well." Mel tosses the last bite of her bagel into her mouth. We both cringe when Camille slams the screen door behind her on the way out. "You didn't have to apologize, you know."

I take in the early morning sun that's done absolutely nothing to lighten the mood. Sigh. "I'm not sorry for throwing the guy out, but I do feel bad about coming on so strong. I should've tried warning her again . . . left her a message or something. Or maybe I should have made us stay behind the door and wait for her to come into the hall."

"She could've been pregnant by then." Mel pushes back from the table and rolls her neck until it cracks twice. "Stop trying to control the situation."

"I was apologizing!"

She holds up one palm. "Yes, you were. Maybe you don't realize this, but that's how you operate. You try to control how everyone thinks and reacts and, in this case, you didn't like Camille's reaction. So you apologized as if that would make everything all better." She stands.

I laugh, not even caring it comes out snarky. "Okay, so now you're a psych major. If I were your professor, you'd have failed that little analysis."

Mel's face softens. "I'm not saying that apologizing was the wrong choice, Tara. You just can't make people forgive you."

"So either way, I'm the bad guy."

She shrugs. "Pretty much. If it helps any, and I doubt that it will, I back you up on this one hundred percent. Camille needs to learn to be a better judge of character." Her chair makes a deep, scraping sound as she pushes it back under the table. "I've got to get to Simka's, but I'll go find out where Camille's off to first. Don't worry yourself. She'll get over it."

Alone in the kitchen, I glance out the window and down toward the sea, where a flock of herons glide freely beyond the rocky cliffs. My breathing slows as I watch them ride the air with such grace, such power despite their narrow, stick-like bodies. Sadly though, if I turn my head a half turn toward the right, I can find a glimpse of Beth's burned-out house. The pretty and the ugly, side by side. Isn't this the way life is?

I reach across the sink and jiggle the wooden window until it slides open. A nippy breeze flows in, raising goose bumps on my arms. And yet the smell of salt and sea and pine all woven together is worth every bit of chill. Despite the turmoil of the past few days, the smell alone is enough to help me remember the pretty things from my family's past and, for the moment, to forget about all the uglies.

My cell rings and with a sigh I leave the open window in search of my purse. I answer it on the fourth ring.

"Tara, it's Josh."

A flutter runs through me, and not from the cold. "Hi."

"I have to see you."

"Um. Okay." Not the sort of reaction he may have expected, but I'm not used to men *having* to see me. Unless they've got a late payment to make on their auto parts account, that is. Sure, Trent and I were together often, but it was more of a "You wanna do something tonight? I dunno, what do you wanna do?" kind of thing.

Josh grumbles and groans. "I can't drive."

He needs me to pick him up. Now *this* I'm used to. I smile. "So you're at my mercy then."

Josh is quiet for a moment. "Sounds like a place I'd like to be."

My heart does one of those flips that's reserved for women on the brink of diving deep into churning waters. Do I really need a man like Josh right now? Someone who is hell-bent on being a daredevil when what I really long for is a calm and steady hand as I continue to delve into my family's past?

He doesn't wait for my answer. "I'm home now. Will you come for me?"

My flipping heart melts at his request and I know the truth. It's too late. I've already taken the plunge. Big time.

I only hope I can remember how to swim. "Guess this means you'll need to tell me where you live."

He gives me directions, the sound of relief in his voice lifting my wavering heart. At least for the time being.

Chapter Twenty-two

Josh lives just minutes from my rental cottage. Minutes. He could even walk over, say, if he hadn't just suffered a concussion.

I pull up in front of what looks like it should be nestled in the mountains somewhere, a cabin wrapped in stained wood with a jacaranda tree in front, its purple flowers nearly spent.

Being here makes seeing Josh again all the more real, and conflicting feelings climb their way through me. When I came to Otter Bay, I wasn't looking for a man; I'd just gotten rid of one, although admittedly, not by choice. Josh has stirred up something fresh and exhilarating within, like a roller coaster that throws in a couple of quick twists after the initial death-defying drop.

The tune of my cell phone jars the quiet. "Hello?"

"Tara, it's Camille."

"Oh, Camille. You okay?"

She sniffles. "Yeah. I am." Muffled tears make it through my earpiece. "I just wanted to say th-th-thank you for saving me from that . . . cr-creep."

My brows crinkle. "Um, you're welcome. Are you sure you're okay?"

She doesn't answer right away, then Mel comes on the line. "Hey, Tara. I found her at the beach, kicking the snot out of Shane." Camille's crying gets louder. "She found him here with naked girl."

"Oh, no. Listen, I'm at Josh's, but I'm going to come home—"

"Don't do that. Camille and I have plans to check out her new school today. Go see Josh. You need something tempting to distract you from all this weirdness."

I sit back. My initial reaction is to protest, to throw my car in reverse and be Camille's cavalry. Isn't that what Eliza would do? I flinch. Eliza. I'm still not sure she should've taken things with her son's fiancée to quite that extreme . . .

"Tara, you still there?"

I shake away my random thoughts. "Y-yes. Still here. If you're sure you don't need me, then I guess I'll just stay with Josh."

Mel's laugh roars into the phone. "You *guess* you'll stay

with Josh! Please. The man's harem-worthy, Tara, or are you blind?" She snickers. "Nah, I've seen the way you run your eyeballs all over him."

"I do not!"

"Yeah, whatever. Try not to get too bored over there. I've got this covered."

She clicks off and I stare at my phone. A movement near the driver's side window catches my attention and I look up. Josh peers in at me. I jerk, slapping the back of my hand against the parking break.

I laugh, but my voice shakes. Is my heart zipping along because of this fright, or because of the man with the magnetic eyes watching me from behind the glass? He taps the door, eyeing me with a mischievous grin, as I unlock it and step out.

"Thought maybe you were second-guessing yourself in there." He reaches for me.

I scowl at him, or at least give it my best attempt. "Were you spying?"

He shrugs. "A little. Let's go in." He lays an arm across my shoulder and ushers me toward his cabin, the ground strewn with slim, purple petals and thick piles of pine needles.

I stop. "Should you be on your feet?"

He winks at me. "Nope."

"You're making me nervous."

"Ah honey, I promise not to ravish you, at least not in my current condition."

I stop again, this time rooting myself in place. His eyes dance along with his dazzling smile. Maybe he's on morphine or something.

"What?" He looks genuinely confused.

"I, uh, didn't come here for, you know, *that*. Not that I don't find you attractive." Now *there's* an understatement! I take a breath. "It's just that, well, I ended a long relationship recently and, uh . . ."

Josh furrows his brows and my heart sinks at the look on his face. I get it. He doesn't want to hear my *no* right now. I can tell. He just suffered a concussion, but apparently head trauma's not enough to stop a man on a mission. He drops his arm from my shoulder, and for some reason this causes me to hold my breath.

"What you must think of me."

I let out my breath at his sad words and turn my chin upward. He continues navigating the path to his front door. "You didn't seem very happy when you left my hospital room yesterday, so I'd hoped we'd be able to sort things out by talking about it." He pauses. "Trust me when I say that I didn't call you over here to seduce you."

I rub my lips together, at a loss over what to say. What is wrong with me? Why do I keep thinking—and saying—the worst? This man is the whole package, and yet something's holding me back.

There's a lift again to his voice as he holds open the screen door for me. "Not that I don't find you attractive or anything."

I step in through the doorway and wave both my hands. "Okay, okay. Truce. Let's not go there." The words have barely rolled off of my lips when Josh pulls me into his arms and kisses me like one very healthy man. Ex*treme*ly healthy. Behind us, the wooden screen door closes with a succinct bounce. A gull caws across the sky. My toes, I believe, have left the ground.

Josh pulls away, his eyes staring into mine. He holds me at arm's length. "I'm sorry."

I still feel the warmth of his kiss on my lips. "You're . . . sorry?"

He rakes his fingers through his hair, his face sheepish. "I got carried away. I really meant what I said, that I didn't ask you here to . . ."

"I know."

"I'm usually very careful . . . uh . . . what I mean is . . ." He lets the wind flow through his teeth. "Tara, I'm not that kind of guy."

My jaw clicks. *And you think I am that kind?* "I see."

He touches my shoulders with both hands and looks upward. "No, I don't think you do. You just bring out . . . something in me." His smile reminds me of a grimace. "Can we start over?"

I nod and he kisses me lightly, one hand barely touching my shoulder. A flutter tickles my insides.

He's smiling at me, a slight shadow stretching across his cheeks, the lines in his face smooth and distinct. "It's good to start again."

The compassion in his gaze startles me. Trent? Trent who . . . ? I'm speechless and no longer offended.

"Tara?"

"Hm?"

"I'm feeling woozy."

"Oh!" I slide my arm around his back and guide him toward the couch until he lowers himself into it. I stand up, my arms awkwardly wrapping around my middle. "You okay?"

His nod is accompanied by a grimace. I glance around, wondering if I should look for aspirin. For a bachelor who's out fighting fires and taking on myriad volunteer projects and other adventures, his house looks well lived-in. Loved, even. A picture of Josh and his parents wearing their Sunday best rests on a butcher-block end table. His furniture is neither ultramodern nor ancient history, but overstuffed and comfortable, in manly beiges—best not to mention that to my color-obsessed sisters. On the coffee table a bar of Irish Spring has been transformed into a baby chick.

He tries to pull himself up and I stop him by sitting next to him. His scent swirls around me. "You shouldn't be up. What can I get you? Aspirin? Some water?

Our eyes meet and we both lean back against the overstuffed couch. "I have what I need. I'm fine. This is normal."

Normal? This is anything but normal for me and yet I know what he means. My body sinks deeper into the cushion as I relax. Being here feels good and right and . . . natural. How could it be that just a few months ago I'd been planning my wedding to another man? Okay, only in my mind, but so what?

A cooing sound escapes me as I daydream, causing Josh to laugh. "I'm glad we kissed and made up."

A shadow falls across us and my eyes flicker toward the door. A tall lump of a man presses his nose against the screen. "Josh. You in there?"

I rouse and Josh shushes me with a whisper. "Maybe he'll go away."

"We have to get it."

Josh's body stays still, but he lifts his chin and twists his face toward the door. "Scram! We don't need any."

The guy scoffs and pulls open the door. When he enters, I recognize him as Billy, the firefighter who's been in the diner lately. "A little bump on the head and you think that . . . oh." He whistles. "Sorry. Didn't realize you weren't alone— that your 'stang out there?"

I extricate myself from Josh's side and stand. "I'm Tara. Yes, that's my car."

He nods, appraising me. "Sweet. Hey, didn't I see you over at the RAG?"

"With my sisters, yes."

We're smiling and nodding and completely awkward. Billy speaks first. "Well, I just came by to check up on Joshy-boy, but I can see that he's being well taken care of."

Josh stays put. "Thanks for stopping in."

Billy walks backward to the door. "But don't let the door smack me on the behind on my way out, right?" He laughs at his own joke. "Between you and Beth, I got nowhere else to go."

Josh's forehead wrinkles. "What about Beth? Things not working out so well with her? I thought you two were together."

Faint pink trails across Billy's face. His grin fades and his eyes dart between Josh and me. "We're getting there. She's having a bad day, though, so I, uh, told her we'd try again tomorrow."

Josh nods and it's obvious to me that he's drawing some kind of conclusion. He purses his lips, his focus on Billy intense, as if trying to decipher what's on his friend's mind. Billy glances at me, then settles a small grin on his face, as if everything's just dandy. He begins walking backward toward the door again before halting. "Wait. I forgot to ask. Junior wants to know if you're bringing a date to his wedding. Luanna's been asking."

From awkward to where's-the-door-and-how-fast-can-I-get-out-of-here? I hold myself still, as if this will somehow dissipate the sudden pin-drop silence. Josh reaches for my hand and gives it a tug. "Haven't had a chance to find out."

I meet his gaze and notice the quirk in his mouth. His expression tells me he's asking me to be his date, but I wait for a more formal invitation. Trent had this irrational belief that I somehow suckered him into asking me out that very first time. The "legend" as it became known, was one of his favorite stories to tell at parties. I got tired and stopped denying it.

Josh's fingers play with mine, but I just cock my head and continue to wait.

Billy laughs and it sounds like he really means it this time. His face has become bright and animated. "Looks like you're gonna have to try harder, my man."

Josh rubs the back of my hand with his fingers, eyes unwavering. "Go with me?"

My reaction reminds me of one of those dreams where you try to say something, but your mouth gets stuck in some kind of warped slow motion. I respond, but it comes out sounding more like a string of half words.

Billy doesn't wait for my official answer. "A week from Saturday," he calls out, his tone light and teasing. "I'll give him your RSVP for two. See ya." His feet pound quickly down the steps.

Josh sits up with a question in his smile. Concussion, my foot. He's as healthy as I am. "Sorry to put you on the spot like that," he says. "Would you really like to come with me?"

"Sure."

His smile breaks out further, but his eyes weigh my answer. "So that was playing hard to get back there, then?"

Hard to get? Like some drama queen? The headiness of these moments with Josh comes to a screeching stop as the reality of my life looms before me. I lower myself into the cushiony couch. I've only known about Daddy's indiscretion—a second one—for about a day, and Mel tore into me when she found out. Then there was last night. I breathe in, trying not to relive the scene with Camille and Shane yet again. Tempting as Josh might be, is this the best time to be risking my heart again?

"What's wrong?"

I kick off my sandals and pull my knees up to my chest. Suddenly I've got no words.

Josh stares. "I haven't forgotten what you said in my hospital room . . . about moving too fast. Is that what you're scared of? I meant it when I said I was sorry . . ."

"I'm not scared. Not really. Just overwhelmed." I glance down at my toes, the need for a pedicure more than a little evident. So much to do . . . to think about. I mentally push aside my worries. "And I wasn't playing hard to get. I just wanted to make sure you were actually asking me." I give him a sideways look. "Don't want to be accused of inviting myself."

"I'd never do that."

My gaze lingers on him. "No, I don't believe you would."

"I want you to be with me. Besides, it's never fun to disco by yourself."

My snort takes us both by surprise. "Disco? I'm so not
doing the Hustle. What is this, 1976?"

Josh shrugs one bruised shoulder. "DJs always seem to
think so." He groans, followed by a slight wince. "It's the
conga line I'm really looking forward to, though."

"Maybe I should've checked my calendar firs—"

Josh reaches over and tugs at my elbow, freeing me from
my fetal position. "Not a chance. You've already agreed, so
you're stuck. I have a witness."

"He left."

"Yes, well." He smiles and begins to pull me into his
embrace but slows, as if he'd just thought better of it.
Instead, we sit together, listening to the breeze through the
pines, as if we've known each other forever.

Chapter Twenty-three

Josh's eyelids keep lulling, the sound of my voice apparently quite the sleeping aid. He wakes for the fourth time with a start and an apology. "S-sorry, Tara. It's not you." He slides lower into the couch, hugging a pillow to his chest, while I stand and pull a blanket over him and up to his chin. I move toward him, tentatively, to graze his forehead with my lips, the kind of simple kiss that I will no doubt replay over and over, but he rustles, as if awake. "Stay away from me. Trouble . . ."

He's *trouble*? Though barely awake, his words are clear. I change my mind about the peck on his forehead and leave for home.

Only I don't make it all the way there. Instead, I pull over to the side of the road, where the cliffs meet the beach. After scrambling down chiseled rock, I sink my feet into an infinite pile of moonstones, their flat, smooth surfaces like a massage to my skin.

In the distance elephant seals bark at each other—Nigel says that there's a rookery not far from here, one that tourists love to visit. I plan to drive up there soon. My feet crunch as I walk along the shore, heading north, with only wind and waves filling my senses. The sounds and breezes flow over and through me, better than the facial Mel talked me into having before Mother's wedding.

Looking westward, I shade my face with my hand. Giant kelp bob atop the water, their dense bodies and bulbous ends making me do a double take, wondering if they're really some sort of creature from the sea. I imagine tiny fish swimming through the maze of kelp, in search of dinner and a night's rest.

The comparison is not lost on me. I too feel like a tiny fish in one big confusing maze. If only I had an inkling of Josh's meaning behind the "trouble" comment, I'd have one less issue to worry over. My cell rings and I groan. Why didn't I remember to leave it in the car? "Hello?"

"It's Mel. How's lover boy?"

"Asleep."

Mel clucks her tongue. "Well, then. Just wanted to let you know that Camille's doing fine. We checked out the school and have been shopping all afternoon in downtown SLO. We'll catch dinner here, so you don't have to worry about fixing anything. I know how you are."

I smile, ruefully. "You don't know as much as you think."

"I think I'm offended."

"Better get used to it."

Mel gasps. "Does this mean you're planning to ditch your family and spend more time with hunk o' burning love?"

I glance off into the infinite sky. "Might."

"Well. Can I give you some advice?"

She startles me with the question. When has Mel ever asked to give me advice? She usually just delivers it like a poke to a bonfire. That's how it's been between Mel and me, for as long as I can remember. Mother put me in charge of a lot of things, and Mel was always close behind, nipping at me, like a puppy jealous over a hound's rag doll.

"Let him lead on this dance. Camille and I actually like this one."

"Explain."

"You're always so uptight and so in control. Or you want to be. Don't do that. Let the guy do some of the leading this time."

"Okay, first, I never do that. In fact, Trent controlled our entire relationship and where did that get me? I'll tell you, it got me an empty ring finger and a broken heart."

"Well, then your heart recovered awful quickly, didn't it. And you only *think* Trent controlled your relationship, when in fact, you two would never have been together in the first place if you hadn't set that in motion."

Here we go. The "legend" strikes again. "Five years, Mel. He promised that after college, he'd propose. And then it was after he got his career started. I wasted so much time with him, that I can't believe you somehow think that *I* was the one controlling things. What I was doing was *waiting.*" My hand clenches over and over again at my side.

"Tara." Mel's voice becomes pliable and warm. She's a regular chameleon. "Why did you wait so long? You couldn't possibly have loved Trent. You just became whatever he wanted, whenever he wanted. It may seem like he was the one in control, but by conforming to his every wish, you were saying that you weren't about to let go—even if he wasn't really the one for you."

"Mel, I have to go." Without waiting for her reply, I power down my phone and stuff it into my back pocket. I pick up a moonstone and flick it into the water, watching it sink rather than skip, as I had hoped. Why does Mel suddenly have to make sense? When Trent left me, I blamed him for being spineless, for being unable to follow through. Why do so many people have trouble with following through on their commitments?

The cool tide washes over my feet and I sink deeper into the coarse sand. Camille's words come to mind, the ones she spoke in the diner, soon after we arrived. Everyone thought I needed a vacation, they believed that just because I'd wanted to do something outside of my norm, that somehow this meant I was heading over the edge. Trent, apparently, even thought I needed some shaking up, as Camille put it.

My eyes spring open wide, hot tears stinging the corners. *Does Trent expect me to change and take him back?* Water flows over my feet again, draining between my toes and washing back out to sea. Without a doubt, my relationship with him is dead and has been far longer than the day he finally walked away. There is no turning back.

A lump in my throat threatens to burst, but I deny it. What's the use of crying away the years given to the wrong man? It bothers me, but Mel was right. Maybe I was the one holding on too long.

Another wave builds in the distance, this one rolling faster toward me than the last. I leap out of its way, then dash up behind a rock, swiping my brimming eyes with the back of my hand. It occurs to me that these budding tears have little in common with those I spilled over a broken engagement. It's true. I recovered from that faster than anyone expected. I knew we weren't perfect together, but I had settled because he was comfortable. Like nubby sweats.

Moving here proves that I'm no longer willing to settle and that, like shifting tides, I'm changing too.

"I USED TO BE a rascal." Nigel lowers his soup spoon into the bowl.

The RAG's quiet tonight, with Peg home due to a cold and Holly off for the night. Trusty Jorge is behind the stove and Mimi's got the dining room covered.

"So you never wanted to come back here? What made you take back the inn then?" I push my salad around on my plate, the dry carrot curls and iceberg chunks not overly appetizing. What I wouldn't do for a toss of Holly's cranberry bib greens.

"A friend sent me letters, many letters over the years, reminding me of how refreshing it was in Otter Bay."

"You'd forgotten?"

"Yes, I suppose I had." He takes a slow sip from his spoon. "Oh, I wanted to be where the action and city night life were. As you know, there is not too much of either in this sleepy town."

I laugh. It's difficult to imagine this genteel, beret-wearing man yearning for something other than the unspoiled coastline of Otter Bay. "I bet your sister was glad to see you return."

Nigel's face sobers for just a moment, before settling back into his signature, peaceful countenance. "She only knows about my return from heaven's gate."

I stop fiddling with my salad. "She passed away before you returned?" He nods and something inside me sinks. How terribly sad for her—and for him. "I'm so sorry."

"Don't be. I have become aware of how the Father has orchestrated the aspects of my life. It's been all for my good."

"Are you saying that God caused you to miss seeing your sister?"

Nigel stops moving toward his soup, as if considering my question. I mean no offense, but it seems to me that God's more interested in the big picture, like wars and famine.

Nigel sits back, folds his napkin, and slowly wipes his mouth with one small corner. "The Lord did not cause me to miss seeing my sister. My stubbornness did. And yet I know with every ounce of my breath that He has worked all things that have happened in my life for my good." His smile is infinite kindness. "I have not always known this. That took some time."

A burst of questions ricochet through my mind. Undeniably, walking into church the past couple of weeks has provided me a sense of grounding, but I've thought it's been because of my family's past within those walls. I've never been able to completely wrap my mind around faith, though. So much of it seems so ethereal and unconfirmed. I want to ask Nigel how he *knows* what he does, but he's a private man, and who am I to ask him for more than he's offering?

The door to the RAG swings open, rattling bells against the glass and announcing the arrival of a large group. There's laughter and spikes of conversation as the crowd pours in, dragging chairs enough to squeeze them all around two small tables pushed together. The spectacle tugs at me. I was such a loner in high school, one best friend and a second for when my other pal wasn't around. I was her fallback friend too.

One lanky boy notices us and jerks up from the table. Mikey walks tentatively up to our table. "Hi, Nigel. Hi, Tara."

"Looks like a whole lot of fun over there." I keep the wistfulness from my voice. But just barely.

Mikey's hands dig into his pockets. He swivels around to look back at his friends before returning my gaze. "Um, just wanted to say I'm sorry for saying too much to your sister. She seemed kinda mad. My mom yelled at me later."

"Apology accepted."

He stands there awkwardly, pivoting on his toes and glancing around. "Was nice of you to go visit Josh. He seems better."

My cheeks heat up at the sound of Josh's name. "He is, I think. I saw him this morning." I avoid Nigel's questioning eyes.

"Cool." Mikey walks backward. "Well, I gotta go eat with my friends."

Nigel's smiling at me. "You bring out the joy in him."

"In Mikey? I don't think so, Nigel. That kid's happy almost anytime I see him."

"No, dear. I was referring to Josh. He's a different man with you in Otter Bay. I may seem like an old man to you, but I have perfect command of my faculties and there is a definite spark between you and Joshua Adams."

I giggle and the sound of it makes me want to slap a muzzle on myself. Camille always giggles too, as do teenage girls and old women who eat truffles and watch chick flicks together. But Mom always said I was the serious type, the leader who didn't need frivolity in her life. Always took a bit of pride in that.

Nigel continues. "And it is very good to see. Very good, indeed. Perhaps you are the answer to the demons that young man fights."

Nigel's words shrink the girlish smile on my face. How can I be Josh's answer when I need one of my own?

Chapter Twenty-four

 It's like déjà vu, except today the diner is bustling with hungry tourists and Peg and Holly are jetting through the place with the intensity of adrenalized puppies. Too bad that underneath Peg's energetic exterior lives a pit bull.

Camille's reflective. "Did you know that celebrities often go commando when they walk the red carpet?"

I blink.

"I mean the women. It's so no one can see their panty lines."

Mel cuts in. "It's because their dresses are sewed on so tight that they can't fit panties or even a thong underneath them."

Sigh. "Is this pleasant breakfast time conversation?"

Camille continues. "One of the classes at the college is on waxing. I'm intrigued by that."

I take another bite of my poached egg. "As in brow and lip waxing? That sort of thing?"

Camille flips a chunk of curls over one shoulder. "And the Hollywood, the Brazilian, all kinds."

I look to Mel, who's wearing a quirky little grin, like she's got a secret. "Think naked in the nether regions . . . or nearly so."

I gasp. "No! Why would anyone want to . . . to . . . ? Ugh. And what does this have to do with fashion design?"

Camille giggles. "Isn't that cool? We designers need to know the different waxing styles we'll be dealing with when planning our designs. This opens up a whole new world."

I gulp my juice, trying to wash down the egg that just got stuck in my throat. "Some worlds are better left unknown."

"What are you girls laughin' about?" Holly stands next to our table, one hand slung into her waist. "Wish I could just forget about workin' and sit right down and have some toast with you."

My back hits the booth. "Believe me, you don't really want to know."

Camille slides out of the booth. "Speaking of fashion—" she brushes something from Holly's shoulder—"these uniforms are pretty, but have you considered changing to a black dress with white apron?"

Holly scrunches her mouth before replying. "You mean not go with white on white anymore?"

Mel gives me a surreptitious glance and whispers, "More like blah on blah."

"The contrast would be stunning!" Camille proclaims. "Or you could go with a savory sage or earth tone, something to give your outfits contrast and warmth."

Holly giggles, reminding me of Camille. "Well now, that's what we need—a little more warmth around this place." She peeks over her shoulder toward Peg. "She's still bein' ornery and it's gettin' old, if you ask me."

"Well, maybe I can talk to her. I'll tell her about my fashion design classes. That oughta give me some credibility, don't you think?" A tap on the window makes us all spin around to find a handsome face pressed up against the glass. His dark, thick eyebrows appear Chaplin-esque and he wiggles them at Camille.

She tosses him a quick wave and looks back to Holly. "Don't you worry about a thing. I'll talk to your Aunt Peg when I get back in." Camille ignores Mel and me when she adds with a low voice, "I've got to go meet someone."

Mel and I gape at each other. *That was awfully fast.*

Holly shrinks away from the table, her shoulders taut. "Gotta go before Auntie comes by and gives me what for."

We eat in silence, Mel and me. We haven't been alone since before that awful conversation yesterday when I hung up on her at the beach. She's not exactly handing out romance advice to our flirty sister, so it riles me that she has so much to say to me on the subject.

Not that I haven't mulled over what she said. I glance out at the busy room of diners, many ensconced in vibrant conversations. A tot twirls in the aisle as her parents attempt to finish their meal. Jorge laughs with a diner behind the counter, until Peg shoos him back to his post. The whole world, it seems, orbits around us, as we sit here dwelling on our own private thoughts.

"Have you thought about what I said?" Peg's sudden presence pulls me out of my reverie.

"Remind me." Eliza wouldn't let someone like Peg bully her, so why should I?

Peg blows out an exasperated sigh. "It's really not the best place for you people to live, knowing what you know about that father of yours. People might talk, so I have an offer to make you girls."

Mel's face hardens.

"And that is?" I ask, but I don't really care all that much.

"I pay your moving expenses. Must be terribly expensive to move all the way across country, so I'm here to help."

Mel clucks her tongue, an eye roll away from laughing in Peg's face. "What is your problem, lady? You think the Sweets'll run just because of a few gossips? It's hard to believe that you and Holly are related. That girl's a sweetheart, but you"—she shakes her head—"you're cut from a different cloth."

Peg's eyes narrow and she gathers wind in her lungs as if readying herself to let loose on us. Before she can, Camille prances through the door and slides up behind Peg, her old bounce back in her walk.

"Hey there, Peg," Camille says, her voice earnest. "I just *love* your new hairdo. Are you growing it out?"

Camille's compliment seems to knock the thrust from Peg's assault, rendering her speechless. Something in her face is unreadable—unlike the curse-filled expression she often darted our way all morning from across the diner. The tension that drove the lines in her face deeper, has let up slightly and I'm more than a little curious. Is this a simple case of catching more flies with honey?

Camille slides in next to me, her focus still on Peg. "And those earrings you're wearing are amazing. You have really good taste!"

Stunned, Peg fingers her right ear. Her eyes don't seem to know where to land. "They were our—my—mother's."

Camille jostles her head side to side, her curls following along playfully. "Well, then, your mother had exquisite taste too."

Peg runs both hands down the front of her apron, as if trying to right herself. "Th-thank you. More lemonade?"

Mel and I exchange a wide-eyed look. Is this the same woman who moments ago tried to pay us to leave town? The one Mel thinks may try to sue us for our father's supposed theft? The transformation is stunning—until she turns to leave and our eyes meet.

Something familiar smolders in them and let's just say, it's anything but the warm fuzzies.

IF YOU HAD SAID a year ago, or even last month that I could be found stepping into church on a Wednesday night, I'd have thought you had suckled the vodka bottle for far too long. Wednesday night. The end of hump day and the day before everything goes downhill. I've always been too busy on that night getting ready for the rest of the week.

Instead of my usual Wednesday night race, though, I make my way to the side aisle of Coastal Christian and take a seat about halfway down. In front would be too conspicuous and, come to think of it, so would being in the back. I settle in, watching churchgoers trickle in, some obviously from work, others from a day at the beach. I, too, worked much of the day, but I just couldn't bring myself to go home yet. Too many unsettled thoughts.

Instead of the quiet sanctuary I was hoping for, pockets of groups form in every corner, some, like the band, set up, while others fall into happy chatter. It's like an old-fashioned town meeting. Unfortunately I'm feeling more and more like the perpetual outsider and I sag into the pew.

To my far left, three men give each other shoulder slaps,

reminiscent of the result of a game of pick-up basketball. One looks awfully familiar and after several quick glances, I realize it is Josh's father. He's livelier than when I saw him last week, but then again, we were visiting his son in the hospital. I marvel at how much he looks like an older, more seasoned version of Josh. The same handsome height, broad smile, though his are timeworn and gracious.

A guitar player tunes up on the stage, minor notes slicing through the crowd. Laughter from the far corner becomes more boisterous, causing me to flick a glance back and forth between those setting up for service and the posse of men who appear to have no plans to take their seats anytime soon.

Certainly not the impression I had of church as a child.

A crashing sound hurls from the corner and I stand to my feet. The men are bent over in a circle, calling out Pete's name. Josh's father has fallen from view. I leave my seat to see if I can help. Already several others have rushed to Pete's aid, but I can't help myself. I'm nearly there when Josh leaps in front of me.

His eyes implore me. "Stay here, Tara."

"Where'd you come from?" I don't wait for his answer, but stretch a look over his shoulder. "Your father. Is he hurt?"

Josh walks forward, causing me to take a step back. "He's . . . he's fine. I'll go check. Just relax and take your seat. I'll handle it."

"Josh!" A voice from the crowd calls out to him.

He turns to go and I follow until Josh spins around and looms over me. "Stay out of it, Tara."

I shrink back, hurt, confused. Conflicting emotions skitter across Josh's face, as if mirroring my own. I flash on the day I first saw him, when he leapt the counter at the diner. Does he want to be the hero again? Or did that conk on the head last week cause him a long lasting bad temper?

He takes a step back, then stops. "Tara . . ."

"Go. Your father needs you." I turn and head back to my seat. By now, the laughter has subsided and several in the group have helped Pete up. He looks disoriented and I'm worried for him, but Josh is on the case and it's not my business. He let me know that all right.

As if nothing out of the ordinary has just occurred, the worship leader cues the band and the music starts. I try to focus on the words of the song that are projected onto a large screen, but all I can think of is that something about Josh just isn't right.

Chapter Twenty-five

What would Eliza do?

I'm out on the deck, rereading the last few days' events of *Quartz Point* on *Soaps Weekly Digest*. It used to be that I would stay up late every night just to catch up on Eliza's doings, but lately, I don't know, it's as if I've been distracted. I rub my eyes until they sting, and the words blur across the screen. Eliza hosted a dinner party for twenty guests, including a new match-up for her beloved son. She wore white and flitted from guest to guest, never spilling one drop on her pristine suit. I yawn, surprising myself. For the first time I can recall, my interest in Eliza's day wanes.

I shut the laptop and sit back against the Adirondack. Josh hurt my feelings today and, if I am being completely candid, he embarrassed me. His order to take my seat felt eerily similar to the time I volunteered to work the cash register at Dexton auto parts. Woody rushed over then. "I'll handle the store, Tara. I will be fine. You stay at your post in the back." *You're not welcome up front, Tara.* He didn't really say all that I am thinking, but it felt as if he did.

"You still up?" Mel pads out onto the deck, her silky robe cinched around her waist.

"'Fraid so. I'm wide awake."

"Try a glass of warm milk."

I weigh the option. "You know I'm not a fan of milk. Unless it's in my morning coffee, that is."

"Worked for Mom."

I smile. "Thanks, but I'll probably just go read in bed." Mel's face becomes clearer as my eyes adjust to the absence of the laptop's light. She looks worried. "Why are you up?"

She shrugs. "No reason, really. I just had a few more ideas for Simka that I wanted to think out and write down before I forget."

"So that's going well? Working with Simka?"

Mel tries to hold back a smile, but a partial one breaks through anyway. She's always so open with her opinions, especially the negative ones. Why can't she share the good things with me too?

"It's all right. Nothing long-term, but something to do while I consider my options." I just nod, knowing full well if I were to ask what options she might be considering, she would continue to be vague. It's as if my asking is an invasion of her privacy. Silence settles around us, except for the occasional burst of wave lofting onto shore.

Mel surprises me by staying. "So the big wedding date is this weekend."

I nod, although I'm not exactly glowing with the luster of anticipation.

"You are still going, right? Simka says the whole town will be there. Apparently the happy couple has lived in little Otter Bay their entire lives." She glances out to the distant sea. "It's nice around here, but I can't imagine staying here *that* long."

"Really?"

"Too much of all this beauty might give me a cavity." She laughs at her own joke, the sound rattling through the quiet night.

"What? Oh, I meant, is the whole town really going to be there? I had no idea. I just thought we were going to a wedding of another fireman."

"Don't worry about finding something to wear. The girls and I already planned on dragging you back to Simka's tomorrow. Sshh. Don't tell Camille I squealed . . . she was going to kidnap you."

I set aside the computer, stand, and begin to pace. "This is perfect. If the bride and groom have lived here their whole lives, then maybe some of their guests have too. Someone other than the Sims family must have known us!"

Mel crosses her arms. "So you're going to take a couples' happiest day and turn it into a fact-finding mission about our parents? What're you going to do? Walk up and say 'My daddy had an affair here, remember that? And oh, yeah, he stole big bucks from Peg, the diner owner from hell . . . whaddya know about that?'" She shakes her head vigorously. "No way, Tara, I wouldn't recommend this at all."

"You really think I'm that callous, don't you?" My eyes shut tight and I hug myself against the coldness of the night. Eliza wouldn't allow such negativity to stand. She'd nip it before it grew any further. Why have I always allowed Mel to get to me? My eyes snap open. "All I meant is that if I'm friendly and introduce myself to people, surely someone will remember our name. I need some good news, Mel. The happy memories of this place"—my voice chokes up—"are beginning to fade."

My sister's brows dip. "But what if the things they say hurt you and us? What then?"

"What is wrong with you? Our father was amazing! Don't you remember him at all, Mel? He loved us and took care of us . . . and what about all those people who came forward at his funeral to say how much they admired him? Have you forgotten?"

Those furrowed brows soften and tears form in the corners of Mel's eyes. Her voice is just a whisper. "I will never forget him. I-I just want to remember him the way he was."

Her statement is like the proverbial lightbulb springing to life in a dark room. I reach for Mel and pull her close, no longer mindful of how she might react to my embrace.

"Yeah. Me too."

"YOU GIRLS HAVE BEEN here only a little while, but gracious, how did I do without you all these years in Otter Bay?" Holly's standing in the middle of Simka's main gallery, the living room of the former residence, her elbow jabbed into her waist and a polka-dot thong hanging from her forefinger.

I toss my head back, defying her. "You don't for a second believe that I would wear one of those."

Holly glances at it. "Well of course I do. Everyone's supposed to be admirin' the bride on her weddin' day. You don't won't want to be distractin' them with your big ol' pantylines, do you, Tara?"

I squint. "Maybe I do."

Holly twirls the thong around her finger like it's a piece of string, which actually, it is. "You're such a fuddy-duddy."

My mouth opens and stays there. Not long ago Camille called me the same thing. Why is it that choosing not to wear trendy underthings that are nothing but mere floss with a pretty design somehow makes me old-fashioned and boring?

Mel takes Holly by surprise and wrests the offending thong from her grasp. "You are barking up the wrong pine tree, Holly. My sister loves her granny panties."

I protest with a sigh and a Camille-worthy eye roll.

Mel keeps moving, obviously intent on returning her prize to the lingerie bin. Before she can, though, Camille skips over and grabs it from Mel, pirouettes and pulls back on the thong like a sling shot and flings it with a snap. It hits Simka on the cheek when she enters the room.

We all gasp.

Simka holds out the thong and considers it critically. "I've always preferred a less geometric design."

Camille bites her lip. "Sorry, Simka."

Simka's bell-like laughter ripples through the air. "No harm done." She turns to me and claps her chubby hands. "Now. I have chosen several delightful gowns for you, my dear. The yellows are my most favorite, except for the bees—bees love yellow, so I have only chosen dresses that use it as an accent color rather than primary. Oh, it is a shame."

"I will keep that in mind. Thank you."

I head to the dressing room, listening as the girls "ooh" and "aah" over Simka's newest summer arrivals. It's a universal phenomenon among women that purchasing a new wardrobe—or even a new dress, as in my case—uplifts the soul. For as long as I remember, though, I've been too frugal and sensible to shop much. Trent hated that about me, but there's nothing more trying than attempting to find the perfect blouse, shoe, whatever, during the lunch hour, when I was most available to shop. That's the time that just about every other shopper, be they retirees, moms of little ones, or nine-to-fivers, seem to flood department stores and take over the aisles and dressing rooms. And have I mentioned the lines that snake through the racks? Not my idea of a lunch break.

Camille's sudden squeal surprises me. "I love these capris! Hurry up, Tara, so I can have the dressing room."

I take her seriously, because if I don't, Camille just might strip down to her skivvies for all the shopping population to see. The first dress I try on has a high waist and wide skirt, causing me to look "with child," more so than someone who truly is pregnant. I step out of it and hang it quickly.

"Hey, Tara, not fair." Holly catches me. "You have to give us all a modelin' show."

"Next one," I shout over the flimsy fabric curtain. Unfortunately the next one hugs me like the skin of a caterpillar and I want to eat my words. The dress is tight, revealing and the worst shade of yellow ever. Like sludge.

I step out and discover, too, that the board-straight skirt provides little room for actual walking. My feeble attempt to strut around is met with suppressed mirth. Camille glances at Holly. "Didn't know there were penguins in these parts."

Holly snorts loudly, and Mel shakes her head, but the smile across her face refuses to fade.

"All right. I'm done with you people." I waddle back behind my fabric barricade. Maybe attending this wedding isn't the best idea. Josh's behavior yesterday still weighs on my heart. If it weren't for my quest to see the whole town in one place, I may have backed out of this date.

Would you really, Tara?

The thought falls across my mind like a shadow. Would I really have the guts to turn down a date with the most eligible bachelor in town, even though his behavior left little to be desired? For some reason I could confront a nonpaying customer at the auto parts company with the evil eye, but when Trent continued to put off our wedding, I acquiesced, as if grateful for the chance to call myself engaged.

"C'mon, Tara. Give us one more chance." Holly's no-nonsense voice shuts down the running commentary in my head. I survey the remaining selections within my tiny dressing room and pluck one from the bunch. The black, white, and yellow print with its double straps and shimmery skirt hugs my skin, but in a natural way. Wearing it makes me feel cool and thin . . . and pretty. I attempt a slow twirl, hoping the girls don't spy my feet beneath the curtain.

"Oooh, Tara likes this one." Holly doesn't miss a thing.

Camille giggles. "Let's see, let's see!"

With reluctance, I slide the curtain to the side and step out. Holly and Camille rush me, their mouths overflowing with adulation. The effect on my heart startles me. Something inside twists a little. I've wanted to be on the receiving end of a man's praise forever, and recently I had been, when Josh's eyes lit up the night of our first date as he noticed me walk out from the hall. It had been a long time since anyone caressed me with eyes that way. If I were to be honest, Trent probably never had.

Simka nods at me. "Oh, yes, yes, yes. And with the right shoes and accessories, you may just draw all the attention away from the bride!"

I laugh, uneasily. *That's about as likely as Peg giving me a warm hug and welcoming me to Otter Bay.*

Mel stands back, though, her eyes assessing me. I suppress the uncomfortable sense her appraising eye gives me, as if I'm standing naked on the beach. "What do you think about this one, Mel-Mel?" I ask, an attempt to dissipate my uneasiness.

An unhurried smile stretches across her face. She gives me a slow, succinct nod. "I think you look absolutely . . . striking."

I run my hands down my hips. "Really? Not too, um, spicy?"

She laughs a from-the-belly laugh, probably for the first time since showing up here in Otter Bay. "It's about time you added a little spice, Tare-Tare."

Her sentiments tickle me, even though it feels silly to admit this. I'm a grown woman. It should not matter if Mel approves of what I wear. *Or approves of who I am.* But after a lifetime of tug-of-war with my younger sister, I realize that her opinion does matter.

And always has.

Chapter Twenty-six

I stand at the counter of the Bayside, resolved and serene—unlike the guest in room 9, who very much personifies the cliché of people with smoke pouring from their ears. He shakes his bill in front of my face, but I'm unfazed. Ever since that moment yesterday when Mel called me by that old pet name of hers, the one Camille occasionally adopts when she wants something, I've felt lighter in both body and spirit. It's as if a heavy crust of stone has fallen away from my shoulders, leaving me renewed and restored.

"The bed was too soft, the closet inadequate, and the rate too high!" A puffy, gray vein protrudes from the bald spot on the man's crown. I focus on it a little too long . . . *What would happen if the vessel burst right in front of me?*

"Well?"

His angry question hangs in the air between us. As a former accounts receivable clerk, I have no qualms about refusing to take this man's guff. I could threaten with the very best of them, although I readily admit that it's easier to do so over the phone.

Or I could do just the opposite—the very thing that Mel has accused me of doing in my personal life—and passively take this man's abuse if only it would make him go away. With me it's always been an either-or situation.

Either I'm a tough accounts receivable rep refusing to excuse a $4.10 charge, or I'm the pushover girlfriend, the one who walks on eggshells in hopes that some day Prince Charming will finally climb down off that horse and book the castle for the wedding of the year.

It occurs to me that Eliza would refuse this man's guff and that she'd do it in such a way that he'd not only pay that bill, but leave her a tip on the way out. *She'd probably overcharge him too.* I shove away that random thought and as it goes another idea takes hold, one that splashes a wash of peace over me, similar to that moment at Mom's wedding when I realized it was time to move to California.

Maybe it's time to put aside my old ways. It's not like they've been much help to me anyway. Really, did making old men grovel for another thirty days do much for my state of mind? Or for theirs?

Just look what an angry countenance has done to Peg.

Dad used to say that gentleness could turn away anger. After hearing a similar phrase during the sermon recently, I am beginning to understand why he believed that to be so.

I take a mysterious peek about the lobby, then lean across the counter. "I know what you mean, sir. A few of the beds are almost ready to be replaced. When I stayed here, my mattress wasn't the firmest."

His chest continues to rise and fall, but his grip on the room bill loosens. He begins to mumble. "And the closet area is just large enough for one suitcase. Where will my wife put all her things?"

"Tell you what. I'll send in a rolling laundry rack. It should fit well between that empty space and the bathroom door. Will that be helpful to you?"

He lays his forearms, which just moments ago had been striking the air, across the countertop. The bill falls from his hand. "My company just announced layoffs." He lowers his sweaty forehead into one hand. "I don't know how secure the job for an old man is. My wife didn't want to cancel this trip, and I just couldn't disappoint her."

"No, sir, I don't suppose you could have." His desperation touches me. "I wonder . . . do you possibly have auto club? Because I can offer you a rate deduction if you are a member."

He straightens and yanks a wallet from his back pocket. "I am—we are members! Hadn't thought about this."

He begins flipping through the papers in his wallet, his hands shaky and frustrated grunts escaping from within. "It's in here somewhere . . ."

I pick up the phone. "While you look for your card, I think I'll have housekeeping send over a board for underneath your mattress." Mary will no doubt grouse about having to retuck all four corners of the sheets again, but she'll get over it.

He lifts his chin. His eyes brighten. "You're a peach." He whips out his club card and smacks it on the counter. "You've made my day, young lady."

After he's gone, I think about the abrupt change in my angry customer's countenance. The thought haunts me. In my old life, I could have turned around dozens of situations if only I'd tried a little understanding. Somewhere along the way, I'd forgotten that.

I'm double-checking the registration cards, laying them out "just so" for Betty who should arrive at any minute. The lobby door opens and I wave her in without looking up. "I'm just about ready for you, my dear . . ."

"I'm relieved to hear it."

I jerk my head up. Josh walks toward me, tentatively.

"I called Mel and she told me you'd be off work soon. Hope you don't mind."

"Hope I don't mind you calling Mel? Or you coming here?" *Did that have to come out so terse, especially after my breakthrough with Mr. Angry Guest in room 9?*

He leans his head to one side, but no grin breaks out. "I want to make this up to you."

"Forget it. You were tense. It happens."

"I'm sorry."

"Forgiven."

"You don't sound like you mean it."

"Are you saying I'm not sincere?"

A small smile curls on his face. "Of course not." His voice slides over his tongue, soft, low. "Not at all."

"Well, good. I hope your father is feeling better."

The door opens again and in stumbles Betty. "Hoo-wee. I'm here, I'm here now."

"Hello, Betty. Take your time. I'm in no hurry."

Josh raises an eyebrow, but I continue with my job, puttering around the lobby, straightening brochures and stacking magazines, fully aware that his eyes follow me. Betty removes her coat—she wears one even on warm days—and hangs it on the rack in the corner. She then fills a cup with hot water from the coffee service and plops in a fresh tea bag retrieved from her purse.

"There. I'm ready for the rest of the afternoon."

"You sure?" I'm barely able to hide my reluctance to leave the inn.

Josh's touch lands at my elbow. "She's sure. C'mon. I want to show you something."

We drive northward along the coiling highway, with far-reaching, unfettered ranch land to our right and breathtaking ocean vistas on our left. Josh's golden hair ruffles in the drive-generated wind. All seems perfect.

"I don't suppose you'll tell me where we're going."

He shrugs mischievously. "I suppose I could."

"Well?"

"I'm taking you to see some of the strongest animals in the wild."

"Really."

He nods and smiles and doesn't say anything more. He doesn't need to, as the views leave plenty to think about. The sky stretches to forever and provides covering to the vast sea. Coal-black rocks mimic sunbathing whales with frothy waves washing over them. Tourists park along the highway and dash onto private land with their knee-shorts and cameras and expectant looks.

I, on the other hand, have decided to have no expectations, to instead live for this moment and see where it leads. I expected Trent to agree to a wedding date; he never did. I expected to find paradise in Otter Bay, and while the cool breezes and sea air provide the feeling of serendipity, the reality is that Mother and Dad found it less than idyllic here.

I glance over at Josh and he smiles at me, that wind still blowing through his hair. Something pulls at me and I want to reach out and touch him. But I don't. Still too many questions in my mind about my family, this place . . . his demons.

He pulls into a viewing point just off the highway. Tour buses hog multiple spaces, while full cars weave in and out, dodging foraging squirrels and distracted tourists.

"We're here." Josh snakes an open spot right at the cliff. He dashes over and opens my door, the wind providing help as it flings back.

We mosey along the dirt lot to a viewing spot overflowing with people speaking myriad languages. It doesn't take long to see what has drawn so much of their attention. Spread out on the sand below lie rows and rows of elephant seals, their blubbery folds encrusted with fresh sand.

I laugh and grab hold of the handrail separating us from the drop to the sand. "They're enormous! Why are there so many out there?"

"They're here to shed some skin. If you look closely you can see mottled brown—the older skin—peeling right off. Look. See the silver skin shining through?"

I nod. "They remind me of oversized sardines!"

Josh throws back his head and laughs. "I've never been a fan."

"What can I say? They're full of calcium—a girl can never have too much calcium, you know."

He wrinkles his nose. "So you eat sardines often?"

I wag my head and laugh. "Never actually tried them. They smell disgusting."

Laughter resonates through him and he shakes his head. "You are too much."

A blush heats my face, but there's a good chance it'll appear like nothing more than the start of a sunburn. I clear my throat. "I tell guests about this rookery all the time, but I always feel like such a fake since I've never actually been here before."

I continue to hold the railing but straighten my arms and sway backwards, my back arching until my chin lifts to greet the sky. The rustle of ocean waters mixed with the buzz of air across my warming face sends me to the past. I'm about six, with no thought in my head that we'd be leaving Otter Bay anytime soon. A group of adults and some older children splash around in waist-high water. Mother sits in her beach chair, a distance away.

All of a sudden, several of the parents walk out together in the surf. I remember my father turning and smiling at me, but when I try to slosh toward him, he tells me no with a quick shake of his head. I look back to Mother, but she doesn't seem to be paying attention. By this time, other children and some adults gather near the edge of the water. A tall man wearing a wet suit takes turns dunking each of the parents into the sea. I remember being afraid, a rising, choking panic building in my throat. But the others around me are laughing and clapping. Dad's smiling too.

"Tara? You still with me?"

I snap out of my memory, realizing I'm suspended above the ground, my arms still hanging onto the railing. "Yes. I'm here. Sorry." I release the railing, landing on my feet, and focus on the squirming, barking mass of elephant seals below. Several massive seals hunker into the water and slap against each other, no doubt males showing off their sparring abilities. "I can see why you'd say they're the strongest animals."

"These elephant seals are strong, but I wasn't talking about them. I want to show you something else, but first"—his voice and features turn resolute—"I want to tell you I'm sorry for barking at you the other day. I was wrong to do that."

Despite my wounded heart, I almost laugh when his apology is accented by air-beating barks from the nearby elephant seals.

"I'm sorry for more than that, Tara."

"Oh?"

His eyes flit around this time, as if trying to gather the right words to say. "My faith is important to me, but with you, I'm making all kinds of mistakes."

"Excuse me?"

"Wait. That came out all wrong."

"I'm waiting."

"All I meant is that I'm trying to live out my faith every day. Not just on Sunday. I'm not sure if our beliefs are compatible. And that's not a judgment on you—if anything, it's more of one on me. You've said more than once that we're moving fast, but I've never felt this way about anyone. Believe me."

"Whoa. I'm a little confused. Are you asking if . . . if I believe in God?"

"Sounds trite, doesn't it."

My eyes scan his face and find nothing but sincerity. "Maybe, but I think I know what you're asking." I breathe in. "I didn't attend church much while growing up, but my father spoke often of God's love and His goodness. He was a praying man—just not a churchgoing one. Anyway, I've believed in Jesus since as long as I can remember, but until moving here, I never considered how that should impact my life. Does that make sense?"

He nods. "Absolutely. And now?"

"Now I want to know more."

"That's what my apology was for. I'm sorry if my affection for you has done anything to keep you from growing in your faith."

Something catches in my throat and I can't speak. *He cares this much about* my *faith?*

Isn't this when he should be attempting to take control in order to get everything he wants from me? Like Maurice would do to Eliza? *And Eliza would do to him.*

And yet here Josh is, apologizing for playing some non-existent part in the weakening of my faith. I squeeze my eyes shut against the wind, hoping he won't see the emotion trying to spill out. When I open them again, he's still watching, waiting. "You're one very different guy, Josh." I shake my head, my voice quiet. "Thank you."

Tenderness shapes his expression. He reaches out his hand, taking a quick peek at the docent who's backed up to us. "C'mon," he whispers. "I want to show you something."

We slip out of the crowd and follow a narrow trail that has been worn into the earth. It's absent of signage, unlike the rest of the area that is lined with trail markers. We reach the point directly below the vista point, excited voices lofting in bursts above us. Other than that, we are alone.

Josh stops. He pulls me to stand in front of him and rests one hand lightly at my waist. His other hand hovers over my shoulder, pointing due west.

"I don't see anything."

"Listen for the tapping sound and look beyond that jagged rock out there." His whispers tickle my ear and I hear tapping all right—in my chest.

"See it?"

I listen. And squint. "There! I see it!" I laugh and slide a look over my shoulder at Josh. "What is it?"

"An otter. Look real close and you'll see a raft of them playing out there. A raft just means the group, it's like saying 'a school' of fish."

I lean forward, conscious of Josh's protective arm slipping further around me. "I do see them. Oh, they look amazing—like wet puppies!"

"My mother always thinks they look like teddy bears, but I can see the puppy resemblance too."

We stand, mesmerized, until the distinct sound of tapping rises above the lull of waves, followed by loud cooing. "What are they doing out there?"

"That's how they eat. They float on their backs and bang hard-shelled food, like abalone, against a rock that's balanced on their chest." His enthusiasm for sea life reminds me of my father's.

"They're the cutest animals I've ever seen—way prettier than those fat elephant seals. Although, they're a sight too." I pull away from Josh. "I want to go closer."

He tightens his hold on me. "Whoa-whoa-whoa. It's too dangerous down there."

I stiffen. Why is it that when I finally decide to try something—anything—adventurous, opposition comes my way? One turn to glance into Josh's face, though, and I'm taken aback by the slight downward curve of his mouth. "So you're serious?"

He attempts a smile, but his eyes give him away. "Even the docent won't come down here, especially now that the tide's coming in. Stay here . . . with me."

A staccato puff of air escapes through my parted lips. "I would just love to see one up close. Don't worry. I can move fast. Promise."

Josh squeezes shut his eyes and then pulls me closer, as if he never wants me to leave. A tingle runs up my arm and ignites, spreading wildly through me. All thoughts of petting lovable sea otters dribble away as I find myself wanting to lean further into him and yet cognizant of his confession moments ago. His eyes open inches from mine and they are like liquid, clear and bright. They elongate when he smiles. "You might be fast, but not faster than me."

Chapter Twenty-seven

 Floating on a cloud does not begin to describe the Pollyannaish bounce in my step as I head into the house. I had walked to work this morning, so after our day trip up the coast, Josh drops me off at home. Mel and Camille are sprawled in the middle of the rather ratty shag carpeting, surrounded by skeins of yarns and patterns, along with pictures and old photo albums.

"My, aren't you the glowing one?" Mel assesses me from her spot on the floor.

"Oh, Mel-Mel, even your snide attitude won't bother me today." I step over her and the accompanying mess and head into the kitchen. "Lemonade, anyone?"

Mel comes up from behind. While I open the fridge, she leans against the door frame. "So. You followed my advice and decided to let the man lead this time? Good girl."

I pour myself a tall glass, plunking two cubes of ice into my drink. I cast Mel a blasé smile. "Whatever."

Camille's voice carries into the kitchen from the living room. "Hey, Mel, Tara. Come see what I've found." She's standing now amongst mess. "It's a picture of Dad and some old cronies of his here in Otter Bay, I think."

I scramble over to her, with Mel close behind me. "He was so young," I say, unable to keep the sigh out of my voice.

"Yeah, Cam, you made him sound so old. He was what? Twenty-three in that picture?"

Camille pulls the picture from me and gives it another look. "Man, poor Dad looked old even when he was young!"

There's truth in her words. For a man so young and with a vibrant life ahead of him, Dad's shoulders slumped far too low in this picture. The issues I'd forgotten, or at least had laid aside, now emblazon themselves like a Vegas marquee in my mind. What was going on in his head? Was he thinking about Peg's money? Another woman?

The thought forces my mouth into a frown, and I turn away. "What are you doing with those pictures anyway?"

"I'm trying to crochet a frame. Well, not a frame, but a cover for one. Thought this place could use some personalizing. Don't you want to look at it again, Tara?" Camille holds the picture out to me. I begin to shake my head "no" when Mel pulls it from her grasp and studies it.

"Check out the James Dean wannabe in the back. Reminds me of Nigel." She tips her chin up. "Did he know us back then?"

I glance over her shoulder. Most of the men in the shot wear rumpled tees and shorts that expose too much leg á la the '80s, but one leans against a burnt tree trunk in the back, looking very much a rebel in his tight jeans and leather bomber jacket. Mel's overzealous observation lightens my mood. "Yeah, that Nigel, always strikes me as the renegade-type." A cackle escapes me.

"It's not impossible."

"Except that he hasn't lived here all that long. He inherited the inn and came back to run it after his sister died. But seriously, Mel, our dear Nigel in bad-boy leather?"

Mel shrugs. "So maybe it's his evil twin." She hands the photo back to Camille, who giggles as she files it in the box with the others. "I'm going outside to watch that sunset you're always fawning over, Tara," Mel says. "Feel free to come along and give me the real scoop about your afternoon with lover boy—he was terribly eager to know your schedule today."

Outside she plops herself into the center Adirondack and I take the chair on her right. The hard slats of wood provide a surprising amount of comfort. Neither of us speaks, as the waves cry out their swan song for the evening. Streaks of fuchsia dash across the sky and from the corner of my view, a bunny feasts on a patchy section of grass.

This. This is what I longed for, what I remembered most about Otter Bay. Not an exact memory, as I was too young to enjoy the things adults often do, but a sense that this place along the coast had the ability to take the wrongs of my day—my life—and in one grand sunset, make everything all better.

"I bet Dad loved these sunsets."

Mel stays quiet. She's often quiet as she's thinking, so I don't take offense. Still, and even though it's a small thing, I hope she agrees with me. After a moment she inhales. "Mom sent an e-mail today."

I pull myself up to look at her. "What did she say? Did she finally get international calling?"

Mel turns, her expression thoughtful, her eyes searching. She shrugs. "She's worried about you. She says that you're going to learn some things that neither she nor our father had the courage to tell you."

I sit back down, taking in the cooling sunset along with our mother's words. "Too late for that now, isn't it?"

"Rather cynical, coming from you, big sister."

I groan. "Maybe. But can I ask you something? Why is it that she trusts you more with information than she does me?"

"Are you kidding? Trust me? Hardly. Mom's always so concerned with you and *your* reaction to everything. I don't know why she tells me so much, but I can promise you it has nothing to do with trust. Sometimes I think she just needs me to be her sounding board."

"Oh, Mel."

"I guess she figures if I don't pass out over her latest news, then you'll be just fine—and that's what matters most."

"You're serious. You really think that Mom favors me." I laugh. "How ironic is this?"

"Oh, really. And why's that?"

I slowly shake my head, hardly noticing as the sun submerges itself into the sea. "Because while you were busy resenting me, I was just as busy . . . resenting you."

"JOSHUA ADAMS, WOULD YOU look at that! It's like you brought Cinderella herself to the ball." Glory Sims, wearing more pink than a flamingo, approaches us from across the lawn, two steps ahead of Burton.

My arm is looped through Josh's, and he smiles. "Guess that makes me the prince."

"I'll say. And you know what that makes me now, don't you?" We all look to Burton, who wheezes between sentences. "The jester!"

We all laugh and nod, and as Josh guides me through the throng of strangers gathering for the outdoor wedding, I realize how very much like a princess I feel. Come to think of it, Camille and Mel were the antitheses of ugly stepsisters, the way they fussed and carried on over me this afternoon. I'd completely forgotten about shoes when I bought this dress from Simka's and it took a bit of searching through Mel's unpacked suitcases and boxes, but eventually, the girls came up with the perfect, shimmering black pumps for me to borrow.

"If the night's a dud," she whispered when Josh picked me up, "just tap your heels together three times—like you're Dorothy."

So I mixed my fairy tales. I'm still in one, as far as I'm concerned.

"Tara, you look stunning!" Norma gives me a hug and turns to a wiry man who resembles Mikey. "I'd like you to meet my husband. Mike, this is Tara, the new friend I've told you about."

"Good to meet you, Tara." He shakes my hand, his grip firmer than I'd expected.

"And you as well. You have a lovely family."

Norma takes my arm in hers. "Speaking of which, may I speak to you for a moment?"

Josh's face registers slight surprise, but he steps back, his smile congenial.

When we're a few steps away, Norma lets go of my arm. "I just wanted to tell you in person how very sorry I am that your private news got back to your sister. I'm so ashamed."

I touch her shoulder. "Please don't be. It was all for the best. Mel needed to know and I, well . . . I was having a hard time figuring out how to tell her."

Norma's shoulders lower as her smile deepens. "So you forgive me?"

I swallow the lump that has formed in my throat. "Yes. Yes, of course I forgive you. No harm done."

"I called my sister this morning and forgave her for snapping at me the other day. She sounded so relieved! We can't receive forgiveness unless we give it first, you know."

I wasn't aware of that.

She hugs me tight. "Find us after the ceremony, okay?"

I promise, and Josh leads me to find our seats next to Billy and Beth, who have apparently come together. The men shake hands while Beth and I just smile our hellos. I try not to notice the long sleeves she wears on this warm day.

Seats all around us fill in as the time for the wedding nears. Peg doesn't notice me, as she strolls down the side aisle, and I almost don't recognize her myself in that smart gray suit with pillbox hat. Funny, but associating Peg with Audrey Hepburn had never come to mind before. It's not the clothes, though, that alter her appearance so much, but the gracious smile displayed across her face. Like she's genuinely happy.

Imagine that.

"Trouble at ten o'clock." Billy's clandestine message may be meant for Josh's ears alone, but I hear him too. Beth's on his other side and seems fairly occupied with the wrist orchid she's wearing, a tender gesture on Billy's part, if you ask me.

Josh groans quietly, a muscle twitches in his jaw. "Can't believe he'd show up here."

"And with her," Billy whispers back.

Like a couple of old women with nothing but time to kill, they each, in turn, take surreptitious glances toward the left front where a striking couple takes their seats. The man's hair, so dark, thick, and wavy, rivals the richest chocolate. And the woman turns heads. Her mane of white blonde locks obediently hold themselves in place, as if they've done so her entire life. They are one of those couples, like Eliza and her first husband, Charles, the kind who know the life they've been groomed for—and never let anyone around them forget it.

I lean toward Josh. "Who are *they?*"

He slides his arm around me and whispers, his lips grazing my ear. "That's Beth's slimy ex-husband, Gordon, and his new girlfriend."

I steal a glance at Beth, who's smiling into Billy's face now. My gaze finds Josh. "She seems to have moved on quite well."

He cocks an eyebrow. "So you're saying I should let it go then."

I let loose a teasing, but exasperated laugh. "I'm not assessing you . . . just making an observation."

Josh quirks the corner of his mouth, then releases a sigh. "You're right. I guess." A small laugh escapes him. "I still think the guy's slime."

"All that hair gel, probably."

He's smiling fully now and running his eyes over my face. Crowd? What crowd? At this moment, all I see, all I smell, all I hear, is Josh.

The familiar notes of "The Wedding March" begin to play, signaling the bride's impending entrance. The crowd stands and, with reluctance, we join them. As we turn to face the center aisle, Josh rests a hand on my waist, sending a quiver through me.

Tears well up behind my eyes as the woman in white, someone I've never even met, takes her place at the top of a flowing carpet of rose pedals. Something about that song always does that to me. I swallow the emotion rushing its way through my body and slide a glance to see if Josh's reaction mirrors my own. He doesn't notice, though, because his eyes are fixated not on the bride, or on me, but somewhere across the aisle.

As the bride and her father make their entrance, and cameras begin to pop and flash, and tissues start to do their work, I follow Josh's line of vision. He's staring at his father, who stands beside his mother, laughing outright in the very last row on the bride's side.

Chapter Twenty-eight

 After the "I dos," Josh's mother kisses his cheek. She offers me a hug. "Such a lovely ceremony, wasn't it?"

I nod.

Josh rubs my back. "Mother, where's Dad?"

Shirley wiggles her hand into the air, as casual as can be. "Oh, you know your father. He's probably found some friends to chat with."

Josh's back rub intensifies, along with the strained look in his eyes. "Maybe you ought to go find him."

Shirley's smile is wide, carefree. "Joshua, you mustn't worry. Your father's just fine. He'll be along any minute." She pats his shoulder. "I'll ask him to stop by your table."

I cut in. "Won't you be joining us?"

She looks to Josh whose masseur moment has ended, as I gently extricate myself. She places both hands on my shoulders. "My word, she's simply lovely, Joshua." She squares her gaze on me now. "You truly are. It seems that the seating has already been pre-arranged—there are place cards at each table. Oh, but I do hope you and Josh will join us for dinner soon. Make him promise you, all right?"

"Absolutely. I will."

Josh squires me away to a table bordering the dance floor. The reception is being held adjacent to the ceremony site, beneath a mansion-sized tent. Thousands of tiny white lights lace themselves around silk trees and flower-laden trellises creating a virtual garden of Eden.

Josh holds my chair out for me and I take a seat next to Beth. Maybe we'll get a chance to actually talk instead of just smiling at each other over our dates. Although he sits down and holds my hand beneath the table, Josh seems distracted. Billy's pouring the wine that had been set out for us, but Josh turns his goblet over with his free hand. Billy's carrying on about some strange call to the station involving burning marshmallows and a faulty smoke alarm. The rest of the guests at our table, two couples in their twenties or so, laugh in all the appropriate places.

"Everybody, I'd like you to meet . . . my girlfriend, Tara Sweet." Josh squeezes my hand and I realize that I'm tottering a bit. Girlfriend. He called me his girlfriend, which I suppose is true considering we've been exclusive for oh, say, two weeks now. Except for those occasional disagreements.

One of the women, a firefighter I soon learn, reaches

across to shake my hand. "I'm Reese. Good to meet you." She gives me one firm pump of the arm, as if I were a hatchet. The men follow suit.

"I'm Thomas. Hi."

"Hey, Tara. I'm Joey." He gestures to the petite woman sitting next to him, who's smiling shyly my way. "And this is Carolyn, but we all call her CeCe." She raises her hand and wiggles four fingers at me.

As the conversation progresses it's clear that most of them know each other from the station. Except CeCe, who sits quietly with a pleasant but rather blank expression on her face. I'm pretty sure we haven't met before, but her name does have a familiar ring.

"A toast!" Billy's standing now, holding a goblet out before him. "To firefighters . . . in love."

Snickers and hoots and laughter erupt all around the table. Joey cinches CeCe in close as she blushes profusely. Reese smacks a loud kiss on Thomas's mouth, and Billy bends down and brushes his lips across Beth's cheek.

Josh just grins and shakes his head. He looks to me and his eyes glow as if all distraction has vanished. "So, am I a liar?"

"How so?" I whisper back.

"The girlfriend announcement. You didn't seem upset by that."

I tip my head up when Billy's voice slices the space between us. "Just kiss her, man!" Billy looks around the table. "What's he waiting for?"

Beth pats Billy's hand, as if to calm him.

Josh grins, dimples sinking deeper into his cheek. He bends toward me and I can feel his warm breath on my face. "Don't want to disappoint them. Or you either." He kisses me then and the crowd disappears.

More crowing and laughter erupts from our table.

"Hate to interrupt you young folks, but I think the missus and I are seated here." Burton towers above us, with his pink-covered wife, Glory, jiggling beside him.

Reese's face alights. "Sit on down, Granddad. We've been waiting for you both."

"Well, my goodness, look at this lively table we get to join!" Glory's perfume infiltrates the group. She takes her seat and glances around the table, her smile deepening the lines that crisscross her face. "You all look lovely," she says, stopping on Carolyn, "but I don't think we've met."

All eyes turn to Carolyn, who's become a blushing machine. Joey pipes up. "Glory, I'd like you to meet my date, CeCe."

"CeCe! Oh, my, what a delightful name! Is that short for something?"

CeCe nods, while Joey tells her, "Carolyn. Her real name is Carolyn."

A befuddled look overtakes Glory. Her lips pooch and a distinct divot appears on her forehead. "I've heard that name somewhere before. Let me think. Gah. I'm an old woman, but I'll think of it."

Billy holds up the wine bottle, a question in his eyes.
Burton offers his empty goblet. "By all means. And Glory
here'll have a pink lemonade when I can flag down one of
those waiters in penguin suits."

A trio of musicians begin to play songs that although
probably famous, I cannot identify. They stir the magical
mood under the big tent, though, and now that all the intro-
ductions are out of the way and dinner is about to be served,
I feel myself relax.

Maybe a bit too soon, because Josh's hand tenses in mine
and I look up. He's staring across the room to an open bar
where his father's tall frame rises from the hovering pack.
I place my hand on Josh's back and push aside the rush it
gives me. "Is everything all right?"

He nods, but doesn't turn to me. Nothing in his face
confirms that all is well.

The rest of the table stays buried in conversation. "Josh."
I whisper his name close to his ear, once again ignoring the
wave of desire that unfurls. "I'm concerned. Let me help."

Josh swivels toward me, his eyes sad and soulful. "I wish
you could." He closes those eyes of his and breathes in deeply.
"My father's . . . got problems."

I pick out Pete from the group and watch him for a few
seconds. He's laughing and carrying on and shoulder slapping as if he's never heard something so hysterical in his
life. My mind moves fast. We're face-to-face, Josh and I, our
conversation as private as it can be in a room full of people.

Suddenly I think I understand. "Does your father . . . is he an alcoholic?"

One look into Josh's grim face and I receive my answer.

ELIZA'S FATHER WAS AN alcoholic too. Only he never laughed as much as Pete does. He was angry and bitter and perpetually out of a job. Which goes a long way toward explaining just why Eliza had become so self-sufficient—not to mention a teetotaler. *And perhaps a tad more of a manipulator than I'd like to admit.*

Glory, who sits just on the other side of Josh's now-empty seat, slathers a slice of bread from the table basket. "Where's he going?"

"Just had something to tell his father. He'll be right back."

She bites into the soft bread, closes her eyes and squeals in culinary delight. "Mmm-mm—oh!" Glory's eyes pop open.

"You okay there, Glory?" I ask.

She turns to Carolyn who slowly chews a hunk of bread while listening to an intense debate between Billy and Joey over which team's the best: Dodgers or Giants. "I just remembered why your name was so familiar!"

All conversations around the table stop. Glory swipes a look at me, a magenta-colored fingernail taking aim in my direction. "It was CeCe! CeCe was the woman that had a thing for your father!"

WHILE IT MAY BE customary, and a high form of politeness, to invite other ladies to join you for a trip to the restroom, protocol had sunk to the bottom of my to-do list. I had to get away. From the first time we met, I knew that Glory didn't have a mean bone in her chubby body. But I'm beginning to wonder if she's missing something upstairs.

I wash my hands for the second time, even though I've done nothing to sully them in the first place. The running water distracts me from the inner tidal wave building within my heart. *You're going to learn some things that neither I nor your father had the courage to tell you . . .*

My mother's words burn. Other women in their taffeta and chiffon and strappy shoes roam in and out, and I wonder just how long I can hide in here.

"There you are!" Norma wanders in, chattering. She stops. "You look like you just bit into a slice of bad meat."

I almost laugh but halt myself, knowing the sound would come out as I feel: sharp and bitter.

"Did you and Josh have an argument?"

I hang my head and shake it back and forth. "Glory's sitting at our table."

"Oh . . . oh!" Norma sighs. "And she has more to add about your parents' problems?"

"The same stuff, really. She suddenly remembered that my father's . . ." I swallow. "The other woman's name was CeCe. There's a woman at our table named Carolyn and . . . oh no." I tip my chin up and stare at the ceiling. "I think I'm going to be sick."

Norma places a motherly hand on the back of my shoulder. "I've got Pepto-Bismol in my car. Shall I send Mikey for it?"

I shake my head vigorously. "Glory remembered the name CeCe after talking with a woman at our table named Carolyn. All we've ever known about my cousin Camille's mother is that her name was Caroline." The comparison careens through my mind and lands with a heavy throb. "Is it possible that my father had an affair with Camille's mother?"

The bathroom door flies open and two young girls hustle in. "Mom's going to kill me! Shirley Temple juice all over me!"

The older girl rips five paper towels from the roll, sops them with cold water and begins to scrub. "You have to be more careful!"

"I was, but that stupid Collin bumped into me really hard." She begins to cry.

Her sister keeps wiping and sighing. She stops. "It's okay. It'll wash. Please stop crying."

The younger girl's tears have been reduced to sniffles, and how I'd like to join her. Mel and I had plenty of similar moments growing up. If only I could go back to dealing with mundane tasks and silly squabbles.

Glory appears in the doorway now, picking her front tooth with one of her dark pink fingernails. "They're serving the food, ladies! Better get yourself on out there, Tara, before those boys start pilfering from your plate." She frowns. "You don't look well."

Norma puts a hand on her hip. "Glory Sims, you need to stop sharing so much of Tara's personal business with the whole world!"

The two young sisters exchange glances before making a quick turn to gallop out the door.

Norma continues. "Seriously, Glory, what has gotten into you?"

Glory lays one dramatically placed hand across her heart. "Whatever are you talking about? All I said was that CeCe was the woman's name. Is it so wrong to tell the truth?"

I pull in a slow, filling breath, my hands still leaning on the countertop, steadying me. I stare at Glory's reflection in the mirror. "My parents may have made some mistakes, but we never doubted their love for each other. They may have had some tough times, but they stayed married and worked through them."

Glory fans herself. "Oh, my, yes. They had tough times from the very start those two, what with your mother becoming pregnant even before the wedding." She pauses. "That must have been with you. Right?"

I whip around, away from the mirror. "What?"

Norma glares at her.

Glory shrinks back, her chin nearly disappearing into her neck. "I-I said that, uh, well, as I recall, your mother—Marilee, is it?—had gotten herself, er, um, pregnant. Oh, dear, you didn't know this. But don't worry. Your father did the honorable thing and married her. Even though that CeCe was still hanging around."

"I don't understand. Are you saying that CeCe was Dad's girlfriend *before* he and Mom got married?"

"Hm. Now let me think a moment. Ah! As I recall it, they were sweethearts before your dad married your mom. Then she disappeared and then—oh, I believe it must have been years later—she showed up in town again."

So much of the mystery is suddenly becoming clear. My parents had a shotgun wedding. Contorted laughter, like a ball of bitter sarcasm, rises in my throat. *I traveled across the country just to learn that I was an accident?* Is this what Dad meant that day we dangled our feet over the rocks when he mumbled, "she lied," over and over?

I push myself away from the damp counter, straighten up, and tuck stray hair behind my ear. "Norma, Glory, I have to go." I take my purse and leave, having no idea what to say to Josh as I set out to find him. All I know is I need to think and I hope he'll understand that.

Chapter Twenty-nine

 The party's in full swing as I return in body, yet not in mind. Guests feast on garlic-infused meals and conversations flow all around as I weave between tables and frenetic food servers, not caring that my less-than-jovial facial expression surely stands out.

I can't find Josh anywhere.

There's a line at the no-host bar, where servers circulate with appetizer trays. Norma's husband, Mike, looks like he's been captured in conversation by a woman with much to say on the subject of mushroom caps. Behind the bartenders, off in the distance where a rock wall meanders along a winding stream, I spot Josh, his father and mother, along with a small gathering of people on the other side of a stand of pines, their branches serving as a wide canopy to stroll beneath.

Surprisingly cool air gives me a chill as I step outside the tent's protection. I wrap my arms about myself and carefully step across the damp lawn. My heels sink into the earth, taking my heart with every step. No one seems to notice me struggling to approach.

Voices ricochet against each other, yet Pete's rises above them all. He's telling a story and laughing more than the rest. I strain to make out what's being said and notice how Shirley bends toward him, her posture admonishing.

"I *hate* you!" Beth's voice startles me from behind. I stop and whip a look over my shoulder. Beth and her ex-husband have just emerged from the tent and are headed down the other side, away from me. I watch as she charges after him, showing more moxie and emotion than I've ever seen from her.

Gordon, the ex, swivels around to face her, and she jerks to a stop. He throws back his head, mockingly, but she doesn't back down. She's shorter than he and he seems to revel in looking down on her. I'm standing unhidden on the gracious lawn, riveted on the spectacle of two people, once so in love, now enemies.

More laughter emerges from the group in front of me and I turn to see that Josh's father continues to be the center of attention. Yet behind me, Beth's tears grow stronger and her voice thicker and more desperate.

"Why?" Beth grabs Gordon's lapels, but he's unmoved, with one hand casually in a pocket and the other holding a martini. "Tell me!"

He says something in a low tone, something that only serves to cause her more anguish. Norma steps out of the tent just then and rushes to Beth's side. She shakes her index finger at Gordon, who laughs her off, just as Beth abruptly makes a dash toward the parking lot. My heart clenches for all the pain she carries—and for Billy, who I fear is on the road to a broken heart himself.

Norma follows quickly after Beth and I nearly join them. My hopes had been so high for this day and I suspect that Beth's had been too. But the past has a way of nosing its way into even the happiest of occasions and I only hope that mine carries no more secrets.

Reluctantly I pull my attention away from them and continue on across the wide lawn, suddenly longing for the comfort of Josh's embrace. Sharp words have begun to punctuate the silence. I pause beneath the stand of pines to check my heels, which no longer sink into mud. Instead, dry dirt and pine needles line my path *and* the wet spots on my shoes.

No one seems to notice me.

"Freshen me up, now Jimmy, will ya?" Pete holds his glass up to a friend with rosy cheeks and a sparse crew cut.

Josh's face smolders with something I've only seen a hint of before. When he tries to take his father's glass, the other man clamps his fist around it.

The pitch in Pete's laughter rises, like a young boy's. "Hoo-ey, you're a feisty one today, sonny." He cracks himself up and bellows, to no one in particular. "My sonny boy needs a good woman to loosen 'im up, if you know what I mean."

Cackles break out and I freeze, unable to move from beneath the pines.

"Now Pete . . ." Shirley's voice unrolls soothingly.

Pete stands and puts a hand on Josh's shoulder. He attempts to say something in mock-seriousness, his mottled red face shaking. Before he can utter a word, he squeezes his eyes shut and giggles, his large hand still pressing down on Josh.

Shirley rubs her husband's back. Pete takes her hand in his then and kisses it roughly. "Now this, this, is a good woman!" He swipes a glance at the group, still not noticing me.

Josh gestures for his mother to move aside. "Let's get you home, old man."

"Old man? Old man!" Pete rises up like an angry grizzly. He seems to tower over his son, only to crumble into a spitting laughter. "Did y'all see my son's face? Sonny boy, you better go and find that spicy thing you brought here . . . what's her name, Shirl? Tessa . . . Tata . . ."

Shirley gently takes her husband's arm and whispers into his ear.

He jerks his arm out of her grasp. "Well, whatever her name is! You go find her, son, and have her give you what you need. You're too uptight."

Josh rushes his father, his back to me. My good sense tells me to leave, now, but I don't. Instead, I approach Josh as he faces off with his father. "You've got everyone here snowed. The whole town thinks you're a hero, but I know better."

My chest tightens.

Shirley takes hold of Josh's raised fist. "Joshua, stop it."

He yanks it away. "No, Mother. *You* stop it. Dad's been lying to us, to this town—to everybody." Josh glares at his father, his eyes larger and more round than I've ever seen them. "You're nothing but a lousy drunk, you know that?" He shakes his head, both hands clenching at his sides. "Hear me loud and clear on this: I am no longer your son."

"Now, Joshua, you take that back." Shirley turns to her husband who's begun to cry like a tired toddler. "He didn't mean that, sweetheart. Josh, tell him you did not mean what you just said."

But it's too late. Josh has already stepped past his parents and their dwindling band of celebratory friends. His mother continues her attempt to console his weeping father, when Pete rises up as if overtaken by a sudden presence of mind. He marches past his friends and after his retreating son, until his foot collides with a large root protruding from the ground. He stumbles forward and reaches out to Josh, but Josh wrenches away, nearly stumbling himself as his father tumbles to the ground.

I swallow a gasp as Shirley and one other man rush to her husband's rescue.

Josh stands still, a mixture of shock and anguish and grief marring his handsome face.

His father stretches his neck upward. "See that boy? Almost lost some footing yourself. You're just like your old man." He drops his head down to the earth again. "Just like him."

Josh's shoulders and chest rise and fall with his silence. He moves closer to his father, whose eerie grin shines from below. "You"—pain radiates from every word—"are dead to me."

Anguish and confusion mar Josh's face. Overcome by all I've just witnessed, I attempt to take a step backward, but stop just as Josh turns and looks straight into my eyes.

MY DATE WAS OFFICIALLY over. Unable to express the tumult of thoughts careening in my head, I left Josh there to tend to his family crisis and found my own ride back. An elderly couple I recognized from Coastal Christian drove me home in their late model Buick, the vast back seat swallowing me up into its wideness. Actually, I asked them to stop at the end of my block, down near the water and they obliged.

I just can't go home yet.

Instead, I slip off my sister's pumps, the ones that already need a good washing from the elements, and tiptoe in my bare feet down the weathered stairs built into the cliff. The tide's high and deep, but a narrow strip of beach remains exposed. I attempt to walk, but the moonstones are piled up all around me, making it difficult to make my way without shoes.

What would Eliza do at a time like this? The thought
tickles my mind, but no answers come to the surface. Once
she screamed at an old lover, "Your absence makes my heart
grow happier!" But somehow that little witticism does nothing for my fragile state at the moment.

That's because this is real life, gritty pain.

The thought sears, even as the tide wraps itself around
my ankles. It's as if I've been pushing against that tide for
years and for what? I'm more confused, more crippled by my
modus operandi—fooling myself I'm in control—than ever.

*Then maybe it's time for real answers—and not just some
lines written by a handful of daytime-soap writers.*

I'm stricken by the thought. Almost as stricken as Josh
just an hour ago when he realized what I'd witnessed.
We stood in that meadow, silently watching each other as
Shirley and Pete's friends tended to the fallen man. "I know
what you're thinking," Josh said to me, his voice deep and
patchy.

But he couldn't have any idea.

I realized that no matter what my parents had done in
the past, I could never hate them—nor worse, wish death
on them. Yet there was still so much to come to terms with
in my life. Like hidden secrets. Past indiscretions. Lies. No
matter what label they wore, they all conjured distasteful
images.

"You left me with this, Dad!" I say into the sky. Now
I have to live with all his regret. "If only you'd have come

clean, all this would be old news instead of something that your eldest has to deal with!" A whimper escapes me, my voice just a whisper. "Was I just an accident, Dad? Did your problems begin with me?"

Yelling at my father when he can't answer back doesn't bring me the closure I'm looking for, nor do I feel any sense of relief from it. Just more anger.

"And thanks a bunch, Mom, for whatever your unspoken part was in all of this." The thought that maybe my mother suffered silently for years nudges me, but I shove it aside.

Water lands on the shore just a short distance from me, a shallow remnant passing over my feet. Staring at the water for hours as a type of therapy comes naturally to me. I sniffle. *You taught me that, Dad.* Long after we left Otter Bay—whatever the real reason—his passion always seemed to be built around water: fishing, canoeing, even the three fountains he installed around our home in Missouri and tended to on his days off.

Glory's revelation filters through me and yet, as I replace her words with real, breathing memories of the man who left us all too soon, all my anger dissipates. Which makes me wonder, could Eliza let go this way? And if not, why would I ever want to emulate someone like that?

Pastor Cole made a reference to "living water" in a sermon he preached recently and the phrase has lingered in my mind ever since, as if it carries with it some kind of faraway connection with my father. While he left so much undone here in

Otter Bay, Dad did love God in his own way. He told us girls about Him, for one thing. Though I'm not sure of all the pastor meant by referencing that verse, I am sure of this much.

Never again thirsting for things far out of my reach sounds awfully appealing.

Chapter Thirty

Tell him I can't talk."

Camille holds the phone receiver against her jeans. "Well, he'll know that's a lie, Tara, 'cuz everybody knows you can talk."

I roll my eyes. It's been three long days since the wedding and, thankfully, Josh has been away, conquering fires. This is the first I've heard from him, but I could have waited longer.

Mel smirks. "You really can't come up with an excuse that's less lame?" She sighs and holds out her hand. "Give me the phone, Cam. I'll talk to him."

I contort in a silent protest.

"Hey, Josh. Yeah, it's Mel. She can't talk right now. Uh-huh. Yeah. Okay, I'll tell her." She sets the cordless phone onto the end table, while I plop into the couch with a suppressed grunt.

"What are you supposed to tell me?"

"He says you're to meet him at the top of the Empire State Building at midnight on Valentine's Day."

Camille gasps. "Oh, that's so romantic of him!"

I slap her on the leg. "That's a line from a movie! Let's not talk about this anymore, okay girls? I'd rather forget the whole, ugly day."

Camille collapses onto the floor into a cross-legged position. "Then can I ask you about something else?"

"Great. Yes. Anything."

She pulls a curved and round swath of crocheted fabric from her bag. Turquoise, gold, and specks of red run throughout. "What do you think of this?"

I take it from her. "Well, hm, what is it?"

Her forehead wrinkles. "You mean you can't tell?"

I see Mel holding back a smile in the background. "Wait a sec. Hm. It's a coffee-mug cover. Right?"

Camille grabs the fabric from me, exasperation on her face. "It's a beanie, Tara." She examines it again, fingering the design. "Guess I'll have to work on making that more obvious."

"A beanie—yes, yes, I see that. It's pretty. Really."

The phone rings again and I dart a glance at Mel, who looks up toward the ceiling and sighs. "I'll take it in the back and I get it—you're not here."

Across the carpet lay some of the most vibrant colors in yarn. Camille's been preoccupied lately with her crocheting hobby and it's good to see. I glance up and Mel is standing in the hall doorway, holding the phone out to me. "You need to take this."

"Mel . . ."

"It's Mom."

Both Camille and I dart for the phone. "Let me talk to her first!" Camille gets there before I do and wrests the receiver from Mel. "Mom, it's Camille . . . how's Europe? Did you see the Eiffel Tower? Tara thinks you're stuck in some dirty hotel, but I told her, 'you're crazy.' How's . . ."

She disappears down the hall. I look to Mel.

"I e-mailed her this phone number. About time she signed up for international service on her cell phone."

"Did she sound happy?"

"Sickeningly so."

"Hm. Enough said." A brief laugh escapes me. "Wonder why she's calling and why now. I mean, I've been wanting to talk to her for a month and she's been so elusive."

"I told her everything we'd heard. She confirmed it all. Dad really took eight thousand bucks from that old battle-ax. She didn't want to elaborate, though."

As is Mom's way. Quiet drapes the room. I run my index finger over and over my thumb, thinking. "I figured you'd talk to her about it. And you know what? I should have done that the minute the rumors began to fly."

"Why the turnabout then?"

"I looked in the mirror."

"What?"

"I heard more surprising news about Mom and Dad the other day—at the wedding, of all places. And as I leaned against a bathroom counter, hiding out while trying to figure out what to think, I noticed that I look old, Mel. Why didn't you tell me how old I was beginning to look?"

Mel's face appears soft. Instead of a haughty glance, or sarcastic sigh, I see compassion in her eyes. "Well, you are my *older* sister." She smiles and I know she's kidding with me. "Tara, like I've told you before. You're the one who always holds things together. Haven't always enjoyed that trait in you. Okay, to tell you the truth, it's the part of you that I love to hate. But lately, you've had me worried."

"You, worrying about me?"

"Don't let it go to your head." She uncrosses her arms and lets them drop to her sides. "This move—this brainchild of yours—seemed so crazy at the time. And so unlike you. But you know what? It's been a good thing for all of us, even though I can't believe I'm admitting this to you."

"You really think so?"

Mel grasps me by the elbows and her eyes bore into me. "Look at Camille. She's going back to school and she was just about to tell you about a new business idea she and Holly have."

"Really?"

"Yeah, really. And this move has helped me too. I've wanted to live in the big city for as long as I could remember, but when you all left me to come here, I lost my nerve. I've always felt like I was the one who had something to prove and then I failed." She glances down at the floor before shoving a harsh sigh from her chest. "I think I'm almost ready now."

"You are ready, Mel. I'm the one who's had a hard time letting you go, but I have no doubt that you can conquer whatever you set your mind to doing."

"Thank you. Now get in there and tell Mom everything you know."

As if on cue, Camille prances into the living room, her face flushed from talking with our continent-hopping mother.

I take the phone from her. "Mom?"

"Tara, darling! It's wonderful to hear your voice again."

"You too. I've read your Facebook, but you don't update it often enough. We need more pictures!"

Mother laughs and the sound feels akin to warm bath water rolling over bare skin. I've missed her more than I knew.

"Camille says you are working, Tara, at an inn? Are you handling the accounting for them?"

I smile. Of course she'd think that. "Actually, Mom, I'm working the front desk. It's just part-time, but I love it. The gentleman who owns it asked me to work for him on our second day here."

"Fabulous. I've always known you'd be good working with the public." I revel in her praise. "This boss of yours . . . is it anyone I'd know? Your father and I lost contact with the people of that town, but it's possible, I suppose."

"Hm. Don't think so. His family owned the place and he came here to run it after his sister died. His name is Nigel."

There's a pause on the line. "Nigel Thorton?"

Something like heartburn drops within me. "You've heard of him?"

"Well, of course I have. Didn't Nigel tell you? He was your father's pen pal for many years. Oh, after he had reformed himself." She laughs lightly. "For someone so proper, he was quite a troublemaker, back when we lived there . . ."

Somewhere after "pen pal" I lost her. Nigel and my father . . . friends? He's been lying to me? My temples constrict, the living room shrinking from view. He might not call it that, but isn't it true that in a court of law omission of fact can be considered a lie?

Nigel must have had a good reason for not mentioning this information. Unless he doesn't realize who my father was.

Right. Not possible.

". . . anyway dear, I'm glad that you've been able to make peace with Otter Bay. Perhaps someday I will too."

Her words touch me. Knowing all I do now, what must Mom really think of these changes in her daughters' lives?

Surely, she's happy with Derrick, but I sense that her tone is bittersweet.

She changes the subject like a champ. "Well. It's very early here and Derrick has made plans for us to tour the North York Moors before the sun fully rises. Can you imagine me, getting up before dawn? Oh, but they say the view of heather, far as the eye can see, is simply too breathtaking to miss."

"But Mom, I've got more to talk to you about . . ."

"Soon, darling. Derrick waits for no one." She's the only one laughing.

Though I've got more to say, experience tells me that Mom is done for today. I can only hope that we'll have another chance to talk. And soon.

"AM I CORRECT IN my assessment that you now know?" Nigel holds his cane in front of him, both hands shaking as they lean on its slender handle.

"Why didn't you tell me?"

"There are things I wanted to say to you that I didn't think you were ready to hear."

I groan. "Why does everybody feel the need to decide when *I'm* ready to hear a little thing like the truth?"

Betty, who's reading a romance paperback, slides it upward in front of her face, but keeps it low enough to see over the top. Her bespectacled eyes don't move from me.

Nigel's eyes sag, his face filling with a downcast smile. Pity? He's got pity for me? He lowers his gaze. "I've prayed hard about when to tell you . . ."

"You've *prayed*? And God told you to just keep on lying? I admit, I don't know God all too well, but it would seem to me that the *creator of the universe* would be above telling His children to keep secrets from one another."

Nigel nods. "Perhaps you are correct." His brow, usually so even and anxiety-free, now has grooves burrowing through it. It glows from moisture.

I tried to avoid this moment, although I'm not sure why. Like my mother had done, I rose up early this morning, just as the sun began to stretch its rays. I padded down to the water and waded through briny thickness, the air heavy, like my mind and heart. Confrontation, although once an energizing event during those drab days at the auto parts company, no longer held any spark for me. Still, it could not be avoided.

Betty chews her fingernails, as if watching a horror flick. I almost laugh, but knowing how wicked it would sound I mentally make myself regroup. "You are the one person, Nigel, who could have kept my father's memory alive in a beautiful way and instead, you chose to let me hear all sorts of terrible accusations." Bitterness stings my eyes. "Were you so desperate to fill a vacancy that you'd resort to this? To allow my family to suffer while you look the other way?"

The spears I throw bring me no cure from the brokenness.

"Tara. Please. There's much I have to say to you. Allow me to take you to breakfast, so we may discuss this at once."

Breakfast at the diner. What had become a mainstay since our relocation, no longer holds any draw for me. I'm not even hungry. "Moving to Otter Bay has been enlightening, that's for sure." I pause, drawing strength from my disappointment. "But it's also been the stupidest thing I've ever done."

"No, no, no, my dear. You mustn't say that. Please. I ask that you reconsider my offer." He takes his cane and turns toward the door, opening it wide in an effort to guide me over to the diner. "Your father saved my life and you must allow me to tell you about it."

Betty gasps. She wears a guilt-ridden smile and turns a page she never actually read.

Nigel lures me with the first positive words about my father that I've heard since we arrived. I don't want to be angry anymore. Nigel welcomed my sisters and me into this town from the very start and this is something I've not forgotten. I wipe my eye with the backs of two fingers. "Coffee's all I need."

As we walk across the parking lot in silence and enter into the daily din of the Red Abalone Grill, I only hope what Nigel has to say will help me to truly understand.

Chapter Thirty-one

 So my father wrote to you all these years?"

Nigel's eyes never leave me. "He never forgot me. He liked to call himself my personal narc."

I swallow. The thought makes me want to laugh aloud. Dad, a narc. It's even funnier hearing the word coming from Nigel's mouth. Still, the implications are frightening. "You were addicted to drugs then, Nigel? That's hard to believe."

"I would prefer to have thrown my old life into the incinerator, but that's not always possible, nor the right thing to do. You see, God has long forgiven my past, but if I were to forget it completely, what use would I be to others in need?"

"So my father was the one who kept you accountable, then?"

"Precisely. He would write, and when I would not write back to him, he would call. Oh, this was before e-mail became so prevalent. I would not have been able to get away with so much avoidance these days."

"Except the way you avoided telling me the truth all this time."

Nigel's usually neutral coloring takes on a faintly scarlet hue.

Mimi's on duty this morning, swinging a coffee pot in her normally frenetic way. I accept another refill and she scoots on to other customers.

The mug warms my hands. "Did Dad ever talk about us?"

Nigel sips his tea, the creases near his eyes deepening. "He spoke of you girls quite often. Your father did not show his emotions readily—unless talking about his daughters. He loved you all so very much. That was always clear."

I sling back into the cushioned seat. "I had no idea. Dad never mentioned you—oh! I didn't mean to insinuate . . ."

Nigel smiles in that soothing way of his. "You didn't. Robert was a private man, except when it mattered."

I lean my head to one side. "When it mattered?"

"He shared his faith with me."

"The prayer. He had each one of us recite it when we were children too. My mother never seemed to take it all that seriously, but for Dad, it was a solemn occasion. Any time he talked of God was a solemn occasion, actually. He asked me often if I believed that Jesus was my Savior and how much God loves me. I always said yes. I guess that's why I've felt so drawn back to church lately. It's like I've needed to know more about my faith."

"Yes, well, I have noticed that you have grown immensely in your beliefs. Your father would be pleased you have accomplished something he so wanted for you. He prayed for this, Tara. For all you girls."

Hope stirs inside my chest. "Really?"

"Yes, truly. Robert struggled with pride—I believe that's one reason he could never find it in him to return here—but he also knew the eternal value in a relationship with God. He told me many times that all I needed to do to get right with God was confess my failures and receive the Lord's forgiveness. And I have done so."

"And yet you lied to me."

Regret, palpable and raw, shrivels his face. His chin quivers. "I'm very sorry."

My eyes skim the diner's ceiling and I draw in and exhale a deep breath. Part of me wants to indulge in some finger pointing, to make sure Nigel knows just how his deceit has discouraged me. The other part of me longs to soak in every detail that he can remember about Dad.

"Tara? Do you remember your father's baptism?"

I squeeze my eyes shut, blinking away trace bitterness. I let out another breath, while digesting Nigel's question. My inclination is to say "no," but somewhere in the far reaches of my mind, a familiar thought resides. Water, my father, he's happy . . . "Nigel? Was Daddy baptized at the beach?"

"You do remember—how wonderful. Yes, your father, along with several friends, was baptized in the ocean. Except for the birth of you and your sister, I believe that was the happiest day of his life. Made him feel like a new man, he always said." Cheer tries to alter Nigel's countenance, but it doesn't last and regret settles back on his features. "Of course, that was before, well, the church hurt your father. Deeply."

I reach my hand across the table. "What do you mean? How?"

"He wasn't a perfect man. Unfortunately you have heard about some of his past sins, things he never denied. However, your father would have stayed in Otter Bay forever, despite his fallen state, except . . ."

"Except *what?*"

Deep rivulets reappear on Nigel's forehead. "Some of the more vocal church members no longer thought he had any right to attend services. He did understand that his indiscretions most probably should disqualify him from teaching Sunday school, but they asked the pastor to send him away. And the man of the cloth agreed—the scoundrel."

The injustice slams into me like a rod to the back. "I'll never go back there."

Nigel shakes his head. "No, my dear. Those people have long gone and with them their ungodly ways. I believe your father would be tickled to know that you have gone back to the church he once loved. Those who are there now understand that the church today should operate much like a hospital for sinners."

I lean my elbows onto the tabletop and cover my face with both hands, emerging only after I've had a moment to think about this latest barrage of news. One secret after another revealed. Just a few months ago, life was unstartling. Predictable. Linear in its approach. What I didn't know, didn't hurt me—but it didn't help me much, either.

On the heels of that thought it occurs to me that I've been reading my beloved *Soaps Weekly Digest* less and less lately. The more I reread the Scripture passages from Pastor Cole's sermon each week, the less interest I seem to have in Eliza. Besides, it's not near as much fun to read when I'm starring in a daytime drama of my own. "Why did you keep all this from me, Nigel?"

"I was fearful. And, perhaps, stupid. You see, after verifying who you were that very first morning, I did start to tell you, but we were interrupted by the delivery of Jorge's fine meal. I wondered if perhaps it was a sign that it was too soon. I feared you would leave before Robert's wish was fulfilled. After some time had passed, I saw the error in my judgment. By then, you had been discovered by Peg and I became concerned that she would fill your head with her opinions."

"So you knew about Peg's relationship with my father?"

"Some, yes. He had made peace with his past, however, so I had hoped she could move on."

I hang my head, taking in his revelations. After a few cleansing breaths, my eyes meet Nigel's again. "Well, you shouldn't have worried because my father's wish *was* fulfilled. He asked me to take my sisters home to Otter Bay."

"That my dear, was only part one."

"Oh? He told you there was more?"

"He did, indeed. Robert hoped that someday you and Mel and Camille would all fully embrace the life of freedom he never had."

"I don't understand."

"Don't you see? He wanted you to *live* your faith and not be ruled by bitterness. He knew what it was to struggle with that and wanted so much more for you girls."

Mother's words spin into my consciousness: *Don't let bitterness guide you, Tara. Forgive and move on and you'll be set free. Make a point to love your life, dear one.*

Nigel's eyes shine with emotion and I reach out and rest my hand on his. "Thank you."

"Whatever are you thanking me for?"

"For being my father's friend." I catch my voice before it breaks, then turn toward voices mingling behind the cook's counter, across the diner. Peg bustles between customers, cracking jokes and offering coffee and napkins. She moves fast, but people seem to enjoy her, their smiles congenial, warm. After Peg sets down a check in front of a guest, she mops her forehead and walks to the far corner of the diner. There she slides into a booth.

"Before you go, I have something I must ask. Will you forgive me, Tara?"

I can't receive forgiveness unless I give it first. Norma's words reopen raw wounds. Who am I to refuse to forgive someone who asks for it? "Of course. Yes. I do, Nigel. I really do." Peg rests in the booth across the diner and I address Nigel. "Will you excuse me for a moment?"

He nods, his features more relaxed, and I leave the diner to call Mel on my cell. We talk, my sister and I, the steady crash of waves as my backdrop. Conversation over, I step back inside the diner and head directly for Peg, whose white-clad feet rest on the seat opposite her.

"May I?" I gesture to the seat where her feet lay.

I slide in next to her shoes. She's neither smiling nor frowning; instead Peg appears tired, loose bags dangling beneath her crescent-shaped eyes. I had hoped to talk to my mother about Peg last night, but as it turned out, our conversation was disturbing enough for one evening.

"You looked lovely at the wedding," I tell her.

"They're good kids. Come from solid stock."

My hands flex over and over beneath the table. "I'd like us to start fresh, Peg."

She looks away, those flat lips pulled against her face. "I have nothing left to say. You have made your decision to stay and that's your right."

"I've made another decision as well. My sisters and I . . . we want to pay you back the money our father took from you."

"You want to . . . pay me back? Why?" She narrows her eyes. "What do you want?"

"Nothing. Well, nothing other than our father's memory to be left intact. He was a good man who made mistakes." I drop my gaze to the table, draw in a breath, and give her a firm look. "A lot of them. But he loved his family—he made a million sacrifices for us. I wish you could've known the man we did. But since you didn't, please allow us to erase the debt he owed you."

"And your sisters have agreed to this?"

I nod.

She places her feet back on the ground. "I've never heard of anything so . . . so crazy in all of my life. Paying your father's debt . . . when you had nothing to do with it."

I spot Nigel glancing around the diner, so I slide out of Peg's booth. "You have my word on this." She doesn't answer, her eyes still carrying a look of bewilderment.

As I make my way back to Nigel, Mel rushes through the door. "Good. You're still here."

"What's the matter?"

She pushes me gently, indicating with a flick of her chin that I should sit.

"Good morning, Mel." Nigel gives her a congenial smile.

Mel sits. "Norma called. I take it neither of you have heard the news about your friend Beth—the one who used to live in that burned-out house across from us."

I shake my head. "What news?" A sickening thought slithers through my stomach as I recall the scene of Beth and her ex-husband at the wedding.

"It's awful. Your friend Norma called right after we hung up. I didn't want to call you with this news."

"Whatever is it, my dear?" Nigel's face registers alarm, rare for him.

"She's in the hospital, and it's bad. Apparently she slit her wrists."

Silence enshrouds our table, the image too terrible to allow for in my mind. Nigel looks stricken, as if physically ill.

Mel's voice continues, low. "She'll pull through, Norma says, but she could have died from this."

It makes no sense. "How can this be?" I ask her. "And her child?"

"Beth's father has him."

The enormity of Beth's pain, deep and raw enough to drive her to such drastic lengths slams into me, constricting my breath. I wonder too about Billy. How is he taking all this?

Mel peers into my face, her eyes stricken. "Let me drive you."

Stunned, all I can do is nod my head in agreement.

THE HOSPITAL CORRIDOR IS jammed. People of varying ages mill about, talking, carrying teddy bears and flower baskets. Have I somehow landed on the maternity floor?

"Tara!" Norma throws her arms about me and squeezes. "I just heard."

Norma's nodding and fighting tears. "I know. I know." She looks around. "Everyone is here to let Beth know how much we care. If only we'd recognized the signs . . ."

Behind a glass partition marked "Waiting Room," Billy sits alone. I tap Mel's arm. "Norma, this is my sister, Mel."

Norma hugs her as if she's known her all her life.

Both sets of eyes look to me. "I'm going to talk with Billy."

They nod and wave me on. Billy sits so still, his arms against his knees, his hair in disarray, his eyes focused on the scuffed linoleum. The very first time I saw him, I thought Billy was huge, yet gentle and funny. Now, sitting there in the corner of the waiting room, he appears small.

And scared.

"Billy?" I sit two chairs down from him. "I'm so sorry."

He quirks the corner of his mouth. "Guess I wasn't enough for her."

"Stop."

"Did you know she'd done this before? This cutting thing? She's been hiding it."

"No." I pause, taking in the depths of this news. "I hadn't heard that, but in the short time I've known Beth, I have heard about some of her trials. Billy, you can't be expected to be the antidote for someone's complicated issues."

He purses his lips and shakes his head. "She could have told me anything. I would have found her some help."

"Why would she do such a thing? Hurt herself like that?"

Billy straightens. "We've been trained to work with people who do these things. Usually it's people who have a difficult time expressing their emotions. Some even feel they've been forbidden to do so."

His tone was flat, emotionless, and I had the sense reciting cold facts helped him maintain control.

"People who hurt themselves are often hiding their deepest problems. Instead of dealing with issues and traumas, they inflict pain on themselves in a variety of ways. Including cutting."

Though his voice remains neutral, his face wears so much pain my heart constricts. "Billy, now that Beth's secret is out, you can still be there for her. You can still find her some help."

"I don't know, I mean, I'd help her in a second. But she's going to have to want it—I can't force myself on her." He stares off into nowhere. "Her father'll get her therapy, but it's gonna be a long haul for the two of us." He sighs, loudly, before standing abruptly to acknowledge someone else's presence. "Josh."

Billy throws himself into Josh's arms and they grip each other. Billy's face crumbles and red splotches spread and fill his cheeks. Choked sobs break through and he buries his face in Josh's shoulder.

I back out of the room to give them their space, but Josh halts me with imploring eyes, turning my legs to quivering jellyfish. How insensitive of me to feel such magnetic attraction during such a tragic time. But no matter how hard I try, I can't stop the visceral reactions I have to this man. My hard heart toward him softens, just a bit, as he unabashedly hugs his big bear of a friend.

I attempt to step back again, but this time, Josh reaches out and grasps my hand. He pulls me closer. We almost look like we're having a group hug. "Don't go," he mouths.

I'm caught in the middle, between the tragic circumstances of this day and the wavering feelings I have for Josh. Billy lets him go and blows his nose on a napkin that's been overused. Josh continues to hold my hand, stroking it with his fingers, as I try to make sense of the tragedy that brought us here—and why I can't easily turn away from him.

"Tara?" Mel steps into the waiting area. "The word is that no one but family is allowed to see her until tomorrow. Do you need a ride home?" She eyes Josh as she asks the question.

I don't wait for him to answer, which he surely tries. "Yes. Absolutely. Let's go."

Josh carefully releases my hand, yet every part of me prickles at his nearness. One turn. That's all it would take and I'd say "adios" to my sister, even though there is too much uncertainty with Josh. He brushes my right shoulder and I can't help but hesitate.

"Life's too short for you to not allow me to apologize. I hope some day you can forgive me." His breath tickles my ear and I close my eyes. It's true. Life can be short and grudges only fill it with bitterness. And yet I wonder at Josh's words.

If you can't receive forgiveness without giving it, then what good will it do for me to forgive Josh . . . when he's never forgiven his father?

Chapter Thirty-two

Mind if we make a stop before going home?"

"Nope." Mel could gun it into the woods and I wouldn't protest. I'm too distracted and muddled to care what route we take.

She turns off the highway and onto a winding, unpaved road. Silence grows like thick kelp. Finally Mel exhales. "Well, I, for one, would love to know what happened between you and lover boy—within reason, that is. I know you haven't been talking, but I'm still reeling from the heat back there."

"Stop it."

She looks at me. "Are my eyebrows singed?"

I shake my head, trying not to laugh. We're driving toward the west along some back road that's lined with horse rail fences and drooping willows and even a few vineyards growing syrah and cabernet sauvignon, among other grapes. "Where *are* we going?"

"Just back to Otter Bay. I discovered this road one day when I took a wrong turn and I like it. It's different." She pauses. "So, you going to tell me what happened between you two?"

I shrug. "Josh has a lot of layers to him. Some more attractive than others."

"Ouch. Hm. But you wouldn't be so indefinite about your feelings for him if those attractive qualities weren't outweighing the others so much."

My mouth falls open.

"Right?"

I close my mouth and glance out over a ridge that disappears into the sky. A red-tailed hawk soars effortlessly after giving itself three measured wing beats. "He scares me."

Mel laughs. "Yeah, well, the best kind always do." She turns left up and over a bump of a hill and we coast down a recognizable street. "Here we are."

"There's . . . Simka's. How fun—we came down the back side of Alabaster Lane." I turn to her. "You're quite the adventurer, Mel-Mel."

"There aren't a whole lot of other ways to fight boredom in this town, you know . . ."

"Stop it right now."

She laughs and parks the car. Something is different at

Simka's. I run my eyes over the grounds and side to side, but can't figure out what has changed.

"You like the fence?"

I blink. "That's what's different. There's a fence out here now and it's such a pretty one. I like the arbor and the pink roses too."

"Those will grow up and over that arbor. We also muted the color of the house—that other pink was obnoxious. This one's more appetizing, like a nice sherbet."

"We?"

She's halfway up the stairs. "Don't you remember? Simka's been consulting with me."

I rub my lips together tightly. I do remember, but just barely. *Where've I been?* "The place looks spectacular. It's a real showstopper now."

Mel's hand rests on the doorknob. "Tell me about it." She opens the door and the front gallery swarms with shoppers. The place is alive with female chatter, a set of twins whining in a double stroller, and several old men getting their patience tested as they recline on an upholstered church pew up against the back wall.

"My idea," Mel whispers. "I told Simka that she needed a place for the guys to sit so they won't rush the women out."

We both laugh and head into Gallery Two or, as I've always thought of it, the dining room. Beneath the window, a sofa table holds an array of brightly colored beanies, similar to the one Camille showed me the other night. Mel picks one up. "So what do you think?"

"About what?"

She plops the beanie onto her head and pulls it down until it's snug. Her long dark hair flows casually down to her shoulders. "About Camille and Holly's wares. Simka's giving them a try here."

"You are kidding! They made all these?"

"Yup."

"Darlings!" Simka nearly dances into the room, her peacock-inspired wrap swishing gracefully about her. "Business has never been better. Never at all. What do you think about these amazing head accessories from HollyCam designs?"

HollyCam? "I'm amazed. I had no idea they had accomplished so much. They're . . . they're beautiful."

Simka takes my arm and leans in toward my ear, as if telling me a cherished secret. "The most fabulous news is that surfers have found them already. Just yesterday, two came in here right off the beach—I had to sweep the sand right out of the store once they left. They bought four total, one for each of themselves and the others for their girlfriends. Isn't that divine?"

I pat her hand, which rests on my forearm. "That's terrific news, Simka. And the store is beautiful too. I truly love that fence."

"Your sister has an amazing gift. Did you know that she spoke with the gentleman who owns the antique shop down the block? He agreed to allow me to place a small, elegant sign pointing the way to Simka's!"

I smile at my sister, who's trying very hard to look nonchalant amidst so much praise. "Good job, you."

A woman approaches Simka. "Excuse me, but may I try this on?"

"Of course you may, my dear. Come, come." Simka turns to us. "Ta-ta, ladies."

My cell rings as we climb back into the car after perusing Simka's place a while longer.

Mel starts up and heads for home and I debate over whether to answer it.

"If you won't, I will," she calls out.

With a sigh, I answer. "Hello."

"Tara, it's me."

A beat passes. "I know."

"There's something I want to tell you . . . something I haven't told anyone. You don't have to meet me—that's your decision. But I'm asking you to anyway. I'm at the cove. Meet me here?"

What would Josh have to say to me that is so private he wouldn't have told anyone before? As he said earlier, though, life's short. Besides, I never turn down a chance to sit by the waters in the cove. "Okay, I guess. I'm almost there now."

Mel lets me out at the top of the stairs. She leans over toward the passenger side. "Do *not* come home before dark."

I shut the car door with a restrained sigh and head down to meet Josh, whose truck sits near the edge. He's waiting for me on the steps. "Here." He reaches out. "Take my hand."

We walk a bit until out of earshot of a few late afternoon beachgoers. Josh ushers me to a secluded cove of sand between two chiseled and towering rocks. His face shows grim. I breathe in. "Did Billy get to see Beth?"

He nods, his eyes squinting against the light. "He did. Actually, I saw her too, briefly." He shakes his head. "She and I developed this bond . . . can't explain it."

"You saved her life once. Nothing can shake that out of a person."

"I've told you before that I don't consider myself a hero."

My fingers play absentmindedly with smooth stones on the beach. "Yes, you did."

"I'm not about to take that back."

"No, I suppose you won't."

"But I learned something new today."

He takes in my face with grief-stricken eyes, and my breath catches in my chest. "Josh? You're scaring me. What is it?"

His Adam's apple moves sharply and he breaks eye contact, looking into the sand instead. "The day of the fire, the day I dragged her out of that house—I thought I'd nearly killed her."

"What? No, no. Josh, everyone in town says you were the hero. If you wouldn't have been there and acted as you did, she might have perished. I heard that she was bleeding . . ." I take in a big, jarring breath. "No."

"It's called self-injuring, and Beth's been doing it for a long time."

"And you blamed yourself for her getting so cut up on shattered glass. Oh, Josh."

"I wasn't on duty that day. I'd gone to a friend's to watch the 49ers play. They won and I decided to celebrate. I wasn't driving, so I had two beers and took off walking."

"I've never seen you drink before. I thought you didn't."

He shakes his head. "I swore it off years ago because of all it's done to our family. I broke my own rule that day."

"Is that when you saw the fire?"

"On my way home. I took a shortcut through your neighborhood and smelled it—I'd know that smell anywhere—it's like destruction. I called it in but couldn't wait knowing that Beth and her son lived there. By God's grace, he wasn't home, but it took me awhile to spot Beth. The smoke was coming on thick."

I touch his back and instinctively massage him with my fingers, trying to soothe away the tautness from his muscles.

"Once I got her in my arms, the operation went well. The front door was blocked, but I had kicked out a side window and helped her through it. That's when I saw all the blood." He pauses, hanging his head between his knees. "Rivers of it."

Nausea climbs my esophagus. I breathe in the sea air, allowing it to fight against my unease. "You saved her from more than a fire then."

"Don't you see? I'd been drinking, Tara. I figured the beers had affected my ability to be sharp, to move accurately." His chest visibly expands and contracts. "Just like my dad."

Scattered dots that have been floating around in my head for the past few weeks connect on Josh's words. I'd understood his embarrassment over his father's public drunkenness, but the fear, deep-seated and raw, obviously ran much deeper. His anger went beyond himself. Josh must have begun to believe he'd fallen prey to the same insidious disease his father had, and that it had affected the job he loved dearly.

"You must've been tortured by the thought. And you've kept this all to yourself?" He nods, gazing out to sea. "Is this why you jump at the chance to take every call—even before finishing a good-night kiss?"

A tender smile stretches across his face, but his eyes reflect regret. "I did that, didn't I?"

I rub my lips together and nod, slowly. "'Fraid so. It's as if you've been trying to atone . . . for something. I didn't see it, but I wondered."

"You wondered what?"

"Why you were such a daredevil. I mean, I know guys tend to be adventuresome in nature, but you always seem to be in the fray. You . . ."

"Didn't even give you a proper kiss good-night."

A blush heats my skin. "Something like that."

A haggard sound drags out of him. "You're right, I guess. I wanted to make up for my mistake that night—or what I thought my actions had caused. Beth's doctor probably could've explained all this to me if I'd asked. But I didn't. I saw the blood and the cuts and was so focused on what I had done wrong that I didn't piece the truth together."

I lean into his chest and wrap my arms around his waist. His arms slide around me and I feel their strength, and yet it's the fragile part of him lying exposed that I long to comfort.

The deepness of his voice resonates against my ear and sends a quick ripple up my neck. "Nothing could take away the pain Beth must've felt, or all those scars and the image of so much blood, but I've been caught up in trying to make it right. For a long time." His lips are inches from my cheeks. "I'm sorry I made you feel second best."

Second best? I release a slow breath. "Oh, Josh, you didn't make me feel that way. I've just been trying to figure you out, to understand where all the anger and need to prove yourself came from."

"Other than that, you thought I was a pretty good guy."

"I knew when you leapt over that counter, and by the way Holly praised you, that you were a pretty good guy."

"If we're going to be passing compliments, then you deserve to be first. You're the one who jumped in and started serving coffee to strangers."

"Crazy, huh."

"No, not crazy—terrific. I saw your heart."

I blush.

He groans. "And now it's your mind that's got me. You're right, you know. I have been trying to prove something. That I'm not my father and I'm not going to wallow in addiction."

"Then something happens to make you doubt yourself. Been there."

He doesn't say anything, but as I lean my head against him once more, his shoulders relax. We're quiet for a long while, and the sea's rhythm lulls us. I roll my gaze upward and he stares at me, his smile rueful. "You've pretty much figured me out, haven't you?"

"I feel like I'm beginning to."

He scoffs, but his eyes still smile. "Well, it's a start then."

"Can I ask . . . have you changed your mind about attending your father's special ceremony?"

His smile fades and he groans again.

I pull back. "You're not going?"

"Nothing's changed, Tara."

"But you just found out about Beth . . . I thought . . ."

"What? That just because I'm not a drunk like my father, I should just get out there and pretend how full of respect for him I am?"

His anger jars the air around us. So much simmers just

below the surface. It's frightening. "You don't respect him
. . . at all?"

"Even when life was normal in our house, it wasn't, not
really. My father wasn't physically abusive, but he knew how
to make me feel small and helpless."

I can't imagine this hearty man ever believing himself as
weak.

"Anyway, I didn't have too many friends come around
back then, like more normal families always did."

"Why not?"

"How would it look if they saw their mayor walking
around our house wearing boxers and a sappy smile? No,
thank you. Just too much shame in that, Tara. Like I said,
we weren't really normal. We looked it, but"—Josh shakes
his head—"it was a lie."

I try to put myself in his place, recalling the unshake-
able embarrassment that goes along, tongue and groove,
with middle school and on into the upper grades. But those
years have passed, along with the unearned shame that often
attaches itself to the unsuspecting. Josh is a well-respected,
accomplished firefighter. Surely he carries no shame for his
father's behavior.

"Have you talked with him about his . . . problem? Other
than . . ."

"Other than our showdown, you mean?" He shakes his
head. "Dad's problem has always been like the elephant in
the living room. My mother's in denial and bringing it up has

always been frowned on. Like other kids of alcoholics, I've learned to adapt. Just don't ask me to face it anymore. I'm finished with that."

"So you won't forgive him?"

A muscle in his jaw shifts. "Didn't say that." He pitches a smooth, flat stone into the water. "Just some things I'm not ready to forget."

Chapter Thirty-three

 Mel yawns as I step into the house. "I left your laptop on for you. I was working on my resumé, but my eyes won't stay open anymore." She rubs her eyelids. "You're glowing. Sort of."

"I listened to you and came home late, but I don't know what to think about Josh and me anymore. After our conversation stalled, Josh and I wandered along the rocks until nearly sunset, mostly quiet, our thoughts as far away as the islands to the south. We found a rare abalone suctioned to the side of a rocky ledge and watched as the waters tumbled back in, drenching the endangered creature. When the sun sank into the horizon and cool air had set in, the night sky became a picture of diamonds on a blanket of navy blue, spreading itself before us calm and clear. Unfortunately, our hearts were anything but, so we called it a night."

My sister leans against the doorway to the hall. "For someone who's become all about setting her mind on what she wants, how can you say you don't know what to think?"

"It's just . . . it's complicated." She yawns again, so I talk fast. "The more I'm with Josh, the more confused I get. He's strong and handsome and really, really good to me."

"Yeah, that would be confusing."

"Good to me, although he did just break our date for the mayor's big celebration. He's got so much anger toward his father. If anyone should get that . . ."

"That would be us."

"You'd think."

"You know what I really think, Tara?" She taps the side of her mouth, examining me. "You've changed."

I cross my arms. Mel, it seems, has rallied against sleepiness and has more of her signature criticism of me to launch. Here it comes.

"You always were a sergeant, that's true. Bossy, bossy."

My eyes begin to roll.

She raises a hand, as if to tell me to stop my usual reaction. "But a happy one. Carefree, kind of. I was always so jealous of that because even now I have trouble carrying out my plans. Anyway, you got so much done, especially when Dad got sick and Mom, well, you know what an avoider our dear mother can be." She distracts herself by examining a fingernail. "Then all of a sudden, you turned sour."

Slowly I uncross my arms.

She shrugs, her mouth a grimace. "Made it a lot easier to keep up with you."

"What does that mean?"

She looks me square in the face. "I didn't have to work so hard to be you anymore. The new 'you' had become angry . . ."

"And boring?"

"Trent was dull. Yuk, very dull. And strangely enough, my once adventurous and happy sister seemed to be okay with that." She wrinkles her brow at me. "It's like you had given up."

Part of me wants to deny her assessment of me, but another part sees the truth in what she says. Life had become a drudgery. My job—boring. Boyfriend—predictable. Day-to-day life—routine. Yet since arriving in Otter Bay, my emotions have careened over and around one oversized roller coaster, and I've felt a shedding of anger with each fantastic twist. No doubt, despite the astonishing turn of events since the move, less and less anger lives in me.

"I think I see what you're saying."

Mel's brows register surprise. "You do?"

"As recently as this morning, I was still wondering if this is where I should be. If moving to Otter Bay was the right choice."

"And now?"

"I'm more at peace with this decision than I've been since day one."

She draws in a large breath and exhales a healthy yawn. "Yeah, me too."

Her yawn is contagious and one finds me as well. "Go on to bed, Mel-Mel. I'll shut down the computer."

She turns to go but pauses. "It's been a mind-boggling week. Don't rush things about Josh. And who knows? Maybe he'll come to terms with things before his father's big day."

If he attends. My body longs to sit in the dark, with only the tick of the clock and the nearby waves as companions. It's what I should do. But as is my habit, I find myself absentmindedly logging on to my *Soaps Weekly Digest* account. Eliza's had another busy day. Vicky the vixen, her son's replacement fiancée, has fallen from her good graces, apparently. That was quick. I read on. Seems Vicky hit it off with Maurice at the soiree she had thrown for her son's newest (and orchestrated) engagement. If only she'd left well enough alone . . .

Where's the reward in this?

The truth smacks me on my usually sensible brain. I realize just how tired I am of Eliza and her shenanigans. Who could survive such a life unscathed? She's nothing but a fictional character who falls into one conflict after another with no sign of reward. And I'd been looking to her for help?

Maybe . . .

Maybe my own life had become so boring that I needed Eliza. Or at least I thought I did.

But Eliza plays with people with no thought to how her actions affect their lives. Their souls. My mind wanders back to Josh and the confusion in his voice today. *He knew how to make me feel small and helpless.* Josh's statement had surprised me. The way he always put himself on the line was impressive, but maybe there'd been another reason for his many sacrifices, for the inattention to his own safety. Maybe his father's brokenness had caused him to internalize the misconception that his *own* life didn't matter much.

The idea pains me to my center and I sit in the silence, all except for the clicking of that clock. Unnatural light glows from my computer screen and I shake my head. Of course his life matters. *Every* life does. Even mine.

I take one last look at the screen, that old familiar longing for the *Weekly Digest* nothing but a pale memory. "Sayonara, my old friend," I say to the picture of a grinning Eliza, her hair in the style I've always envied. "It's just that there's been enough drama in my old life lately, much of it avoidable."

She keeps on grinning, as if she hadn't heard a thing. A sigh flows through me and I keep talking to the static picture. "You don't care and you never have. And you know what? I need more than that in my life. I need people, Eliza . . . and I . . . I need God."

Saying the words aloud, rather than just thinking them in some fleeting, happy way, moves something fresh and active within me. I. Need. God.

Can it be as simple as that?

With all of me, I know the answer, and it stuns me, but in a good way. At the same moment, Nigel's words from the morning jolt me: *Those who are there now understand that the church today should operate much like a hospital for sinners.*

"Eliza," I say to the quintessential drama queen. "Get thee to the church."

With a click of the mouse, I unsubscribe to the site and click *close*.

"YOU DID THE RIGHT thing." Camille's wielding a crochet hook and sharp eye toward the yarn in her hand.

"You were out surfing when I called Mel to talk about it. I didn't want you both to feel obligated, so I figured it could come out of my portion."

She looks up. "Is Mel kicking in?"

I look at Mel. "Yes, she is."

"I still can't believe Dad would've done stuff like that." She shrugs. "But you know what you're doing. You always do. Count me in too."

I send Mel a questioning glance and she takes over. "So you're cool with us paying back Peg all of the money?"

She doesn't lift her eyes. "Uh-huh."

"Camille?" I rest one hand on her shoulder. "Is something bothering you?"

She works faster and with more intensity, her full curls bouncing against each other as her crochet hook does its thing. I'm wondering if she heard me when she misses a loop and lets a curse word slip out under her breath.

Mel catches my eye and gives me a reassuring nod. She leans toward Camille and gently removes her crochet project from her hands. "Talk to us."

Camille shuts her eyes tightly, something she's done since a child. She smothers her face in her hands and lets out an uncharacteristic howl. "I'm so confused!"

Mel and I exchange a bewildered glance.

I reach out to her. "By what? C'mon, Camille. Talk to me."

She throws herself into my arms and we roll over onto the carpet together, like a couple of roly-poly bugs caught on their backs. Mel stands over us. "You girls need some help?"

We lie there on the floor, looking up into the wood beamed ceiling, our chests rising and falling in the silence.

Camille speaks first. "Do you girls think I'm insensitive?"

I roll over and take in her precious face. "I've never once thought that of you."

"That's it." Mel drops to the floor. "Give it up. You're beside yourself and you need to tell us why."

"I don't miss them."

She's speaking in riddles. "Who? Who don't you miss?"

"My parents!" Camille stands and hugs her waist. "I don't miss them at all. I'm horrible! How could I not miss them?"

I'm at her side in an instant. "Oh, honey." She falls into my arms. "You were just a baby when Uncle Grant died. And your mother left even before that. You couldn't possibly remember them. Don't beat yourself up."

"Yeah, kiddo. If it helps any, we don't remember life without you."

"How did this come up all of a sudden?" I ask.

A dramatic sigh flows out of her. "Holly. She's got all these pictures of her mother and some magazine cut-outs of men she thinks might look like her father in an album with all kinds of stickers and captions. It's kind of sad. She dreams of some kind of reunion someday, like she's Annie."

I rub her back. "You two have become good friends, haven't you."

"Yeah. I feel so bad for her. All she's got is her Aunt Peg—and you know what a bear she can be. I hate to say it, but what happens to her when Peg, you know, passes away?"

Mel clucks. "She'll throw a party?"

"All I'm saying is that Holly loves two people she's never known. I'm so worried about her because a reunion may never happen—and then she'll be alone. And that makes me feel guilty, because honestly, I don't ever think about my birth parents."

"Never?" I'd wondered, on occasion, what it would have been like for Camille to have been simply our cousin. The thought always chilled me, like a cold snap in winter. And for that, I always felt guilty. Somewhere within me an idea niggles at me, bringing on that same sickening chill, followed by the guilt of my own selfishness. Camille's mother could very well show up here in Otter Bay.

"Well. Maybe not *never*. I used to wonder about my real mother. And you know how Mom always likes to tell stories about how funny my father was." She shrugs again. "I have happy memories of him only because of what Mom has said. I don't remember him. Anyway, I never felt like I didn't belong and I've never really wondered 'what if.' If anything, I've been counting me lucky stars. Sheesh, Dad treated me no different than you two!"

I swallow the lump growing at the base of my throat. "*We're* the blessed ones . . . so, so blessed to call you our sister." Another reason to offer thanks instead of curses to Dad—and to Mom.

Mel socks Camille on the shoulder. "Yeah. Don't feel bad that you're not mooning over your parents, kiddo. Things worked out the way they were meant to."

Mel's words strike me to my center. Was Uncle Grant meant to die in a motorcycle crash? Was it God's plan for Camille's mother to abandon them both? Hard to imagine either of these scenarios as God-designed, but now is not the time to argue the point.

I hide away these thoughts and muster up a smile for Camille.

Chapter Thirty-four

Déjà vu pays a visit as I look for seats amidst a buzzing crowd. Same crowd, same venue, different event. It's all very weird. If I hadn't told Shirley I'd come, and if Nigel hadn't coerced me into accompanying him with the promise of free tapas and a day off, I might very well have just mailed a card.

A female volunteer—I can tell by the word VOLUNTEER emblazoned on her name tag—hands us a program, and Nigel and I find our seats. Up front, Pete and Shirley Adams sit regally as a variety of residents gather around them to offer hellos and congratulations. Nothing looks amiss as Pete's charismatic smile greets his admirers.

"It's a lovely day for an outdoor ceremony," Nigel says. "Wouldn't you agree?"

I glance at him, aware of how angry I was at this gentle man only days ago. "It's beautiful, Nigel. The ocean, the trees, the warm air—the perfect day to be outside." I don't mention how fierce the waves sound against the otherwise blissful day.

A squeal, followed by an infectious giggle, draws my attention. A tiny girl, dark-skinned and chatty, spins in the center aisle as her mother tries unsuccessfully to coax her into a folding chair. The child catches my eye and lunges toward me, one of her petite hands clutching a single flower.

"I sit with you!" Accent heavy and drawn out on the *you*. I smile and scoop her up, as if doing so is as natural as the unfurling of waves. She's on my lap, beaming like a pixie, her own attention caught between the seaside daisy in her hand and the features on my face.

"Mia!" The girl's mother utters apologies as she climbs over several people in order to exit her row of seats and reclaim her daughter. She crosses the aisle in haste and looks to me, her brow scrunched. "I'm so sorry. Mia, you need to stay with Mama."

I smile. "I don't mind at all. She's adorable."

Mia takes one last look at me and hops from my lap, dropping the daisy onto the grass and scampering away before her bewildered mother can catch her. The woman heaves an exasperated sigh and dashes off.

"You will make a tremendous mother some day, my dear."

"Mm. Thank you." Nigel's sentiments are like lotion to a burn. No doubt he's aware of our mother's often flighty ways. Oh, she loved us and made sure we had what we needed to live, but there was always this underlying sense that her mind was in some other place. I glance off toward the west, where a hawk glides with ease. *Maybe Mom's ways had more to do with all the secrets locked up and left behind in California.*

Why two clowns juggling live fire take this moment to enter from the side with no warning whatsoever I'll never understand, but when they do, children flock near to them, leaving seated parents looking harried and torn. The ludicrousness of flying flames at the mayor's celebration catches me off guard, bringing out the giddy teen in me—who knew one existed?—and I begin to giggle. Slowly at first, since I rarely giggle, until the bubbling peals light a fire of their own, sending me into all-out laughter, the kind that's difficult to cover in polite company. I try, but that only serves to make the laughter build until a wet sheen covers my eyes.

Nigel hands me his hanky and I'm barely able to control myself. "I had forgotten all about that laughter, but now that I hear it again, I remember it well."

My breathing slows from a sprint to a jog. I can feel the patter of my heart. "You . . . you remember my . . . laugh?"

"Oh, yes. Your father always said it sounded like happiness to him." He pauses. "He depended on you for that."

The breeze cools my face, my breathing close to normal. Soberness wraps me in its oversized blanket as memories of our world here continue to catapult me into the past. The clowns fade away and in their place I'm lost in yesterday until Nigel pulls me forward.

"Excuse me, Tara dear. Would you take a look at this program? I neglected to bring my reading glasses with me and I cannot find Josh's name here. Surely he will take part in the ceremony."

Dread fills my chest. I peek at Nigel and then at the program in my hand. "Certainly, Nigel. Okay, let's see." I scan the paper, but despite my own 20/20 vision, Josh's name does not appear. "Apparently Josh is not part of the program today."

Nigel's eyes widen. "No? Dear me. Perhaps it is just a terrible oversight. Joshua would never miss such a fine celebration to honor his father."

Not unless he's too tired of the charade to care.

We watch as members of the community pour in, spilling into the seating area. Cheryl, our realtor, wiggles five fingers at me in a friendly greeting. Nigel and I wave to Tina, who's on maternity leave. Contrary to how we parted, she now appears serene and motherly as she tends to the newborn in her arms. The clowns disappear and, in distinct contrast, a violinist appears onstage dressed in shimmering peach. Voices hush and she begins to play, the music a soothing accompaniment to the distant crescendo of pounding waves. I push Josh's absence into the farthest corners of my mind.

The emcee takes the stage and I recognize him as the choirmaster at church. He stands at the front, meaty hands folded across his middle-aged belly, a patient grin on his mouth, waiting. When the resumed chatter and background music stops, he waits a beat, then begins.

"Welcome, beautiful citizens of Otter Bay . . ."

A latecomer takes a seat to my far right. It's Billy, walking with a hunchback, as if sadness weighs, like an oversized feed sack, on his shoulders. He slides in next to a group of men I don't recognize. Hm. Other firefighters, maybe?

"And we have much to be thankful for here in our community . . ."

A Vanna White look-alike takes the stage, just to the left of the emcee. She's holding a stack of papers, certificates presumably, and looks as if she's about to confer diplomas on the graduates.

"Our first recipient today, for his achievement in keeping our community lit well throughout the winter . . ."

The honoring has begun and no Josh in sight. A squirrel darts through the grass, setting off a cacophony of muffled squeals. Another recipient receives an award, this one for the seasonal light-post décor on Main Street. An especially boastful wave hurls itself onto the rocks, flicking sea spray into the far section of the crowd.

Programs crack and rustle as the line of honorees dwindles. Pete's honor is saved for last, the icing on the cake of this celebration. In the past hour I've learned just how much Otter Bay loves to honor its champions, in everything from town beautification to heroic rescues. *Did my parents love the quirks of this town as much as I've come to love them?*

Josh's absence grows ever more obvious, and I swallow back my sinking heart.

"And now, it is my pleasure and honor, to introduce to you this year's recipient of the OBECA—that's the Otter Bay Exemplary Citizen Award—for his many years of faithful service as our town's Mayor: Pete Adams!"

The applause begins, joined by people on their feet and children standing on chairs, the gentle roar surprising and uplifting. Pete climbs the stairs from where he'd been waiting with Shirley, his gait confident, his smile wide. I only wish . . .

I blink. From the left of the stage, my wish comes true. Josh appears just as his father shakes hands with the emcee.

"I have invited our very own—and in my humble opinion our next Battalion Chief candidate—Joshua Adams to say a few words."

Josh strides across the stage in his blue uniform, taller than I'd remembered, purposeful. His hair shines lighter than his father's and has that same I-don't-do-a-thing-but-it's-beautiful-anyway wave in it. He shakes hands with both men, lingering slightly over his father's greeting.

When Josh faces the crowd, he looks more assured and more determined than I've ever seen him. And yet gentle as a shore bird. He leans one hand onto the podium and my eyes cannot look away.

"Life," he says, "is full of dysfunction . . ."

Oh, Josh.

His expression is not without emotion. "And it starts with me."

There's a catch in my throat.

"I'm honored to be here with you all today"—he nods at the honorees in row one—"and with my father." Josh's intense eyes scan the crowd. "I've been doing some reading lately, reminding myself of things from the past, and one of the worst things that can happen, I've come to believe, is to allow history to repeat itself. Especially in my own life."

Even the children sit quietly.

"You see, the Israelites who wandered in the desert all those years ago, well, they made a lot of mistakes—weeping and gnashing of teeth, if you will."

Snickers of agreement travel through the crowd. Some of the older women are nodding their heads.

"The Lord appeared to them anyway and promised to build them up again. He told them they would be fruitful and filled with joy."

A voice from the crowd calls out, "Amen!"

"What He didn't say was that the people would suddenly become perfect. Some were still lame, some blind, all—in my opinion—ornery at times." A slight smile curls up the corner of his mouth. "But they would come together, gathered by God's hand, even as some wept, unable to clearly see the blessings He laid out for them. And as they prayed, the Lord promised to lead them beside streams of water. He promised that their path would be level; that they would not stumble."

Something twists inside my heart.

"I've been stumbling around a lot lately, but I've been reminded that it's time to stop and accept the rewards of this life graciously." He looks to Pete. "My father's not a perfect man."

I hold my breath. Does anyone else around me feel a swell of air within their own chests?

"But he's taught me everything I need to know." He pauses. "Like how to carve an outstanding frog from a wedge of soap."

The woman in the chair next to mine sends a loud clap into the air and drops her head forward, laughing.

"He's taught me the wisdom of remembering to bring the toilet paper on a campout." With a tip of his head, Josh acknowledges his mother. "By the way, thanks again, Mom, for not being sore that I once came back with the sleeves of my flannel shirt missing."

Roars of laughter spike the air. Giggles hopscotch through the audience.

Again, he pauses. "He taught me that there is great reward in hard work and toughness and fighting fires, both literally and figuratively—but that it must be balanced by pursuing faith, chasing after it when necessary. Especially when one's head is of a particular thickness." His smile is wry, conciliatory. "He's impressed upon me the idea of hope, only it's not just an idea, but a reality to be cherished. Today I read in the Bible: 'There is hope for your future . . . your children will return to their own land.'"

I'm taken aback. The words sear into me, deeply, with permanence. As if they are meant specifically for my sisters and me.

"God was talking to the Israelites, of course, but He left those words behind for a reason. I don't know about you, but I'm glad for His promise of hope. And I'm glad for this land." He sweeps one arm from left to right. "This land *is* my own; it's become a part of me that I never want to leave. And you all have become significant in my life." He turns then and faces his father. "Thank you, Dad, for spending your life protecting this town and these people. And for teaching me all that is really important."

As the townspeople leap to the ground, clapping and whistling, Pete, obviously overcome, crushes his son to himself. Even Nigel rises up, careful to place his cane firmly in front of him. Warm, salty tears stream down my cheeks. Contained within them is a mixture of appreciation, revelation, and another obvious ingredient, the one I'd diligently avoided acknowledging until now.

Love.

Chapter Thirty-five

I hoped you would come."

Josh looms next to me, bigger than life, his voice all at once soothing and thrilling. My "date," Nigel, reclines beneath the shade of a pine talking with Tina. "Well, after you stood me up, I had so many suitors clamoring to escort me, I figured 'why not?'"

Josh clutches his heart. "I'm grieved that you'd think I would stand you up. But, you're a traditionalist. I love that about you." He pauses and watches me for a moment, as if wondering whether I could seriously forgive him. "Can we talk somewhere . . . somewhere quieter?"

"What kind of woman would I be to just run out on my date?"

A grin alights his face as he glances at Nigel and catches him politely stifling a yawn. He looks back to me. "Merciful?"

I giggle. "You're funny. You really are very funny."

Josh quirks a brow. "You say that like you're surprised."

I smile, coyly. "The tide's out."

He returns the smile and offers me his arm. "I can always rely on you for accurate maritime information, can't I?"

We walk along the section of beach just below the event grounds. Here the sand is finer and softer to the touch than other beaches in the area where pebbles dominate. With each step my toes dig deep into the massaging smoothness. Josh's strong arm firmly hugs my waist as we walk in silent contentment.

I breathe in. "That was one amazing speech you gave back there."

He tenses, slightly, before relaxing back into me. "I meant it. All of it."

I stop. "It touched me more than you know. It felt like a confirmation of what I've been feeling about our move out here."

"You've been questioning that?"

I nod. "All along, especially considering all that we've learned about—well, you know. Prior to coming out here, I'd been so restless. The other night, though, I sensed that it truly was the right decision, only now it feels like more than that, almost like a call. It's like God's telling me that not only was this the right move, but that there's hope for the future as well."

He sighs, looks into the sky, and pulls me into his

embrace. I breathe him in, his scent warm and familiar. "There is hope," he tells me. "It's always been in front of us, but sometimes our fears make us blind."

I think about Dad and how he embraced faith while here on earth, but never really got to experience all the peace that comes with it. Such a shame. It's difficult to admit this to myself, but Dad made some bad choices. Terrible ones. Maybe this is one of the answers to the questions I struggled with the other night, as Camille and I lay on the floor, staring into the knotty pine planks above. Our choices bring on consequences that we have to deal with, or in Dad's case, run away from. Either way they can work against God's plans for us.

I raise my head from his chest. "Is that why you had a change of heart about your dad's honor?"

"That's something I want to talk to you about."

I pull myself back a little more, so I can see his face clearly. "Okay."

"Peg told me about your offer to pay her back the money."

It takes a few slow seconds for his announcement to filter through my ears and to my brain. "She did?"

"That's one of the most selfless things I've ever heard."

"I'm surprised she said anything." Why would Peg suddenly want us to be seen in a positive light?

His eyes caress me. "I'm glad she told me. It knocked some sense into me about my father, about a lot of things.

My dad needs help and I'm going to see to it that he gets it. Ultimately, it'll still be up to him, but I should have insisted on that long before this." He pauses. "Tara, it's your loyalty to your father that has always struck me."

"As I recall, you weren't keen on it."

"No. I wasn't."

"You thought I was naïve."

He surrenders a sigh. "Maybe. But your devotion to your father, despite what you'd discovered about him, got under my skin. It made me squirm. It exposed just how angry and unforgiving I've been. I didn't like that feeling very much, but it didn't really make me stop." He shrugs. "I'm not saying these feelings are totally unwarranted. Kids of alcoholics often carry shame around and I'm no exception to that. It's understandable, I guess, but either way I wasn't all that easy to live with either."

"Is that what made you change your mind and come here today, Josh?"

"No. It was you."

"Me?"

"I'm humbled by your loyalty to your father, Tara. It wasn't based on his innocence, because he wasn't, but on pure and all-out love." He captures me with his eyes. "Do you know what a rare thing that is?"

I look away, remembering how I'd tilted my head to the sky not too long ago and chastised my father for what he'd left behind for me to clean up. "I'm not a saint."

He chuckles. "You sound like I did every time someone tried to call me a hero."

I sigh. "First of all, you need to know that the other night I gave my dad a good 'talking to.'" My eyes stay on the sand below. "And I've been unfair to you. I've no idea what it's like to grow up in your shoes . . . it must've been so rough on you."

Josh catches my chin and lifts my face to meet his. "The truth is, my father kept his problem in check for years. While I have memories of him being extraordinarily 'happy' at some inappropriate times, it wasn't until he retired and began to feel like his usefulness was gone that he lapsed into the worst of it."

"I'm sorry."

"Don't be." His hand lingers on my cheek for just a moment. "I've realized some things about my dad. Did I ever tell you that his own father ran away to start another family when Dad was young?"

I shake my head, crestfallen at the thought.

"Yeah, it gets worse. My grandfather not only started another family, but he moved just one block away. So here was my dad having to grow up in a neighborhood with his half-siblings and a father that barely acknowledged him."

The sting of a father's rejection clinches my heart. *Daddy, thank you for never abandoning us!*

"It's helped to examine my father with eyes of compassion. Until you, I don't think I'd ever done that. I called and asked him to forgive me."

There it is again . . . forgiveness. "You did?"

"And I told him I forgave him too. Still some things to work on in here." He thumps his heart with his fist. "But it's a start. A really good start."

"I'm glad."

"I've been reexamining a lot of things lately."

"Like . . ."

"Like Beth. She's always been so in control of herself. If anything ruffled her, most of us didn't know it. I've been like that most of my life too. Always thought it was a good trait, an admirable trait."

"And now?"

"Can't speak for the rest of the population, but for me—and I suspect for Beth—hiding our emotions just got us into deeper trouble. We end up being time bombs, ready to explode. Somehow I don't think this is the meekness Jesus referred to in the Bible."

"I'll need a little time before understanding that reference."

He smooths his thumb down my cheek, gently, lovingly. "All I mean is that dealing with hurt is not a one-man—or in Beth's case, a one-woman—proposition. Kindness is all well and good, but when we're in trouble, we need to belt out our need for help. The next time I'm tempted to give into shame and despair, I've got to get on my knees first."

I cock my chin, still trying to gather the meaning of his words. "And . . ."

Both of his hands now cradle my face. "And trust God to work out all the details. I'm not saying it'll be easy. I often jump into problems and ride them out on my own adrenaline."

I nod. After all, I recognize the pattern all-too-well from my own life.

"I don't expect perfection and, for once, I'm okay with that. Changing long-held ways doesn't happen overnight, especially for a hardhead like me." He laughs and his eyes go right along with him. "No pun intended."

"I don't know what to say, Josh. Everything you've said, all of it, is just beautiful and I'm trying to understand it all . . ."

Before I can finish, Josh runs his hands down my face and shoulders. He runs them alongside my arms and they settle at my waist. "Let's say we start fresh, right here, right now." He smiles into my face. "You in?"

I nod, because no words will come. The wind and the spray of waves swirl around us as we stand barefoot in the sand, gazing at each other. Josh's arms wrap me tighter and I'm floating on a potent mixture of breathlessness and contentment.

He cinches me closer, and when he speaks his breath tickles the tips of my ears. "I love you, Tara."

The words, although I've heard them before, sound different coming from Josh. Full and heady and charged with anticipation. And longing. He pulls back and implores me with his eyes.

Not long ago I admitted to myself just how much I wanted a man's love in my life. Until now, though, I hadn't realized the exhilaration of loving that man back.

I lift my chin toward Josh, barely able to contain my smile. "I love you too, Josh. Very much."

And I mean it with everything in me. Not a drop of doubt remains.

I could stay here forever . . .

"I WOULD LIKE TO come in." The woman standing on our porch at half-past ten wears a full-length wool coat and a befuddled frown. One hand continuously squeezes the fingers on the other.

I push on the screen-door latch, speechless.

All three of us are still up, although barefoot and dressed in pajamas as varied as our personalities. Camille's wearing pj bottoms and a cami, Mel is in silk loungewear, and I've slipped into a pair of fleece sweats. Before the doorbell rang, we'd been sitting on the floor, feasting on bowls of Camille's favorite ice cream: fudge crunch.

Peg steps into our cottage, her flat lips pulled into her face. She glances around at the walls, yet appears to notice nothing.

Camille hops up. "Is Holly okay?"

Peg's eyes widen on Camille, as if she's just been awakened from a frightening dream. She makes a visible effort to calm herself before speaking. "Holly's good. She's at home watching the Food Network. Has some crazy idea about putting something with chorizo on my menu." Her voice, usually coarse and raspy, trails off.

"So why are you here?" Leave it to Mel to set things straight. It has not gone unnoticed, at least by me, that my sister's back stands as rigid as an ironing board.

Peg puffs out a firm breath, her eyes more focused. She stares at the three of us, an expression of determination on her face. Yet it's not the ornery one I'm used to. This one is more of resolve. "May I sit?"

Her polite tone confuses me. "I . . . sure . . . of course. Why don't we head into the kitchen?"

Leaving our half-eaten bowls of ice cream behind, Mel and her crossed arms lead the way, followed by Peg, me, and Camille scampering up from her comfy spot on the floor. We slide into the booth and I realize my faux pas. I've loved this room for its warmth and cozy feel, but discomfort crawls up my skin like a spider. Our father's nemesis sits with us in the place usually reserved for sisterly banter.

"I suppose you're here for your money." Mel's voice bristles against my raw nerves.

Peg gapes at Mel. "You hate me."

Compassion swells within me. Peg's a victim in this situation, but her daily demeanor has clouded that fact. This night, however, she sits before us looking sad and somewhat lost. "We don't hate you, Peg. We're just sad that we even have to have this conversation."

She nods, her chin moving up and down like a pogo stick on slow. "Yes, well. I'm sad too." She finds my eyes with hers. "And ashamed."

I shrug. "You probably didn't want to be reminded of what happened when we all lived here all those years ago. Your anger was, uh, understandable."

She leans her head to one side, narrowing her eyes. "You know what happened then?"

I let down an exaggerated sigh. "Dad took money from you. I'm not happy repeating that, but if that's what you want to hear . . ."

Redness tinges her eyes and they fight to stay open against the fluttering. "I meant, oh, I meant . . ."

Camille slips an arm around Peg and the moment freezes in my mind. For all her less-than-thought-out decisions and sometimes immature ways, Camille's treatment of Peg is childlike, precious.

Peg rocks in her arms, whispering, "I'm so sorry. I . . . am . . . so . . . sorry."

Mel looks away, while I reach my arm across to touch Peg's sleeve. I'd forgotten to take her coat. "It's okay. Really. I was planning to pay you a visit tomorrow with a cashier's check." I slide out of the booth and stand. "But if you'd like, I can write you a personal check tonight."

"Stop!"

No sound can be heard except for the refrigerator's cooling unit, coaxing itself to keep working.

"Sit down. I have much to say."

That look of resolve, the one I'd noticed in the living room, has reappeared across Peg's face. Slowly, I sit.

She continues. "Your father paid back every cent he owed me."

"He did . . . what?" Mel lunges forward, as if ready to inflict physical justice.

"Peg? I don't understand." My mind tries hard to accept this new and very welcome truth.

"Sometime after he and Marilee took you girls to Missouri, I received a check in the mail in the full amount, plus interest. I did not expect to ever hear from him again."

I whip a look at Mel.

She appears just as shocked. "I never thought to ask Mom if he'd paid it back! And she never offered that nugget either."

My eyes implore Peg. "But you led me to believe that he still owed you a debt. Why? Why in the world would you keep the truth from me?"

"Because I wanted you to leave!"

"But *why*? Just because of old memories?"

Mel fumes. "I'll tell you why. It's because she figured we were all cut from the same cloth. You thought we'd somehow get into that till of yours, didn't you?"

Camille has pulled away from Peg, her hands resting in her lap, her chin pulled downward.

Peg steps from the booth, standing in the kitchen, glancing around as if searching out an escape route. "Your father—and my sister—were close at one time. It was because of her recommendation that I hired Robert in the first place, to handle the books for my diner." She rubs her wide lips together, moistening them. "My sister had problems—many, many problems—and so she left this town for good. That's when Robert and Marilee started dating. Your mother, well, it was obvious to the entire town how hard she was falling for Robert. Very affectionate, that one. She hung onto him everywhere they went, and her face, well, it looked like a full moon the way it glowed. The man could pass a burp and she'd swoon!"

Camille stifles a giggle, but a queasiness sinks into my abdomen.

"It wasn't long before the two were engaged, and everyone knew it was because Marilee was with child." Peg peers at me. "That was you, Tara."

The queasiness continues to quake my insides.

"I accepted it, you know. My sister, well, she had made her choice and Robert couldn't wait forever. Marilee seemed like a nice girl, flighty, but nice."

Mel sighs. Loudly.

"Everything was going along, me running the diner and your family growing like those grasses out on the dunes, until CeCe came ridin' into town, looking like Rapunzel with all that flowing, curly hair. And she had one thing on her mind."

CeCe . . . was Peg's *sister*? Confusion binds up my heart and mind like a knotted web, but before I can work to untangle the mess, I have something to say. "I need to stop you right there, Peg." I glance at my sisters, the muddiness of guilt in my gut. "I meant to tell you about something else I had heard recently, but never actually got around to it."

Mel's eyes are hard, like marbles. "Spit it out."

I meet them with my own, hoping to soften the edges with a look of desperation. "I've heard that Dad wasn't always faithful to Mom. That he, uh, might have had an affair with CeCe."

"Gross." Camille sticks out her tongue.

Mel's expression matches Camille's.

Peg goes on. "It was commonly believed back then that Marilee trapped Robert into marrying her. Still that's no excuse. In my opinion, a man knows what he's doing when he . . . well, you know." Peg pounds one rounded fist into her open hand. "Anyway, CeCe's presence around town again got the man confused and they dallied—more than once, she told me."

I close my eyes against the sheer pain of learning so much about the intimate sins of my father. Somewhere in my mind's cluttered recesses I realize that the woman standing in our kitchen, if she is truly CeCe's sister, is also our beloved Camille's aunt.

"She wanted him to leave you girls, to jump on the back of her motorcycle and ride away to who knows where with her. But your father"—she shakes her head—"to his credit, he wouldn't do anything of the sort. Her ultimatum changed him. Everybody could see it. If I didn't know better, I would have thought he'd hit his head on the rocks and finally come to his senses."

Camille's interest piques, but she seems wary. "What happened then?"

Peg meets Camillie's gaze. "That's when CeCe took up with Grant, Marilee's brother."

Camille is still. "My . . . father?"

I can't take it and grasp Camille's hand from across the table. "CeCe was Caroline, your mother, Camille." My eyes implore her. "I never knew she was related to Peg."

"Is that so bad?" Peg snaps.

Camille appears dazed. "Wait. That would make you . . . my aunt?"

"Yes, it would seem so."

"So that would make me . . ."

Mel cries out, incredulous. "Holly's *sister*."

I gasp. "Oh, of course. You're Holly's half-sister!" A glimmer of silver lining appears in the sober room, the thought of dear Holly and our cousin being related by blood. "Is this what you really came here to tell us, Peg? That Camille's got a sister . . . and an aunt?"

"There's more."

Mel slams a hand down on the table. "For crying out loud, how much more can there be? You've just about turned this family upside down! We're like characters in some bad soap opera! What else could you possibly say that could be any more surprising?"

Peg's shoulders and chest rise and fall as she gathers strength. She eyes us all. "Robert—your father—was Camille's father too."

Chapter Thirty-six

Silence.

We all turn our gazes on Camille, who has been sitting in a stupor. It's all too much for her. She doesn't make eye contact with any of us, but stares into the grain of the wood table, her fingers pressed against her puckered brow.

The magnitude of Peg's pronouncement is only beginning to fill my consciousness. "Camille?"

She shakes her full head of curly hair before slowly rising from the table, whispering a high-pitched, "Excuse me," and dashing out of the kitchen.

I spin back to Peg. "Are you certain about this?"

Mel grunts. "Let me out." She flicks her head toward the doorway and I slide out of the booth so she can follow after Camille. She brushes past Peg, who has yet to answer, and stops. She speaks to Peg without looking at her. "Did our father know this?"

Peg's voice sounds weighed down. Remorse? "No, I don't believe he did."

"Well. Then you've got a lot of nerve keeping this from us. Our father *died* not knowing Camille was his. What's *wrong* with you?" Mel doesn't wait to find out, but marches from the kitchen. We can hear her feet pounding against the floorboards as she heads down the hall.

Peg's head is dropped forward, but her eyes remain level, watching me. "I didn't know. I swear it. Two years after you all picked up and left town, CeCe showed back up here with another bundle in her arms and no plans to stick around to raise her."

"Holly?"

She nods, her face grim. "My sister was a cruel woman— selfish, addicted. I don't even know if she's still alive." Her wrenching sigh fills the quiet. "Grant, your mother's brother, was a rebel, just like CeCe. It was obvious she used him to taunt your father. When she left baby Camille with Grant, I was busy taking care of my sick husband, Hal, God rest his soul. Then Grant went and crashed his Harley, getting himself killed." She shakes her head slowly. "I was relieved that Marilee offered to take Camille in. I just couldn't do it at the time."

Pity draws on me.

"Your father really couldn't afford another mouth, though. That's why he took the money."

I stare at her. "Really?"

"Really." She shoves her hands into the pocket of her coat. "I hated him for getting mixed up with my sister. I think maybe I blamed him for her problems. After my husband died, though, I felt very, very alone." She slides back into the booth, facing me. "Two years later, when CeCe showed up with another child, I felt grateful, as sad as that may sound. I'd already lost Camille and I was being given another chance. I said something to that effect and that's when CeCe told me that Robert was Camille's real father. Apparently, she didn't sleep with Grant until after finding out she was pregnant with Robert's child."

My mouth has gone dry. I'm awash in grief over careless lies and time lost. *Oh, Daddy, did you ever suspect this?* Instinctively, I know. He must have wondered. He always treated Camille like one of his own, whether or not he knew for sure. "So she left again?"

"'Fraid so. And I've raised Holly ever since."

"Then why? Why weren't you happy to see us? Camille's your niece too, after all."

Regret fills Peg's face. "I've been a stupid woman. When you all showed up here a few months ago, I was more scared than a hog at butcherin' time."

"Scared? Of what?"

She looks me square in the eyes. "That if you knew the truth, you'd take my Holly from me."

The idea's unbelievable to me.

"Your faithfulness, though, to pay back your father's debt"—she shakes her head—"that touched this bitter old woman straight down to the core. I could not, in good conscience, keep the truth from you any longer."

Despite the shock and the grief of the last hour—of the last few months really—hope lingers. My eyes never waver from Peg's. I see a woman beaten down by her own poor choices, and yet, did she ask to have those decisions foisted on her? Silence falls between us. We each grapple with what to do next, when Camille appears in the doorway, fresh tears staining her cheeks.

"I—we need to talk to Holly."

The ball of emotion in my chest nearly bursts. I reach out to Camille, and she falls into my arms.

"Yeah, we do."

She rests her mane of curls against my shoulder and sniffles. "I called her. Her food show finished so she's coming over."

Peg's face pales. "Now? Holly's coming now?"

Camille nods and Peg falls silent. Mel remains AWOL, and I'm nearly numb. The clock on the old stove beats a steady rhythm as we wait for what seems like a lengthy passage of time. Yet only ten minutes later, Holly's rubber-soled shoes, the ones we've heard rocket across the diner floor since the beginning, flap up the stairs to our front door. Camille flies from my arms, throws open the door, and stands rooted in place, gaping at Holly.

Our visitor throws out a nervous little laugh as she enters the room. "Now what's got you girls in a stir this late?" She turns and halts, her eyes finding Peg, stoic and still, on the bench just inside the kitchen doorway. "Aunt Peg?"

Peg extends an arm toward her. "Come here, Holly."

Camille wraps an arm around Holly as they walk toward the kitchen. Holly gasps. "Oh my word. Who died?"

For the first time all evening, Camille smiles. "Nobody. We just have something to tell you."

As the girls squeeze around the table, I take another glance toward the doorway. Mel needs to be here, but I can't force her to join us. The old me would drag Mel from her room, but I'm no longer the girl who needs to be in charge all the time. Truthfully, I never really was in control.

Peg shifts and clears her voice. "This needs to come from me." She purses her lips and pulls in a deep breath through her nose and huffs it back out. "Holly, your mother was my sister."

Holly cocks her chin. "Oh Auntie, I know that—I have pictures, remember?"

Peg nods and her cheek twitches. "There's more. Your mother had another child too. Before you."

Holly's eyes widen. "No kiddin'."

Mel appears and leans on the door frame, her eyebrows knitted toward each other, and her forehead bunched.

Peg glances at Mel, and then thrusts her chin toward Camille. "She's right there next to you."

Holly flits a gaze my way, her mouth agape. "Tara?"

I shake my head. "No . . . not me. Camille. Camille's your sister, Holly."

We watch as Holly turns to find Camille's blotchy red face staring back at her. A beat of silence passes before Holly's surprise fills the room. "Well I'll be dipped in buttermilk! *How?*" She grabs Camille by the shoulders and hugs her tight, her voice thick with emotion. "By the looks of you girls, I thought someone had kicked the can, but this . . . this is the best news I've heard ever in my whole life." Holly pulls back, and holds Camille at arm's length, her face glowing. "I . . . I have a sister of my own."

Mel and I glance at each other, our eyes full.

We know just how Holly feels.

Chapter Thirty-seven

Two Weeks Later

You know those times in your life, when your world crumbles and you think you'll never be able to think about anything else ever again and then some time passes and along the way you realize that you have fallen in love—honestly, for the first time ever—and while all issues may not exactly be resolved, they're better?

Much, much better?

That's the way it is for my sisters and me. And I did say, *sisters*. Peg's pronouncements threw us all into a spin for several days, but slowly we emerged from the turbulence, our new sisterly bond a beautiful display—like a pearl-holding clamshell, pried open and laid out in the sunlight.

Thankfully I had my job at the inn to keep my mind occupied during those first few days of shock. Nigel regaled all of us with more stories of our father and, eventually, we found ourselves laughing more often. He admitted to us that although he and our father never spoke of it, Nigel too had suspected that Camille belonged to Dad. We let Holly digest her news, and then explained to her that we too had just learned that Camille was our sister on our father's side.

Now it's Monday. There's no fog in sight while Mel, Camille, and I lounge outside, listening as the roll of waves provide backdrop music to our banter. Instead of facing the west, however, we've dragged our Adirondack chairs to the street-facing, northward section of the porch. From this spot we watch as a gang of town locals begin the slow process of restoring Beth's burned-out house across the street. There is much to do.

"Do you think Beth will ever recover from her injuries?" Camille's flip-flop-shod feet rest atop the porch railing, her voice hopeful.

"Norma says her counselor is amazing," I tell her. "She knows a ton about what Beth's going through. Apparently, self-injury can actually feel like relief to those who practice it."

Mel's eyes are closed against the sun. "Even though they're slowly killing themselves."

"Well," Camille leans back, "I hope she gets lots of help and moves back in. We should invite her to dinner sometime. Holly can cook for us!"

I smile at my sweet sister, grateful to know the truth

about this young woman whom we've loved all these years. Equally grateful to welcome Holly into our family. Whether or not she plans to grace us with her culinary charms is another matter.

"And we should keep her in our prayers too."

Camille swivels her head in my direction, her body still in a lounging position. "About that, Tara. I think I'd like to go to church with you next week."

Hope stirs in my chest. "Sure. I'd like that."

"Only, do they have a later service? I'm not an early bird you know."

Mel yawns. "Unless a surfer's involved."

Camille glares at her, but it's obvious the way a smile tugs at the corners of her mouth that she's only half serious.

I laugh. "Yes, they have a later service. I'll drink a second cup of coffee while waiting for you."

"You know how much I'd love to join you girls"—Mel's trademark sarcasm lines her words—"but I ought to be on my way across the country by then."

Several tendrils of my hair lift on the breeze, tickling my cheek. "You're really going this time, aren't you, Mel-Mel?"

She answers, but her face is turned toward the beach, as if she's hiding. "I am. I really am."

I keep my eyes on her anyway. "Well, I, for one, think you'll do great! Simka keeps raving about your eye for marketing and your resumé looks perfect—Future You is waiting out there, Mel."

It's obvious how much she doesn't want to smile at this moment, but she does. A little. "Well, then. You know how glad I am that you approve, big sister."

"Ha, ha." I smack her chair, lightly.

"Actually, I'm serious. Your opinion matters to me, Tare-Tare." She rises from her chair as our mail carrier, Bea, climbs the steps and hands her a stack of mail. I glance over at the bushel in Mel's hand as she sits back down. It's good to see something in the pile other than ads directed to *Current Occupant*. Mel holds up an envelope stamped *Par Avion*. "It's from Mother."

Camille pulls herself up slightly, craning her neck for proof. "Mom wrote a letter? Like on paper?"

I cringe. I've called and e-mailed her many times over the past couple of weeks, even leaving a message for her to return my call when someone answered her phone with a foreign accent. Her lack of response has unnerved me. I figured that either Derrick has her climbing the Alps, in which her silence might be somewhat explained, or she's angry. Mom always pouts when she's angry.

Mel rips open the letter, sent by priority mail. We watch in silence as her eyes scan the page. She looks up. "They're coming home."

I gasp. "Which home?"

Mel looks as surprised as I feel. "To Otter Bay."

"No way!" Camille straightens up. "What else does it say?"

Mel sighs and leans against the seat back. "She got all your e-mails, Tara, but both of their cell phones were stolen when they stayed at a hostel in Prague. Well, that explains it. Anyway, she and Derrick agreed that they need to come home and help us deal with all the latest news." Mel glances at us both. "She says she thinks she has some explaining to do."

I don't say what I'm thinking, that she might have warned us that our history in Otter Bay consisted of more than splashing around in tide pools with Dad and collecting moonstones at sunset. That she could've saved us from the pain of facing revelation after revelation about her and Dad.

But then again, I've come to see and hear and feel God in the midst of all this craziness. He has used past lies to draw us to the truth. I've discovered that the truth is more than the uncovering of secrets about my family—it's also about learning to live a life of hopeful, active faith. And to do it one minute at a time.

My father's mistakes may have clouded his judgment, keeping him from living the life of freedom God meant him to have here on earth, but his death was not the end. It's a new beginning. Just like God used Josh to help rescue another soul, even in brokenness, He used Dad too.

I just know Dad's living it up right there in heaven.

As Nigel told us, Dad prayed for his daughters often. Just the thought warms me to my toes! Pastor said the other day that God works all things together for those who love Him.

I think my dad would agree that things worked out as they should.

Camille, who just a moment ago was her usual human-pogo-stick self, even from a sitting position, now has a pensive frown etched into her face.

I turn to her. "You okay?"

"I was just wondering if Mom's feelings have changed any now. She must be disappointed that Grant's not my father."

I shake my head. "Mom's been in love with you since the first time she saw your little bald head peeking out through the top of a pink blankie."

"And what about Holly? Will Mom accept her as my sister? Still feels weird even saying it."

None of us notices Holly standing on the second step to the porch until she clears her dainty throat and speaks up. "Feels weird even sayin' what?"

"Holly!" Camille lunges for her newfound sister. She hugs her tight, curly head to curly head, before looking into Holly's face. "It was nothin'."

They already look alike, and now they're even beginning to sound alike. Pretty soon their female cycles will be synced up and that's when their sisterhood will truly be official.

After they embrace, Holly leaves one arm around Camille's shoulder. With her other hand, she thrusts a basket of brownies toward us. "I brought you girls some of my newest creations. They've got butterscotch *and* chocolate in 'em, plus some coconut and pee-cans. Aunt Peg's lettin' me try them out on people."

I jump up to grab one and tear away at the plastic wrapping.

Holly giggles. "Gee, Tara, you're like a foraging raccoon!"

I'm already picturing Thanksgiving with a table full of Holly's creations, many that I neither had to buy the ingredients for nor spend hours baking. Oh, the possibilities!

I'm licking my fingers when a familiar rumbling announces itself from down the street. It's Josh, and something in my own heart rumbles too as he pulls his truck up in front of our home. There's a heap of something tied down in the bed, a tarp protecting it from the elements—and from prying eyes.

I watch in unguarded delight as Josh hops from the cab wearing Levis and a T-shirt that'll need a few washings before it can be considered worn in. The smile he sports could light up the sky on a moonless night.

"Hello, ladies." He jogs the stairs and heads straight for me with not one hesitation in his step. He rests his strong arms on the sides of my chair and leans himself forward to steal a kiss, lingering just long enough to bring out a snarky response from Mel.

"Oh, brother, get a roo—"

"Mel!" Josh wiggles his eyebrows at me as I break away from him to scold the middle kid of the family.

He leans against the railing, next to Holly, grinning. When he reaches for a brownie, Holly playfully slaps his hand. "Use your manners, Mr. Adams," she says with a giggle.

He purses his lips, a look of mock offense on his face. "After all I've done for you."

One of Holly's hands digs right into her waist. "Oh, yeah. And tell me, Joshua Adams. What exactly is it that you've done for me?"

He holds a fist to the chest, looking pained, but turns and winks at me. He offers me a hand, pulling me out of my chair. "You, Miss Holly, are about to find out. Tara and I will be right back."

As we head down the stairs toward his truck, Josh lets go a sharp whistle. One of the volunteers working on Beth's house turns around and jogs toward Josh's truck, meeting us there.

"Don't you go butterin' me up for my brownies, Josh! I'm a businesswoman now!" Holly's still hollering from the porch, her arm a bent triangle. Mel and Camille are laughing.

We reach the truck. "Is it all painted and everything?" I whisper.

Josh kisses my forehead. "Yes, dear."

"I was just asking . . ."

He laughs and climbs up into the bed of the truck, causing it to lower under all that muscle he's wearing. The other guy hovers near the back as Josh unhooks the straps from the tarp. "Grab the other end, will you?" Josh squats to lift the item and swivels his face in my direction. "You just stand there looking *fine*."

His helper buddy grunts, a goofy grin on his face. "Spare me."

The guys carry the item across the lawn without removing the tarp. By now, Camille and Mel have joined Holly, who's hanging over the side, at the railing. "What you got under that tarp, Josh?"

He wags his head and looks to me. "She's an impatient one," he says with a grin. "Gonna have to get used to that."

I crack up.

They set the tarped item on the deck, next to the row of Adirondacks that have served the girls and me well over the past couple of months. In them, we've rested and wrestled and reflected on all that's happened. I get down on my knees and began pulling away the masking tape that secures the tarp. Before I can get even one piece removed, the other girls, except for Mel, begin ripping away at the covering. For her part, Mel stands back, a radiant grin shining on her face.

Camille pulls the tarp off first. "It's . . . a chair?"

We stare at each other for a beat. "For Holly. So we can all hang out here on this great deck. Together."

Camille gasps and throws her skinny little body into my arms. "You're the best sister ever!" Her arms still hang around my neck as she whips a look back at Holly and Mel. "No offense, girls!"

I laugh. "You're welcome."

Camille takes the basket from Holly. "Sit down, sit down. Let's see how you fit in it."

Mel shakes her head. "Her rear end is smaller than mine. She'll do just fine."

Camille flicks her wrist at Mel. "Silly."

Holly moves toward the new Adirondack, her lips pressed together. She glides her fingers slowly across the newly painted armrest. "I . . . I don't know what to say." Her pale golden eyes, the ones that remind me so much of Camille, fill with tears. "You really don't know how much your doin' this for me means."

Camille grabs Mel and pulls her toward us all. "Group hug!" We all laugh and hug and well up a little before collapsing into our row of Adirondack chairs. Josh's grin couldn't get any bigger, as he stands against a deck post, his thick arms crossed across that molded chest of his, watching me.

Longing ripples through my veins and I look elsewhere, afraid my emotions will give me away. Only Josh will have none of it. Playfully, he calls out a low "psst," and I respond simply because I can't *not* respond to him. The headiness of this moment with the girls—beautiful as it is—fades the moment my eyes lock with his. He leans forward, still gazing intensely into my eyes. "You're an amazing woman, Miss Tara," he says, his voice a husky whisper.

"Yeah?"

His smile is confident. "Yeah. Walk with me down to the water?"

Mel flicks a nod toward the sea and mouths, "Hurry—go."

I take in the view—my sisters on the deck, Josh in front of me, a clear shot of the level path leading straight ahead to the sweet waters at the end of the road. It occurs to me that nothing turned out like I thought it would.

I didn't marry Trent.

I no longer work behind a desk doling out auto parts to men twice my age.

I've learned that moving on requires letting go of everything—except my faith. That's something I am pursuing with gusto.

No, things turned out nothing like I had planned. Josh's hand reaches for mine. Actually, they turned out better. Much better.

"Ready?" Josh asks.

My hand curls into his. For a long time, I've been the serious one, the leader of the bunch, or, as some might say, the one trying to control everything. Now, however, I'm content to follow where this road may lead, with Josh pulling me along. As we stroll together, edging closer to the shore, the laughter I hear reverberating through the pines . . . is mine.